IN MY FATHER'S NAME

By the same author

Family of Strangers
Mothers and Other Loves

IN MY FATHER'S NAME

Wendy Oberman

GRAFTON BOOKS
A Division of the Collins Publishing Group

LONDON GLASGOW
TORONTO SYDNEY AUCKLAND

Grafton Books
A Division of the Collins Publishing Group
8 Grafton Street, London W1X 3LA

Published by Grafton Books 1990

Copyright © Wendy Oberman 1990

A CIP catalogue record for this book is
available from the British Library

ISBN 0-246-13622-7

Printed in Great Britain by
Mackays of Chatham plc, Kent

All rights reserved. No part of this publication may be
reproduced, stored in a retrieval system, or transmitted,
in any form or by any means, electronic, mechanical,
photocopying, recording or otherwise, without the prior
permission of the publisher.

For my son Benjamin

*and for my father Barney,
my mother Lily,
and Bella*

*and for Tracy and Debra,
Robert, Ruth, Daniel, Jennifer,
Karen and Meir*

In My Father's Name
would never have been published without
the care and guidance of my agent,
Gill Coleridge, and the support
from Mary Shields.

CHAPTER ONE

In the early dawn of a Turkish morning, Fae Whiteman lay in a small white bed and dreamed of her lover. The sweetness of illicit love flowed into those dreams, the beauty of his lips, his fingers. She shifted in her sleep as if to cleave to him, anticipating him.

A single scream of terror sliced through her pleasures, jerking her out of her ecstasy. Fae heard it again and her eyes opened. She sat up in her bed, but the velvet sleep still claimed her and she wasn't sure that there had been a sound. Then it came again, the shout, the fear. Jumping out of her bed, she ran from her room, down steep stone stairs. As she reached the bottom step she saw to the left black hooded men, with guns, trying to drag her father out of the house. He was struggling, desperately trying to lock his foot around a bright orange and blue beach umbrella that was sprawled across the floor. He couldn't cry out because the biggest of them had a hand clasped over his mouth. Her father stumbled, falling to his knees, anything to impede them; they pushed him up, he slipped – his feet were his only weapon – but like some terrible dance they got him up again.

It was her brother Fabrizzi, just eight, who was screaming. In a daze Fae saw one of the men turn away from her father and lift Fabrizzi up, putting him into his mother's arms, almost as if he were trying to calm him. For a mad moment Fae remembered her father lifting her, when she was eight, high above his head, his strong arms never faltering, his black hair gleaming. Suddenly Fae absorbed what was happening: they were kidnapping her father. She flung herself at them; she was like a wild woman, trying to aim where it would hurt most. One raised a gun. She knocked it out of his hand, but another, behind her, punched her hard and she fell.

Through it all she heard Fabrizzi crying, 'What are you doing to my Daddy? Where are you taking my Daddy? Please leave my Daddy alone!'

They were putting a blindfold on him.

'Don't,' Fae screamed. 'He can't bear to have his eyes covered.'

She grabbed an ankle and bit it, sinking her teeth into the flesh. The man swore and kicked her hard in the stomach. It hurt like hell. She wanted to cry but she couldn't cry in front of them.

'Don't touch my sister,' Fabrizzi yelled, straining to break free of his mother. Innessa – an Italian woman some twenty years younger than her American husband – held on to him, shushed him, rocked him as if he were still a baby.

Fae pulled herself up from the floor: she was groggy and her stomach throbbed. They were getting her father out of the house. He was tossing his head one way, then the other, trying vainly to get the blindfold off. By now there was a gag on his mouth. She pushed past her stepmother and her brother, trying to reach him. He was already in the car. She watched, helpless, as he was driven away from them.

Her brother began to sob. Fae reached out a hand and stroked his back, and gently kissed his shoulder.

'We'll ring the Embassy, they'll get him back, they'll know what to do.'

'You do it, Fae,' Innessa said. She was still rocking Fabrizzi.

The phone was answered quickly. The flat nasal American tones were a long way from the horror about her.

'This is an emergency. My father is a professor at Bosphorus University. His name is Sam Whiteman. He has just been kidnapped.' She quickly explained where they were.

As she put the receiver back in its old fashioned cradle she realized she was naked.

Half an hour had passed and Fae, dressed in a black T-shirt and trousers, stood with her back to an open fireplace. At twenty-eight years of age she was beautiful. Although she was the daughter of an English woman who could trace her ancestors back to the Vikings, she took after her father – she had his ink-black hair. She wore it long and full around her small face, her eyes were of a soft hazel colour, her nose neat and straight.

Innessa and Fabrizzi were sitting together on a dark blue couch. Fabrizzi, in his favourite Arsenal football outfit – a gift from Fae – held his soccer ball in his arms, cradling it. He was a small boy for his age, with his father's thick black hair, but his mother's almond skin and her light green eyes. Innessa herself, tiny like her son, had naturally fair hair. She bleached it white blonde. One of her arms encircled her son, holding him into the curve of her body. The other was free to smoke her cigarettes, one after the other.

'Sam hates this habit, he's always trying to make me give it up. You know, Fae, I just can't believe this. We were in bed, there was this huge shouting. Sam went down to see what it was. Fabrizzi, you woke too, didn't you darling?'

The boy nodded, frowning. Fae could see that he didn't understand the need for talk.

She couldn't believe that any of it was real. It was as if she had read it in a book, or a script somewhere, and they had just played the scene. Someone, soon, would shout 'cut' and it would all be all right. But no one called out the magic word. Sam was no longer in the house, Sam had been kidnapped.

She reached for one of Innessa's cigarettes, lit it, feeling the hot harsh tobacco as it hit her stomach. She coughed, she never liked smoking, but at least it kept her fingers busy.

The little villa was swarming with police. They had arrived, stiff with guns, and even a white armoured car flashing a blue light, in what seemed minutes after Fae's call. They were led by an Inspector in a mint green shirt, sharply pressed dark green trousers and a peaked cap. With his thick curly black hair he might have been handsome, if it weren't for the hardness about the small button-brown eyes. He was polite to Innessa, respecting her position as the wife and mother, kind to Fabrizzi – and insolently flirtatious with Fae.

She glanced over to her stepmother. Sam was God knew where. Was he still alive? She dared not ask that question, not in front of Fabrizzi. Instead she said, 'Who's got him?'

'It could be anyone,' Innessa said. 'You can choose any group you like, Fae, right or left. But I can tell you, they all have one thing in common – they all hate the Americans.'

'Dad knew that, he told me. He wrote me a letter about it, just a few weeks ago.'

'Did he?' Innessa's tone made Fae curious. Fae wanted to know more, but she was distracted by the Police Inspector conferring with his men outside the window. With a wave of his hand he seemed to dismiss them, but two of them took positions by the front door.

He walked purposefully into the villa, neither knocking on the door, nor excusing his arrival. He stood over Innessa, addressing her, clearing his throat before he spoke – the gesture irritated Fae. She was like an overwound clock, the mechanism going too fast, the arms on its face, her arms, whirling around madly. She checked herself, she had to try and calm down. Deliberately she swallowed, slowing the image down, making the clock tick normally. The policeman was speaking.

'We have finished our enquiries here. I will make my report to my authorities.'

'Your authorities!' Fae exploded. 'You won't make any reports to anyone you don't make to us. We're the ones who have to know what is going on.'

'My instructions are to report to . . .'

'Bugger your instructions! You tell us.'

Someone else came into the room. Fabrizzi shouted, 'Richard!' and Fae saw a slender young man, obviously American. He held out his hand.

'My name is Richard Marks. You must be Fae. I'm a friend of your father's. I was at the Consulate in Izmir and as soon as I heard I got a helicopter down.'

'A helicopter. Is it still here?' an excited Fabrizzi asked.

Richard put his arm around him. 'It couldn't drop me here. I was let out at an army base not too far away.'

'Oh,' said the boy. He was disappointed.

Richard looked at Innessa. 'I am so sorry. But we'll get him back. No question.'

Innessa did not raise her eyes to Richard, she concentrated on Fabrizzi, and then she stood up as if she knew what was expected of her.

'Would you like some coffee, and some breakfast?' she asked Richard.

'Thank you.'

'You too, Fabrizzi. You must be strong for when Daddy comes home. Inspector?'

The Turkish policeman, infinitely relieved that some sort of order had been imposed by the arrival of the American, smiled his thanks. 'I am Chief Inspector Varh,' he said to Richard.

Fae sat down on the one chair in the room, leaving the settee to the two men. She knew enough of game playing to understand that this would give her a status, and she had the feeling she was going to need all the advantages she could get.

The policeman acknowledged her with a nod of his head, then turned his back and spoke directly to Richard.

'I believe the abductors are Kurds. They are vicious, unprincipled terrorists who would stop at nothing. They are probably holding Mr Whiteman hostage whilst some trial or another is going on.'

'And when the trial is over . . .?' Fae said.

'They will see there is no point in holding Mr Whiteman.' He continued to make his remarks to the American.

Fae spoke again, determined to make the policeman acknowledge her.

'You said they were unprincipled terrorists. Are you saying they will kill him?'

He twisted around to face her. The contempt in the hard brown eyes was obvious.

'Miss Whiteman, I am sure you are very distressed. Why don't you go and help your stepmother prepare some breakfast? It will be easier for you.'

'You're talking about my father. You can't possibly expect me to leave the room. Mr Marks is a family friend, but I'm his daughter.'

'Mr Marks is a member of the American Government,' Inspector Varh responded quickly.

'No, I am not with the Government. I am a lowly body at the Embassy. Commercial attaché,' interjected Richard.

Fae wanted to be polite to Richard Marks – he was obviously a close family friend, but she needed to make it clear that the Turkish police had to inform her what was happening, not anybody else.

'Mr Marks may be with the Embassy, but, Inspector, as my father's daughter . . .'

'As your father's daughter you are obviously concerned, but you know nothing of the ways of Turkey. Should you wish to get your father back alive, you must let us deal with the situation as we see fit.' He got up from the settee and walked towards the door. 'Do try and control yourself, Miss Whiteman,' he said, and before Fae could say anything more he clicked the door shut behind him.

Enraged, Fae got up from her own chair, ready to run after the Turk, but Richard put his hand on her arm, detaining her.

'I understand how you must feel,' he said, 'but it won't help, getting mad with the Turkish police.'

'I actually don't know how I feel,' Fae said. She needed to get out of the room, out of the house. She felt as if the walls were closing in on her. 'Excuse me,' she said, but as she spoke Innessa arrived with a tray full of hot coffee and warm rolls.

'Cara, are you all right?' she said, putting the tray down. She moved towards her taller stepdaughter.

'I'm OK.' Fae had to smile at her – how must she be feeling? 'I just need to be on my own for a moment.'

She didn't wait for an answer, just continued on her way out.

She walked to the beach where, just the day before, she and Sam and Fabrizzi had swum in the deep turquoise water. She loved to watch her father swim, he cut through the water with such ease, each stroke neat and precise, so unlike the man himself who admitted that he lived by instinct rather than order.

'It's what you feel, Fae,' he always told her. 'That's the only thing that matters, because that's what you are.'

She choked against unexpected tears. She glanced at her watch, it was 9.15 A.M. Most of the holiday makers would be getting up. Soon the long white beach would be dotted with umbrellas and towels and mattresses. She would go then – she didn't want to face anyone. Sam, her master magician, her father . . . the man who fixed her life, the man who made everything all right, had been kidnapped. Why? Who would do that? Where was he? And the worst question of all, was he safe? She felt sick with fear for him.

The terrible part was that they had only come to Kuşadasi because Fae had run to her father, as she always did, because her life was a mess. Sam had said he was going to sort her out. Sort her out – that was a joke, it was he that needed help now

. . . he could be shut up in a cell, or worse. Oh God, no – she mustn't think about it. She had to get him back, it was better to think of that, but how? Who was going to help her? Sam was the only one she could ever rely on.

Fae didn't live in Turkey with Sam, she lived in London where, after an adolescence spent in a girls' boarding school and a coming of age at an English redbrick university she earned her living in the film industry. She wanted to produce her own feature films, she wanted that very badly indeed. But she wasn't sure she was good enough, so she made an image for herself – a creative woman, a woman of energy. She hoped that in that way, like the hand that fits the glove, she would slip into it with ease.

None of this was far from the reality of what she really was, but Fae was unaware that flowering can not be bought superficially – it is an organic growth, it has to come from within. So on the night she saw her lover with his wife she turned back into the little girl who needed her Daddy.

Nick Newman was a television director. They had met when she was just twenty-three. He was thirty then, married, with two children. Shocked by an unbidden passion for each other, the loving was to be only 'this once'; but it survived the layers of guilt and longings, even coped with the birth of the third child, a conception he did not admit to until another 'friend' passed on the happy news. Fae should have ended it then, or Nick should have ended it. They tried, and stayed apart from one another until Fae, weak with yearning for him, and Nick, because he did love her, succumbed to their wanting. He told Fae in the agony of the bittersweet coupling, 'We have to stop. I am going to hurt everyone I care about, I am going to hurt you. I can't leave them, they have to come first. And you deserve more than I can give you.'

Fae didn't care, caught in such a love she would take what she could when she could. She made rules for herself. Never expect a future. His wife comes first. She must never intrude on their time. Unaware of how much damage she was doing to herself, she held on to him and wouldn't allow herself to think about Sally, the wife who shared his nights.

The lovers had been together in an early evening of snatched excitement when tongues searched for flesh and caressed and licked and devoured, when fingers stroked and tantalized. At the hour when the subtle shift from commerce to exploitation changes the feel of Soho, they parted with promises of 'soon' ringing in both their ears.

'I'm sorry, I have to run,' he said, his eyes lingering over her, heating her up. 'Take care of yourself.' A dry kiss on the lips. 'I'll call.' He turned on his heel – a tall man, a good looking man with blond curly hair and a slender body. She wanted to ask when, but he was gone, lost in the people of Soho at dusk.

Fae could have gone back to her flat in the Docklands which she shared with her closest friend, Emily, but Emily was entertaining a new lover because Fae had assumed she would spend the evening with Nick.

From a phone box she rang two other friends, Tom and Helena, who saw her through all her traumas and mostly kept their tight-lipped disapproval of the married man to themselves. They were not at home. Not wanting to scour her Filofax she thought about a movie, but she couldn't face sitting alone in a cinema full of couples. She looked at her watch. Nine o'clock. She'd eat something and then go home. She called Emily to warn her.

'I'm sorry,' her flatmate said. 'That man is a shit.'

'He didn't say we could be together this evening. I just imagined we might. He probably had a meeting.'

'Will you be all right? I mean, I might go back to Jeremy's – after dinner.'

'Yes. I'll be fine,' Fae lied, hating the tight knot of envy that looped its loops. She wanted to cry. She didn't. She bought *Variety*, the trade journal of the entertainment industry, at one of the late-night shops and walked into a crowded Italian restaurant on the corner of Romilly Street. The head waiter eyed her as she waited to be seated. She wanted them to think she was a clever businesswoman grabbing a bite to eat after a heavy day, and wasn't that just what she was?

'Alone, signorina?' he asked.

'Alone. It's been a long day.'

He smiled, flirting.

She ordered pasta – fettucine alfredo – a salad and half a bottle of wine. She had drunk the first glass of her wine and was eating her fettucine when he walked past her table, hand in hand with an elegant blonde woman who matched his step with her own.

Fae couldn't help but watch him. He sat close to his wife, head on one side, a nice indulgent smile on his face. Fae felt sick and hurt.

'What about me?' she wanted to scream, but she had no rights. She was the baddie, the woman who wanted another woman's man. She couldn't eat any more. She had managed a coffee whilst she asked for the bill. Averting her eyes, she slipped out of the restaurant, into the dark night and then she cried.

She got back to her gorgeous flat, studiously ignored the remains of a dinner for two and avoided the low beam that ran across the centre of the huge living-room.

Without sitting down she had picked up the receiver and dialled her father, sobbing her loneliness.

'What do you expect from the man?' Sam bellowed. 'Either accept that your lover has a wife, or find a new lover. You had better get over here, sweetheart. We'll go to the coast, ten days with Innessa and Fabrizzi. We can swim and eat and drink – have a little fun, and then you and I are going to talk.'

She travelled in cream trousers and a cream jacket, her huge hold-all packed with a few holiday clothes, a lot of manuscripts and as many presents as she could fit in. There was the football outfit for Fabrizzi, a smoked salmon, all pink and plump in its sealed, airtight container, champagne – and the latest Tom Wolfe for her father. For Innessa she had bought perfume and a silk nightdress from Marks and Spencer. The bag weighed a ton. The strap, such a clever idea, the sales lady had told her, bit into her shoulder.

Fabrizzi came to Istanbul Airport with Sam. He threw himself at his big sister. When he was born, Fae was a third year English student at Manchester University, in love with Ralph, the leading light on the undergraduate newspaper, and not very sure about babies. But from the first time she saw Fabrizzi, she felt an extraordinary attachment. She had bent down, picked him up and told him she would be his friend forever. Sam had laughed at her.

'You are a sentimentalist, my darling.'

'Absolutely, and I learnt from you.'

The homecoming, for that was how Fae liked to think of it, was crowded with hugs and laughs and the presents. Innessa flaunted her silk nightdress and Sam unpeeled the smoked salmon. The ritual of carving it was left to Innessa who was better at that kind of thing. They were gathered in the little piece of America that Sam and Innessa had allowed to invade their apartment in one of the original wooden houses in Bebek, a beautiful part of Istanbul overlooking the Bosphorus, just down the hill from the University where Sam was a professor. There was a sink disposal unit, a double Westinghouse refrigerator and freezer, a microwave, a toaster and juice extractor, a food mixer, an electric can opener, a garbage crusher and a dishwasher, all fitted inside sleek white and black Italian units.

Fae, who was actually quite tired, and feeling the difference between a damp June day in England and the dry heat of Turkey, was sitting down on one of six black chairs that were positioned around an octagonal table. Her case was at her feet, her clothes and manuscripts littered around her. Innessa put them back in the case in an orderly fashion.

'I wish you lived with us,' said Fabrizzi, dancing around her.

'Fae does live with us,' Innessa said.

'Not all the time.'

'That's because I have my life in London. And you know I want you to come and stay with me. We could go to a football match.'

'Arsenal?' Fabrizzi yelled.

'Soon,' Innessa said. 'Soon he will be old enough.'

'I'm old enough now,' Fabrizzi said, and Innessa smiled at him indulgently.

'Will I have a room of my own, like you do here?' Fabrizzi asked Fae, jamming his mouth full of several slices of smoked salmon that his mother was carefully arranging on a platter.

'It's not big enough. You will have to share with me until I get a place of my own.'

'Or find a husband,' Innessa commented, carefully covering up the space that Fabrizzi had made on the plate.

'I can't see myself married,' Fae said quietly.

'Why not, Princess?' Sam asked. He was opening the champagne and pouring it into three tulip-shaped glasses. As he fetched some orange juice from the refrigerator, and a tumbler from the glass cupboard above the pristine white sink, Fae replied, 'Maybe it's because the men I want don't want me.'

'That's because you don't really want a man in your life at all, so you choose the ones that you are sure will reject you,' Innessa commented.

'And why would I do that?' Fae watched her father as he poured a little champagne into the tumbler and filled it up with a lot of orange juice for Fabrizzi. He used to do that for her when she was little.

'Because you are happy the way you are,' Innessa said lightly.

Fae turned to look at her stepmother. Innessa's blonde beauty never ceased to amaze her. When Sam had first married her, Fae was just seventeen, and had had to admit to a certain jealousy – but it seemed that Sam was always careful never to kiss her in front of his daughter, and never to hold her hand.

'Did you mind?' Fae asked Innessa, after she had fallen in love with Nick.

'There was not much I could do about it. You and Sam, you have an exclusive relationship – all of us are on the outside when you are together.'

'But it isn't like that now. I have my own life. And Sam has you and Fabrizzi.'

'Yes, he does. But it's probably a good thing for you and Sam that you live in England.'

'Probably,' Fae said, and she laughed.

Later, in the bedroom that had been hers when she was a child, Sam came to talk to her. It was a white room with a wonderful carpet woven in rich brick reds. She had purchased it herself at one of the hundreds of little shops in the Grand Bazaar at Istanbul, negotiating the price over an apple tea with a courteous but wily seller who knew the price she would pay from the moment she walked in. The window, like all the windows of the house, was flanked by wooden shutters. Through its clear panes she could look out over the straits of the Bosphorus and dream her dreams. When she was little she would lie in her bed whilst Sam told her a goodnight story, which was always a tale of a beautiful young princess in an act of great bravery – usually rescuing a handsome prince in distress, locked into the tower of the great grey Rameli Fortress that had once guarded the entrance to Istanbul. The prince would want to marry the princess but as often as not she would decline, choosing to return to her wise teacher.

'Perhaps that's why I never wanted to get married.'

'Until Nick,' said Sam kindly.

'No, I can't marry Nick. He has a wife and children. Our relationship is based on the fact that they come first. That's the way it is.' Fae didn't look at Sam, but bent down and examined her instep.

'He's using you.'

'No, no, he's not. I know the score. He's made it clear. It's my choice.' She made herself look up at her father.

'But even so, you have to stop seeing him. It's not good for you – it makes cheats of everyone, and you are sold short. You can stay away from him, Fae. It'll burn, it'll hurt, but I'll be there to see you through it.'

That was their last real conversation. Fae couldn't help the wave of self pity and fear that racked her. She lowered her head and gave in to the tears. She sat, her knees clasped tightly to her chest, her head curled over – a black-clad doll on a white beach. She stayed like that until the hot sun burnt through her thin T-shirt and the perspiration wet her long hair. Even then she wouldn't have left if it weren't for the first well meaning intruder.

'Excuse me – are you all right?' It was a female voice, with the heavy accent of a German speaker exercising her English vowels. They saw the woman on the beach every day. She usually made a point of talking to them and Sam was always friendly, but then Sam was a friendly man.

Fae couldn't deal with idle conversation, however kind, but even so she didn't want to be rude so she managed an 'excuse me' as she stood up. She walked quickly over the hot sand of the beach. The clip clop of her feet sent little sprays flying either side of her. She made her way up a small dry mud path between wild uncut grass. Worn bare by many feet it led directly to the holiday villa which Sam had been assured looked directly on to the beach. Well it did, almost, apart from the small, normally deserted road that lay between the grass and the house. Now the road was packed with cars of all descriptions, some police vehicles, two limousines, several taxis – all dwarfed by an impressive Lincoln, low, sleek and black, flying the Stars and Stripes, parked right outside the front door. Inside it was a driver who looked neither to the right nor to the left. A group of men and women, journalists, she presumed, were also gathered outside the house. She would have said, 'You were quick', if she had been able.

'That's the daughter,' someone said.

'Hey, Miss Whiteman, what is happening?'

'Can you tell us anything?'

'No, no, I'm afraid I can't,' she said.

She made her way into the house. Innessa was sitting on the floor playing a card game with Fabrizzi. A bullet-headed man with a crew cut and an obvious walkie-talkie earpiece glanced at her, establishing her identity. Richard stood in attendance on three men. Two were obviously Turkish, dressed in well cut suits, both with sleek dark hair, the smaller wore a moustache. They, with Richard, were grouped attentively around a third man who lolled against the wall, his arms folded in front of him, shoulders hunched beneath a lightweight black cotton jacket above grey trousers and a white shirt. At Fae's entrance the man straightened up, and extended his hand. He had silver grey hair, a good face, tanned with wide cheek-bones, green eyes, a good mouth.

'Miss Whiteman. My name is Bob Brockwell. I cannot tell you how appalled I am at what has happened here. I can assure you that we will all,' he gestured to the two Turks who nodded gravely, 'bring your father home.'

He was a strong, confident man, it marked him – Fae recognized it. For the first time since her father's abduction she momentarily lost her sense of panic and held on to his hand for possibly a little longer than she should have.

'Are you with the Embassy?' she asked.

'No, I'm a visiting fireman,' he glanced briefly at Richard, 'but as soon as I heard I wanted to come and find out what was going on for myself.' He smiled at her.

'I've known your Dad for a lot of years you know. We were at college together. He didn't take much notice of me then. He was a track star and I just about played basketball.' Fae doubted that Bob Brockwell 'just about played' anything . . . but she nodded politely, knowing that he was playing the right game. As long as Bob Brockwell got her father back, she could cope.

And cope she did – at least for the next twenty-four hours, until the kidnappers released a video tape of Sam.

* * *

Richard had decided they should return to Istanbul. 'You'll be more comfortable at home. And we'll make sure the kidnappers know where you are.'

To that end he organized a press conference at a four-star holiday complex that the Whiteman family had pointedly avoided as not being part of the Turkey that suited them.

They hadn't even gone into Kuşadasi much. Sam didn't like the pretty town that had once merely been a stopover for travellers on their way to Ephesus. Now it was a hive of tourist activity that had little to do with a pilgrimage to one of the great cities of ancient times. The leather shops and the carpet shops and antique bric-à-brac were there to lure the passengers from cruise ships with the promise of a 'good deal' and an apple tea.

Innessa and Fae were paraded in front of the world's media, but not Fabrizzi: it would have been too much for him. Seated under the glare of television arc lights, behind a battery of microphones at a table covered by a green baize cloth, the continual click of shutters and the cutting brilliance of the flashes orchestrated the barrage of questions . . .

'Where were you when it happened?'

'Have you any idea who might have done it and why?'

'How is your little boy?'

'Were any guns fired?'

'Did they harm you?'

'Have there been any demands yet?'

And then a man from NBC asked, 'Have you any idea why your husband was kidnapped, Mrs Whiteman? Was he CIA?' Innessa looked flummoxed. Richard cleared his throat, but before he could speak Fae replied to the question. 'Of course my father isn't a spy. He's a professor. I can't, nor can my stepmother, understand why anyone would want to kidnap him. All we can do,' Fae continued, deliberately lowering her voice – years of working in television production had not gone amiss, 'is to appeal directly to the kidnappers. Please, we have no quarrel with you, just let my father come home to us.'

It was calculated, her appeal, but as she spoke, Fae felt her throat close up. For what seemed the thousandth time she asked the same question. Where was Sam, was he all right and – the worst question of all, did she dare even ask it? – was he even still alive?

Innessa reached across the table and took Fae's hand. 'I have an eight-year-old son,' she added. 'He wants his Daddy.'

There was nothing more to add, the hacks had the day's headline.

Richard brought the press conference to a close.

'As I am sure you realize, the family are under enormous pressure. We ask for your good will. They are going back to Istanbul today. If you could plant that in your copy it would be helpful. We want everyone to know where they are.'

'But it's political,' a CBS man said. 'They won't be dealing with the family.'

'I've told you,' Fae said, leaning forward to emphasize her words, unaware that her tanned skin glowed under the open neck of her white silk shirt. 'He isn't political at all. He is just being used.'

As they walked out of the dining-room which had been used for the press conference, Fae noticed some children swimming in the hotel's pool. A father pulled a small boy away from the edge. The child cried, the man picked him up and comforted him. Fae averted her eyes, she couldn't bear the sudden stabbing hurt at the sight of a father comforting his child. Someone – a woman, elegant, with dark blonde hair, a wonderful face, kind but strong, was watching her. The woman leaned forward as if to comfort Fae. She had never seen the woman before, but there was something about her, a compassion perhaps, that made Fae want to respond to her. Before she could put her hand out to the woman, a rifle butt separated them. The woman was pushed back. There was a lot of shouting and confusion. Richard and some other Americans hustled her away.

'What's going on?'

'It's no problem. The woman is actually the wife of the owner of the hotel. She's OK.'

'I know that. I could see it in her face.'

'You can't trust those kind of reactions any more, Fae. You just never know. You have to be very careful now.'

It was then that the real horror of the situation actually hit Fae. She felt sick. She turned her head, looking for the woman, anxious to see she was all right. And funnily enough, wanting some sort of eye contact. But she couldn't see her, the press were crowding after them, their cameras snip-snapping, their voices braying this and that, the police herding them on. Who were the victims now?

They flew from Izmir, but there was no waiting around in hot and crowded departure bays. They drove, with Turkish police as outriders, along the dual carriageway that sliced through the lush countryside. As they travelled from Kuşadasi the crumbling clay-red soil and its clumps of green foliage gave way to small sand-coloured villages dominated by their mosques and by the little cafés where the men sat and talked, and the village girls, their heads covered with checked kerchiefs, worked the fields, tending the coming harvests. They passed a huge military complex, its gates guarded, its fences sprouting iron bars, and all the time the rich blue sky over Turkey presided over a relentless heat. At the road block leading to the airport, the white police tanks that loomed threateningly over any would-be traveller gave way, and the convoy sped past the steel-faced men with their rifles.

As they drew up to the departure building, Fae noticed the queues of tourists waiting to get through the security check at the doors of the airport. They would have been part of that jostling line if Sam hadn't been kidnapped. Instead they were taken to a side door. A courteous and very kind Turkish Airlines stewardess took Fabrizzi by the hand and ushered them into the VIP lounge. There was tea in the tulip-shaped glasses, or coffee to be had – served in a little bronze long-handled jug, the thick sweet grains swirling to the bottom. There wasn't a long wait, a private plane was at their disposal. If she had been in the mood, Fae would have appreciated the studied comforts which contrasted so strongly with the undignified rush to the plane on the usual flight to Istanbul when the prayers of the devout performing their religious obligations did little to compensate for the absence of life-jackets.

The exhausted women and bemused child were glad to be going home. They anticipated a return to some sort of order, and perhaps there was even a feeling that the nightmare would end once they were back in the normality of their own surroundings. However, when they actually reached their home they found it swarming with activity. Men were reconnecting telephone wires, placing the right devices in the right places to ensure that if the kidnappers made contact the call could be traced. Policemen were milling around the house: one stood right by the front door. The press were already camped on the other side of the road and, even worse, a woman from the American Embassy had installed herself. Innessa and Fae were told that she was just a helper, there to answer the phone if it rang. Fae had no idea how Innessa would cope with the intrusions. She found it horrific.

'How are you going to stand all this?' Fae said.

Innessa shrugged and eased her shoulders and Fae could see how tired she was. She wanted to put her hand on Innessa's shoulders but the Italian woman was already taking Fabrizzi to bed.

'Shall I help you?' Fae asked.

'No, thank you. Sit down, have a drink – and please pour me a brandy.'

'I'll do it,' Richard said as he carried the bags in from the car. Fae wished he'd go away. She wanted to sit and talk with Innessa. Her stepmother was smiling at the American.

'Thank you, Richard, we're so grateful you are here.'

Fae shrugged, she tightened her lips and tried not to mind – after all, Richard was a family friend.

'Goodnight darling,' she called to Fabrizzi. She saw Fabrizzi stumble. Innessa bent down and picked him up.

'He's whacked,' Fae said to Richard.

'It's a terrible trauma for him.'

'Yes. It is,' she replied quietly. She was worried about her little brother.

Richard walked to a slim black unit that housed books and records and drinks. Fae remembered that when her mother lived in the house there had been a mahogany glass-fronted cabinet on that wall. The room that was now the palest pink and grey with elegant black wood once had squashy settees in pale green and comfortable armchairs in soft rose. Huge bowls of glorious multicoloured flowers and silver framed photographs had crowded every spare surface. In the mornings, when the house was cleaned, the day's papers would be placed by the chair that Sam used. By the end of the day they would be scattered by his feet, several books – his latest reading – would be on the floor too. Once Innessa redecorated the house, Fae noticed, Sam's newspapers and Sam's books were confined to his study and the flowers in the room were always white roses – just a few, carefully arranged in a sculptured pale pink vase on the black bookshelves above the black cupboard where Richard now found the drinks. Richard poured two brandies, and then asked Fae what she would like.

'The same please,' she said, feeling her loneliness.

After about ten minutes, Innessa joined them.

'Fabrizzi is asleep,' she told Fae.

'Innessa, what can I do for you? I feel utterly helpless.'

'So do I. We just have to try and be strong for each other,' Innessa replied. She took Fae's hand briefly. She had cool slender fingers. Fae could feel her heavy gold wedding ring. She hoped Innessa would sit next to her on the pink sofa but her stepmother moved away and sat, legs crossed neatly, next to Richard on the opposite side of the low black coffee table.

'Surely we must hear something soon,' Fae said.

And they did. Some three-quarters of an hour later a motor-cyclist roared into the overcrowded road where the Whiteman house was situated. The driver, without slowing his speed, tossed a package directly at the front door. The Turkish police fired their guns, the hacks yelled and ran for cover, the cameras clicked into activity – too late.

The package contained a video tape of a statement from the kidnappers. They announced that they had kidnapped Samuel Whiteman because he was an American spy and would be tried for the torture of three of their compatriots, students at Bosphorus University in Istanbul, and the murder of one of them.

The faces of the young people, Ayala Kaplan, Mustafa Doganay and Ali Keles, who had been arrested by the Political Branch of the Turkish Police, accused of membership of an organization trying to establish the domination of one social class over others (Article 141 of the Turkish Penal Code) and taken to DAL, Ankara Police Headquarters, appeared on the screen. Nothing more had been heard of them until, several months later, it had been announced that Ayala regrettably killed herself – the two boys, it was claimed, were on hunger strike so their families were denied visits. Samuel Whiteman admitted that he had passed their names on to the police and they had videotaped his confession.

Both the women watched in horror as a man, still blindfolded, who but twenty-four hours previously had been powerful, energetic, appeared on the screen, unshaven and crumpled, his voice shaking as he spoke: 'I confess to being a spy in the employ of the Central Intelligence Agency of the United States.'

How could that happen? How could it be that in one day a man could change so dramatically and admit to being a CIA spy? It was madness, where was the hero? Sam had always been a hero to Fae. It wasn't any particular event, it was just the way he was. Oh, Fae knew he was a good teacher, he was very careful and protective of his students, they were always in the house. And he wrote books, he was a minor celebrity – people had heard of him. After he published a contentious tract analysing Christopher Marlowe's *Doctor Faustus* in relation to his supposed atheism, the BBC devoted a whole programme to him. All that made her very proud of him, but it was the way Sam was to her that made her value him.

Ever since she was a little girl, Fae knew that Sam was the provider, and Sam made the decisions. He did all that very well. He made her feel safe – just as long as Sam was there nothing could really go wrong. Even after she grew up she still turned to him. She was Sam's princess. But where was that father now? 'They must have kept him in that blindfold. He couldn't bear that, he was locked up in a cupboard when he was a child with his eyes taped shut, so he could never stand anything on them.' Fae knew she was burbling, but she had to explain – perhaps to herself most of all.

'I know that,' Innessa said gently. Her face was white, her hands were shaking a little.

'But I don't understand why he said he was CIA. Is that what they do, force people to say things that aren't true?' Fae knew her voice was loud, she could hear it herself, but there was nothing she could do about it.

CHAPTER TWO

The very worst day of Fae Whiteman's life – until the kidnapping of course – was when she learnt that her parents were going to get a divorce and she was to go to live in England with her mother. She had just celebrated her twelfth birthday.

There hadn't been any monumental happenings. It was simply that her mother, Barbara, finally decided that she couldn't live with Sam any more. She always admitted he was a charismatic man, but over the years the inflection in her tone had changed from awed love to indulgent passion and finally to fatigue – she no longer even cared about the other women. There had always been other women. In the beginning it had hurt a lot.

Barbara missed her English way of life, she missed England itself. Sam would never contemplate living there. He hated the rain. Nor would he live in America. 'It has no past, and I need a past to have a future,' he told the doting Barbara in their months of courtship in Greece.

They had met in Athens, at a café in the Plaka area where teeming tourists mingled in tiny streets and ate at crowded cafés under raffia roofs draped in vine. Barbara was a law graduate, Sam a newly arrived assistant lecturer in English at Athens University.

Fae was born ten months after they had met, and just six months after a pretty wedding had been solemnized at the English Church. From the moment of her birth she was cherished by her doting father. When she whimpered in the night it was Sam who took her into his side of the bed. It was Sam who helped her take her first steps, it was Sam who picked her up when she fell, it was Sam who taught her to swim, it was Sam who fed her delicious morsels of kebabs and baklava when she wouldn't eat – sweeping away the sensible minced chicken and carrot and potato, without salt, that her mother thought best for her.

As she grew up, Sam stayed constant. He banished the fears of the first day at school, the first pony ride, the first exams. As long as Sam was with her, Fae never understood the meaning of the word 'can't'.

But then Fae went to England and her mother claimed dominance in her life and the gut-rotting English weather robbed her of her father. He wrote, of course, and even telephoned. She spent her holidays with him, but she no longer lived with him.

In time Barbara married a nice Englishman, Max Claremont, and lived in a gracious house near Godalming in Surrey where apple blossom framed the house in Spring, and roses bloomed in Summer.

Barbara flourished in Godalming and Fae pretended not to mind the gut-rotting rain.

When Fae was eighteen, Sam told her to find a lover.

'It's time, Fae,' he said.

Fae searched, and finally Fae slept with Matt, a fragile young sculptor, hot foot from oppression in South Africa. Clever hands aroused, a hard mouth excited, but when he entered her she stopped feeling. It was the same with Hal, an American law student, and with François, a French actor. None of them had the power of Sam, that was what she was looking for – she knew it.

As a young woman of twenty-five she examined her father's influence over her life. 'I think I'm fixated by him,' she told Emily. Emily was different from Fae – she didn't have Fae's sensual earthly quality. Emily was a girl with luminous charcoal-coloured eyes and mouse-brown hair cut very short. She was thin and pale and wore suits cut like a man's. She and Fae had met at school – an establishment of some repute near Godalming. Their friendship was forged over a mutual loathing of mashed potatoes and steamed puddings. They quickly learnt to pool their resources: Emily did Fae's maths homework and Fae wrote Emily's essays. It was Sam who warned them both, when Fae took Emily on a holiday to meet him, that they ought to impart some of their skills to the other, or else the truth would come out in an exam. They taught each other well enough.

But natural preferences always surface, and when Emily went to work in the city, Fae joined a publishing house. The excitement of working with words evaporated all too quickly. No one told her that the work had less to do with the art form and more to do with deal making and marketing, and brushing writers' egos whilst correcting their grammar. She did well and lived the obligatory lifestyle of a rising young editor – mostly late nights over badly written manuscripts. Fae stayed the course for two years, then she went into the film industry and discovered real paranoia where grown men and women pursue the task of make-believe with varying degrees of integrity but always with passion. That's where Fae felt at home.

When she met Nick she fell totally and utterly in love with him. He filled her waking moments and even her sleeping ones. She did her job as well as she could, not just because of her own needs but also because that was something she could share with Nick. She diligently read scripts for as many people as she could, typed her reports and prayed that her judgement was right. Eventually she was rewarded by a job with a real tycoon, running the development side of his film company. In America she would have been called a 'D Girl'. It was said it was just a step away from being a producer – after all, the D Girl scratches and scours to find the new story, the seed to spawn the next blockbuster – but the D Girl doesn't have to find the money.

Work gave the shape to Fae's life, Nick gave it the magic, Sam gave it the security. And now there was no Sam, and without him the structure would crumple. She wanted Nick, but the immorality of wanting the man, the uselessness of it, hurt her.

And so, on the night her father confessed to being a CIA spy, she would not be held by the man she loved, she could not be private in her father's house, nor could she even go out of the house without attracting the attention of the world's press camped beyond the walls.

She sat in a chair opposite Maise Montgomery, the appointed guardian of their house. Maise, who was making a quilt, looked up and smiled, her needle flashing in and out of one piece of fabric which she interwove with another piece of fabric. Fae watched silently. She herself didn't sew, in fact she had no hobbies. She wondered if she ought to try to use a needle, maybe she could make a tapestry, it might calm her. She fidgeted with her hair, and wished the woman sitting opposite her with her quilt on her knee would go away and not keep smiling at her. But Maise Montgomery wasn't going anywhere.

Earlier that evening Fae had spoken at length with her mother, and Barbara was coming to be with her. She was glad – even if she did not share the same intimacies with Barbara that she did with Sam. But Barbara was still in England, and Fae did not want to be alone. Both Richard and Innessa had gone to their rooms early. Fae glanced at her watch and wondered if Innessa was asleep. She would go and see and perhaps, if she were awake, Fae would make them some tea and they could talk. She padded quietly down the corridor; she did not want to disturb Fabrizzi.

The night was punctured by the glare of the sounds and lights of the temporary squatters in the road outside. She gritted her teeth against the intrusion. She knocked on the door, there was no response. She decided not to knock again and simply opened the door. In the gloom of the bedroom she made out the bed and, quickly enough, the two figures silently writhing . . .

'Yes,' the woman's voice said, 'yes . . .'

Fae turned from the room and walked out, shutting the door behind her. She didn't slam it, but the click was decisive . . . she saw, under the crack, that the light had gone on.

She felt her cheeks burn, she was embarrassed – and angry, she couldn't help herself. Sam was somewhere – who knew where, in what state? – and his wife was in bed with his friend. Fae knew Sam was hardly the faithful type, but she was sure that if the positions were reversed and Innessa had been kidnapped, Sam wouldn't have invited anyone into his bed.

She meant to walk straight back to her own bedroom; instead she went to Fabrizzi's room. The boy lay under the covers, his head under the pillow, but he was not asleep – his silent, heaving shoulders gave him away. She lay down on his bed, her head next to his.

'Oh Fae, where is Daddy?' Fabrizzi cried.

'I don't know darling, but he'll be found, I promise.'

'I want him,' the little boy said.

'So do I,' said Fae.

At breakfast the next morning, Fae found it difficult to look at

Innessa, but she tried to be civil – for Fabrizzi's sake. Richard did not present himself. Fae was glad about that.

She spent her day waiting, she waited all day for the kidnappers to call. She managed to avoid conversation with Innessa, she managed to avoid Richard completely. People came, members of the Embassy staff, the Turkish police, the men from the foreign ministry . . . There was some talk about a hostage negotiator but Fae left it all to the others. She couldn't concentrate, her nerves were stretched tight. She was anxious, her heart felt like a bird trapped inside her, fluttering its wings to get out – to be free. She kept looking out of the windows – almost as if she were waiting for someone.

At five o'clock, Fae could stand it no more. She had to get out of the house, even though she knew the journalists were still there. She could hear them. She wondered if Fabrizzi might like to go up to the University: they could walk under the trees, find a space where they could kick a ball – it would be good for him. For the first time that day she spoke to Innessa, who was playing poker with Richard, and Maise Montgomery.

'May I take Fabrizzi to play some football?'

'I don't think he should go out, Fae. The press will hound him – don't you think it's better for him to be protected from all of that?' It was Richard who answered.

'Are you our protectors or our jailers?' Fae snapped.

'Have you looked outside?' Innessa asked.

'No, I haven't wanted my face all over the front pages.'

'Exactly.'

They were right: it would be madness to let Fabrizzi out of the house. Fae let the breath out of her mouth slowly. 'Of course, I didn't think it through properly. But even so, Fabrizzi can't stay cooped up in the house all the time,' she said.

'I know. That's why I am taking him back to Italy. My father has a summer house near Positano. He will be safe there.'

'Is Richard going with you?'

'No, of course not.' Innessa's voice was hard, discouraging any more questions.

Fae actually didn't mind, she wasn't prepared for confrontation, she couldn't deal with any more emotion.

The telephone rang. There was a sudden silence. For a

moment no one moved, no one spoke, and then Maise Montgomery reacted – she answered it.

'Hello. Just a minute please.' The receiver was held out to Fae.

'It's for you. Emily?'

Fae was shaking, her heart seemed to have come out of her chest. Did she mind that it was just Emily? Yes, she supposed she did, but even so her friend's voice was a comfort.

'Fae, how are you?'

'Just glad to hear your voice. I should've called you.'

'No, you shouldn't. I can't imagine how you must feel. Do you want me to come?'

'No, but thank you. The house is crawling with people. Most of them CIA.'

'Yes.'

'What do you mean "Yes"?'

'I mean it's to be expected, isn't it?'

'He isn't a spy, Emily. They made him say that.'

'I know. Everyone's called, they all . . .'

'Everyone?' The tight bands binding Fae's chest snapped a notch tighter.

'Yes, everyone. Nick called late last night.'

'What did he say?'

'Just that he was thinking about you.'

When she finished the telephone call, Fae put the receiver back on its cradle and walked up the stairs to her bedroom. She carefully shut the door behind her. She lay down on her bed and reached out to Nick. He nourished her, made her whole and warm, even as the pleasures mingled with the hurt of the separation from him. For that brief moment, there was no room for anyone else – not even Sam.

In a small, dank stone room with a concrete floor, Sam Whiteman switched about and turned on an iron bed. Still blindfolded, the edges held tight with sticky tape that hurt, he shouted out to no one, for no one was there: 'For God's sake, please someone just take the blindfold off, please!'

His knees still ached from hours of kneeling and his ears still vibrated from the high-pitched music that had assailed him through earphones someone had clamped to his head.

His kidnappers were a small group of dissident students. Three of their number, two men and a girl, sat behind the closed door of his room and drank Coca Cola from bottles.

'I didn't like what we had to do to him,' said one of them, a thin, tanned boy with a sharp nose.

'We had to disorientate him quickly,' the girl replied.

'How long is this going on?' the same student continued. His name was Adnan Karkaus. He was the son of a policeman – he came from the south-eastern part of Turkey. His father's job had secured him a place at the prestigious Bosphorus University, but neither his father nor his father's employers knew that he was a Maoist, originally attracted to the illegal Turkish Communist Party as a protest against his repressive father. He'd been an easy convert when he'd first arrived at Bosphorus University and had found himself out of step with the sons and daughters of the upper classes.

'Let them all sweat some more. And as for Whiteman, he's weak, that one. A blindfold and a kick and he quivers like a baby,' replied the other man. Fae would've known him, he was the man who hit her in the stomach. His name was Hayri Gurbuz and he was an engineering student with a politically active background. His father had been arrested in 1981 after the junta had taken power. He had been accused of being a member of the Communist Party and tortured. The irony, Hayri always told his friends, was that his father would have committed the same atrocities himself, had he been in power. He taught Hayri that ideology always justifies the means. As it was he died in prison and he was turned into a humanitarian martyr. His son followed his course. The men's emotions were easy to read. Hayri was tense – his voice was sharp, and he kept moving his position on his chair, shifting one way then the other. It seemed he had difficulty in sitting in one place, but even so he kept his shoulders straight and his fingers were relaxed, as if he were trying to keep up an appearance.

Adnan, however, made no attempt to hide his anxieties: 'Look, I don't think we should just sit around here and do nothing. We should move him. Someone may have seen us bring him in here. Perhaps we should force the issue,' he said.

It was the girl who spoke, her voice cutting through the nervous blather. 'We don't do anything yet, Adnan, we wait for a while. Let everything simmer down. They'll bring in a hostage negotiator, we wait for him – and then we begin.'

She was sitting quietly, dark, with thick hair, and blue eyes. Faroud Boaz was also studying at the Bosphorus University – she was allowed to do that because her brother Rashid was a student there too, but for her it was just a token law degree, her father had already planned a marriage for her, to a relative of a cabinet minister, close enough to secure the presence of the Prime Minister at the wedding. Faroud always appeared to be a dutiful daughter, because it suited her – the less people knew of her real self the better. She made her jump to the creed for herself. There was no love affair with a man, no idealistic teacher, she simply felt that Maoism offered a better way of life, particularly for a woman – there was freedom from exploitation.

It was Faroud who introduced her brother Rashid to her thinking. Rashid, a handsome man with eyes bluer than hers, and skin whiter than hers, and jet black hair shinier than hers, was the true love of her life. Faroud adored him, and she made him head of the cell, arranging important journeys to see important people in far off places – just to fuel his ambitions. The coup of coups was when she discovered a sympathetic friend at the very head of the University itself . . . a man whom Rashid Boaz respected. With his blessing the little group prospered, they didn't do anything very dramatic, just attended meetings and published pamphlets when they felt it was necessary. Then Sam Whiteman discovered their existence and they ceased to operate. When three members of another group were kidnapped – and Ayala was killed – it was Faroud, acting on her own, who decided that Sam Whiteman had to be the bargaining point for the release of the other two. She was gambling that the kidnapping would make its mark in Turkey, and in America.

But it was not just America and Turkey who found the Whiteman case interesting. In Whitehall, London, the home of the British mandarins, one of their number, Martin Godfrey, perused the Whiteman report on his desk.

'I don't think we should leave all this to the cousins,' he told his private secretary. 'I'd like to have one of our people in place.'

The press were interested too: the tabloids wanted exclusive interviews, so they sent their hounds in.

* * *

At nine o'clock that evening a British Airways Boeing-747 landed at Istanbul airport. One of its passengers – an elegant grey-haired woman with a fine face and startling blue eyes – collected her hand baggage together: a small alligator case containing her make-up and a collection of short stories, and a matching handbag. She excused herself as she manipulated her way past a man of about thirty-five who had brown hair and glasses and who had been particularly charming to her on the flight. The man watched carefully as she walked over to an air hostess who was obviously waiting for her. He overheard the hostess say, 'Good luck, Mrs Claremont. I hope you have good news soon.'

'Thank you.'

The young man waited until the passenger disembarked. The waiting car had swept into position, and the policeman had jumped out of the front seat and opened the back door for her. As the car swung away from the plane the man smiled at the air hostesses.

'Thanks for a nice flight. You treated us very well.'

'It's our job, sir.'

'You were kind to Barbara . . . It's very hard for her. Max is very concerned that she is here on her own.'

'Are you a friend?'

'I'm actually a friend of Fae's.'

'Poor thing. Terrible strain for her.'

'Yes. It is. I'm just grateful her mother is with her. I'll join them later myself.'

'The house must be under siege from journalists I would expect.'

'That's why Max wanted Barbara to stay at the hotel.'

'Yes, and I think he's right. And the Hilton is a good place, I told her that I know people are snobbish about Hiltons, but I like them. At least the plumbing works.'

'Absolutely,' he said, smiling. He had realized that the air hostess was a safe bet for a bit of indiscretion as soon as they'd boarded the plane. It was her assumed intimacy with Barbara Claremont that had told him.

He waited till he was through customs before he made a telephone call to his night editor.

'Mike, Simon Palling here,' he said by way of an introduction.

'The mother is staying at the Hilton. I'll check myself in there and see what I can do.'

'Lucky bastard. All that luxury is going to really bother you, isn't it?'

'Well, you know me, I'll try and cope. It'll be hard though.'

Simon Palling replaced the receiver and dialled another number. When the phone was answered he tutted, it was an answering machine. He waited for his own message to end, then he talked.

'Katie, it's me. The mother's at the Hilton, so I'll be staying there. Give me a call when you get in. Listen, do me a favour, you know the daughter works in films? Just as a long shot, that old girlfriend of yours who's married to that director, what's his name . . . Nick Newman, give her a call, will you? They may just know her. Oh, listen, I spoke to Blackie before I left, the fireplace isn't in properly, it's not symmetric. If you look at the . . .' The tape clicked. He'd run out of time. Should he ring his wife back? No, he'd tell her about the fireplace when he spoke to her. He smiled to himself, picturing his wife holding a gin and tonic in one hand and a cigarette in another, listening to him droning on, as she called it, about the renovations to their flat. It was lucky that he knew that her apparent lack of interest was part of their particular game of marriage.

Katie was a journalist too, working in features. She was good, very good. He had to work to keep the edge.

By the time Simon Palling had reached his hotel, Barbara Claremont was reunited with her daughter. She had driven straight to the house.

'My God, it looks like a siege,' she said as the car honked and crawled its way through the mass of hacks who, galvanized into activity by the arrival of someone yet to be identified, barged towards the momentarily stranded vehicle. After a barked command in Turkish, the driver revved his engine and drove straight on. Barbara shut her eyes and prayed that she would not have to ring the doorbell.

There was no such indignity: a good looking man, an American, ushered her out of the car.

'Hold on to me, Ma'am, and you'll be with your daughter in just one moment.' Barbara, grateful for his presence, did exactly as he said, whilst – albeit momentarily – wishing he was British.

Fae was waiting for her – longing for the flurry of skirt and the smell of familiar perfume. When her mother swept through the door she brought back normality, and even some sort of security. Fae clung to her.

Barbara stroked her hair and tried not to dwell on the thought that she had never held Fae like this – not even when she was a child, not even when she was sick. Fae had always wanted Sam. She cradled Fae until she felt she had had her fill of the physical touching. Only then did Barbara step back from her and turn to Fabrizzi, who was hovering, uncertain, behind his sister. Barbara didn't try to embrace him, she merely reached into her alligator handcase and took out a small computer game that she had purchased at the airport. She knew boys liked those kind of games. Maxwell's grandsons loved them. She offered the package to the solemn faced little boy.

'Thank you, Mrs Claremont,' he said gravely.

'Do you know how to play it?' Barbara asked him.

'Yes.'

'Bet you can't score twenty-five,' Barbara said.

"Course I can,' Fabrizzi said. 'Klaus has got one at school. Not as good as this, though. Thanks.' He grabbed the game and, whistling for the first time since his father's kidnap, he marched into the kitchen and the beep beep beep of the computer game filled the house.

'Thank you, Barbara,' Innessa said.

'And how are you?' Barbara replied. The two women had met just once before – when Sam had come on a very brief visit to London to celebrate Fae's twenty-first birthday. She took the Italian woman's arm, trying not to notice that Sam's second wife was still so much younger than her.

Not far from the Whiteman reunion, in a typical Turkish house built of rich varnished wood owned by Ichmet Golabi, Rector of Bosphorus University, and Sam Whiteman's closest friend, a young man watched the news on a sophisticated slim-line television operated by remote control.

'They've reported that the first wife – the English woman – arrived last night.'

'Good. It is time I paid my respects,' Golabi said. 'Will you call my car, please?'

The young man immediately rose from a soft sofa where he had been reclining. He was graceful with rich black hair made more dramatic by the pale skin and bright blue eyes – Rashid Boaz bore a startling similarity to his sister Faroud.

'Shall I drive you?' he asked Ichmet.

'No, thank you. But later I will arrange for you to meet with Fae Whiteman, the daughter. I think it will be helpful.'

Despite being only five feet four inches in height, Ichmet Golabi at the age of sixty-five was a man of stature. He had white hair and a round tanned face lined with the excesses of age, his dark olive eyes under white eyebrows were never still. The son of a Turkish aristocrat, he was raised in a privileged society and as a very small boy had a memory of the harem. An early disgust with the despotism of the Sultans had propelled Ichmet Golabi's father into becoming a follower of Mustafa Kamel, known as Ataturk, the father of Turkey, who became the first President. Ichmet's father was a fervent supporter of the Westernization of Turkey, he had travelled to the villages and taught the peasants to read and write Roman script in place of Arabic script – just as Ataturk had done. As a young man, Ichmet agreed with his father, but in his later years he had begun to question Western values, and had talked for many hours with his friend Sam Whiteman on the ethical question of grafting alien cultures on to an indigenous way of life. They had agreed, both of them, that such actions were misplaced.

Ichmet Golabi had few regrets in his life. One, however, was the need to walk with a cane. He disliked the necessity of dependence which is why, despite a great pleasure in women, he had never married. If he had a pride in anything material it was his car, a large black Oldsmobile, circa 1956. He would watch his chauffeur polishing it and was not above criticizing him when he felt the chrome work was not up to standard. He used to love to drive the car himself, but his doctors, since a heart attack, had forbidden that exercise. He would have ignored them if common sense had not told him that an attack at the wheel might kill others apart from himself. So he endured his chauffeur and tried to be polite as the man manipulated the heavy car through the overcrowded streets of Istanbul and drove him to the Whiteman house.

Unaware of Ichmet Golabi's impending arrival, the true

victims of Sam Whiteman's abduction shared a difficult lunch of pasta and salad prepared by Innessa with her customary skill. The strain of the kidnapping was the most obvious reason, but various other tensions did not help. Fae and Innessa were awkward with one another, neither wishing to participate in anything other than perfunctory communication. Even more obviously, Fae tried not to speak to Richard at all. The situation between the two wives was not comfortable either. Barbara did her best, but the role of a first wife is never an easy one. Both women have an intimacy with the husband, both have a status.

'Tea, Barbara?' Innessa asked.

'Are you not having coffee?' Barbara replied sweetly.

'Yes, but I presume that you would prefer tea.'

'Only at tea time,' Barbara replied.

Richard managed to bury his laugh in a cough – but not before Fae had noticed.

The coffee was being poured into the small cups. The pungent smell and the dribbling stream of liquid on china were unaccompanied by pleasantries when Ichmet Golabi came into the fractured, fragile group, bringing calm and a sense of order with him.

Although he had never met Barbara before, he treated her with a deference that did not devalue Innessa.

'Mrs Claremont, I am Ichmet Golabi and I wanted to express my feelings of outrage and of solidarity with you all.'

Then it was Innessa's turn. 'My dear,' he said, 'this is a nightmare from which, Allah willing, you will soon awake.'

A grandfather's voice told Fabrizzi, 'Soon, my boy, your father will be home and this will be a bad dream.'

And to Fae he said, 'How hard it is for you, my dear – I know how close you are to Sam.'

After the niceties, Innessa ushered Fabrizzi from the room and Fae addressed Ichmet Golabi: 'You have known my father ever since he first arrived in Turkey. Did you know he was an agent for the CIA?'

'How could I, my dear? It is too incredible to imagine. I cannot understand him admitting to such a thing. The authorities – what are they doing?'

'We have . . .' Richard tried to answer, but Fae interrupted him.

'The CIA have taken us over, they have bugs on the line, they have people here who answer the phone. The press are camped outside. It's almost as if we're prisoners too.'

'There must be news soon, but,' Golabi said, he was now sitting in a straight backed chair, holding his cane in front of him and managing to do so with such elegance that it appeared as if the ebony staff were part of him, 'I think it is very bad for you to be cramped in this house. Can she not go out?' Golabi asked Richard.

'Yes, of course she can, but the press . . .'

'You will ask them, in return for a few photographs, to allow her some freedom.'

'Yes . . .' Richard replied.

'Good.'

'But where will I go?' Fae asked.

'I will arrange for a young friend of mine, Rashid Boaz, to drive you around a little. You will be comfortable with him, he is one of Sam's students.'

'That would be nice.'

'You are absolutely right, Mr Golabi,' Richard said. 'The more normal one can be in this kind of situation the better. It's important, you see, because this could go on for some time,' Richard said.

'The kidnapping?' Barbara asked.

'The silence,' Richard replied.

Fae felt sick. Barbara reached over and squeezed her hand.

'We're bringing in a hostage negotiator. He's a good man, he'll be able to help us all through this. His name is William Fairchild. He's ex-Agency, but now he's an independent negotiator who works for underwriters.'

'What can he do that you can't?' Fae asked. 'After all, you've got the God Almighty CIA on your side.'

'This man is one of the best, inside and outside of the Agency . . . that's why we want him. I have to tell you it has taken a great deal of effort to get the Turkish authorities to agree to someone other than themselves to talk to the kidnappers. But we felt it was essential – to get their trust – so we can get Sam back. It's our best shot.'

'Let's hope it is the best,' Fae said sharply.

The night before Innessa's departure, Richard invited representatives of the press in for a photocall – just the agency photographers and two television news crews: one Turkish and one American. This time Fabrizzi was present, curled up on his mother's lap. Innessa, dressed in a cream linen dress, Barbara in a pink floral two-piece and Fae in her black silk trousers and a black top.

'How are you feeling?' asked a CBS man.

'Bloody,' Fae replied.

Simon Palling stood at the back of the room, waiting. When the allotted time was up he made his way over to Barbara and shook her hand.

'How are you?' he asked kindly.

Barbara remembered him from the plane. The nice young man, she thought to herself as she offered a hand.

'I'm all right.'

'How's your daughter?'

'She could be better.'

'It must be very hard for her,' he said, and Barbara thought how comforting it was to hear an English voice. 'I am staying at the Hilton. If there is anything I can do for you, please don't hesitate to let me know. I don't mean as a journalist.'

'That's very kind of you. As a matter of fact I am staying at that hotel myself.'

'Why don't we have breakfast together tomorrow? That is, if you breakfast in the restaurant.'

'Of course I do. And it would be very nice not to eat it alone. I shall see you there at eight o'clock.'

Simon Palling managed a smile – he had been going to suggest nine o'clock.

So the following morning, at exactly eight o'clock, Barbara Claremont, dressed in a yellow linen sundress and matching shoes, walked into the overcrowded air-conditioned luxury of the Hilton coffee shop. She knew that Simon Palling was courting her for information – she'd discussed his invitation on the telephone with her husband Max.

'But it will be nice to be out of that house for a few hours. I suppose I shall have to stay there once Innessa leaves, and frankly I am dreading it.'

'The sooner you can bring Fae home the better,' Max told her.

'I agree.'

Simon rose as she reached the table and pulled out a chair for her. At her request, he ordered her some orange juice and a lightly boiled egg, and began the dubious business of courtship. He allowed himself the one luxury of wishing that he were with Fae – she was certainly a most arresting woman. He had not failed to notice that she had wonderful breasts.

He steered the talk away from Sam. Instead he talked of harems.

'How degrading for those women,' Barbara remarked as she neatly sliced the top off her egg.

'Did you know that the girls were brought into the harem when they were tiny? They were trained in harem schools of music and literature and behaviour before they were offered to the Sultan. The older ones administered the harems themselves . . . all under the watchful eye of the Sultan's mother, of course. And after nine years they were allowed to leave, and even marry if they wanted.'

'I had no idea they could get out. I thought that once they were in a harem they were there for life.'

'For most of them luring the Sultan and pleasing him was the ultimate aim, because then they could, like the courtesans in Europe, wield the most extraordinary power.'

'It interests me,' Barbara said, spooning yellow and white egg into her small pink mouth, 'that we women still use our sexuality to get what we want. But I suppose it's all part of the game of life. The exercise of power, in and out of the bed, don't you think?'

Simon realized that this woman, who was some twenty-five years older, was flirting with him. He shifted on his chair and settled to a more interesting breakfast than he had perhaps envisaged.

Whilst Barbara and Simon drank their coffee and enjoyed their breakfast, Fae tried to cope with Innessa and Fabrizzi's departure. The little boy held his teddy bear and his football. His eyes were downcast, as if he knew this was an ending – at eight years of age one is not prepared for endings. Innessa looked tired but Fae recognized that her stepmother was relieved to be leaving. As for herself, she was experiencing a sudden, horrible panic which made her legs seem like jelly. Her stomach hurt, and her heart beat at a terrible rate. She didn't want Innessa and Fabrizzi to go: once Innessa had taken Fabrizzi, she would be alone. Momentarily desperate, she tried to think of a way to stop them leaving, at least to delay them.

She grabbed Innessa's arm. 'What if Sam needs you?'

'I will return, but it's better for Fabrizzi to be away from here. Sam would want him out of this, you know that.'

Fae nodded, she let go of Innessa, bent her knees so that her head was level with Fabrizzi and put her arms around her little brother. He hugged her – but she recognized that it was a perfunctory gesture and she understood.

Richard bid Innessa farewell politely, but Fae saw him caress her fingers – Innessa did not respond. A flicker of pain grazed the face of the normally impassive American. Longing should weave kindred care, but still, after Innessa had left, Fae did not allow for any pleasantries.

'What is going on between you and my stepmother?'

'We've been having a relationship for the last few months.'

'Is she going to leave my father?' Fae was standing by the front door as if to block his exit. He had to answer her.

'She was going to.'

'And now?'

'I don't know, Fae.'

Richard's desolation was so obvious that Fae felt a sudden sharp sympathy.

At the appointed hour for their rendezvous, Ichmet Golabi's young friend Rashid arrived to collect Fae. As if she felt the need for a chaperon, his sister Faroud insisted on accompanying him.

Dressed in a white blouse and a pleated skirt, complete with what seemed to be the obligatory headscarf, she seemed a very formal person. She took Fae's hand politely and expressed her sympathy with the family's distress, but Fae noticed that she did not comment on Sam's abduction. Rashid, however, was altogether more appealing.

'I greet you as a sister – for Ichmet Golabi is like a father to me and he speaks of you with fatherly concern. I know it is impossible for you to put aside your concern for your father, but perhaps some air and some space will help a little.'

Fae could not help but be charmed by such courtesy.

The press were kind when she left the house. The rat pack clicked their shutters but the TV crews, alerted by Richard, left her alone, and the CBS man waved.

'Glad to see you out, Fae,' he called.

'Thanks,' she called back.

Rashid drove up to Ramali Castle. Built of grey stone with huge towers, it had once guarded the Straits of the Bosphorus. Rashid helped her out of the car and they walked down the grass parkland that lay beyond the walls. Rashid told her stories of brave and stupid heroes, allowing her, briefly, to forget.

'There was a Venetian galley that refused to pay its taxes to the Commander of the Castle, so he fired cannon balls and hit the vessel. Slowly it sank into the water. Look, Fae,' he pointed out towards the water, 'imagine the proud ship as it sank slowly beneath the waters. Can you see it, the sailors screaming, can you hear the noise of the cannon, and the fire – sweeping through the canvas sails?'

So persuasive was Rashid's voice that Fae shivered in the heat. She wore her black trousers and shirt, but now her hair was covered by a huge straw hat with a wide black ribbon securing it. She had dark glasses on, to protect herself from the sun and prying faces. Suddenly from nowhere a photographer appeared, aiming his camera, shouting his question. 'Is that your boyfriend?'

Rashid, with elaborate courtesy, rushed her to the car, and drove her away. Fae was shaking.

'What's happening to me? Oh God, when will this nightmare stop? Why, why, did these people do this to my father? He's a good man,' she was shouting at the Turks, she couldn't stop herself.

'He has confessed to being a CIA agent,' Faroud said from the back of the car.

'I can't believe it. I don't believe it. I've lived with him. I know him. For God's sake, he is my father. He's no spy. He doesn't approve of the things that America does – the bombings in Libya. We talked about it.'

'Does one really know one's father?' Rashid asked.

'I know him. I love him. He is incapable of a bad deed – he cares about people.'

As soon as Fae left the Whiteman house, Richard Marks drove himself past the Dolmabahçe Palace and the square matchboxes that Istanbul's town planners believe have more value than the graceful façades of a previous time. He turned up the winding street that housed not only the American and British Consulates, but also the visiting places for those needing the skills of the ladies of the night. But behind its iron gates, the American Consulate, despite its ugly barrack-like visa section, sported the same gracious charms as the British Consulate. The Marine checked his credentials and swung open the gate.

He greeted his colleagues, but discouraged any passing chat. He needed some quiet. He let himself into his office and sat, with gratitude, at his desk. He picked up two photographs in silver frames that he kept prominently on his desk – they were of his two young daughters, Caroline aged four and Natalie, a plump little two-year-old. He kept duplicates by the side of his bed, and there were two smaller copies in his wallet. He liked to be surrounded by their faces. He didn't see them very much: their mother, Camille, had divorced him when Natalie was three months old. There had been no acrimony, they had simply fallen out of love with each other and Camille had fallen in love with someone else – an army man. Camille liked service life. That was one of the reasons why she was originally attracted to Richard – she'd believed he was a Marine Officer. Long months alone, and the lack of ceremony and support, had turned the loving to a distant thing, and even before Natalie's conception they had both known there was nothing left. Richard rather liked his successor, Jim. He knew the soldier would be good to the girls, he'd be there. Richard preferred the single life; at least that was the way it seemed until he met Innessa.

Massaging his own neck and temples, he tried not to think of his personal crisis. But he couldn't help it, he had been in love with Innessa from the first time he had seen her – he had been appalled by Sam Whiteman who bragged of his young wife as if she were a possession. If he were honest with himself, Richard would admit that he had never liked Sam. He found the man insensitive, even crass. He had wondered why Innessa had married him.

'Sam wanted me, Sam takes care of me, Sam tells wonderful stories, and Sam tells my father to go to hell,' she told Richard the first time he touched her breasts and sucked her nipple, feeling it hard and sharp in his mouth.

'Does Sam make you feel like this?' he asked, his mouth against her skin.

'He used to before I had Fabrizzi.'

'And now . . . ?'

'To him I am a mother – no longer his whore.'

'What do you want to be?'

'A whore,' Innessa had replied. Richard felt his erection rise at the thought of Innessa's tight hard body against his and he cursed Sam Whiteman's kidnappers and he cursed Sam Whiteman. Did he want him back alive? He didn't know and he was very grateful that the decision did not rest with him.

His intercom crackled into life. It was the dry crisp voice of the Ambassador's secretary.

'The Ambassador and the DCI are here from Ankara – can you go to them, please.'

The sun shone on the Ambassadorial carpet of eau-de-nil, highlighting Robert Brockwell's black, highly-polished shoes. The Ambassador, dwarfed by his huge desk and the furled Stars and Stripes America, was insignificant. Robert Brockwell, the youngest Director of the CIA, an army man, seated in a Louis-Quinze chair set against the wall, was the man who mattered.

'What do we have?' he asked Richard, who was more used to a less significant superior.

'Nothing.'

'That's ridiculous. We can't have nothing.'

'There has been no contact made, sir. But they'll have to make a move soon. They want those guys out.'

'And they'll want publicity, and they'll want money.'

'And if we don't give them what they want, they'll kill Whiteman.'

Brockwell stood up and walked towards the window. Richard watched the man's back.

'Whiteman is just a piece of merchandise who will be traded if he is of value. I don't like the way he's cracked, but who knows how any of us would react. The press already know too much, the family are involved.'

Brockwell turned back from the window. With the sun behind him, in his dark suit and his white shirt he was almost, momentarily, God-like. 'I want him back. When they contact us, Marks, we'll trade.'

A hooded hostage, unshaven, crumpled, stinking of his own urine, was led out of his bare room, bundled into the boot of a car and driven some miles over the Bosphorus Bridge to Üsküdar, the Asian part of the city where the middle classes lived in comfortable apartments, shopped in elegant shops, and drank in smart cafés. The driver of the car, Adnan, operated a remote control device and drove straight into an underground car park. He carefully placed his car near a lift. He got out, opened the boot, hustled Sam Whiteman into the lift, and pressed the button for the second floor. Sam was alone in the lift, but he saw nothing, he was still blindfolded. When the lift reached its destination he was collected by another young man dressed in army fatigues, and pushed into a plush room furnished in heavy wood and red velvet where other men sat in a circle waiting to judge him. A video camera whirred in the corner. A microphone was adjusted so it picked up every word.

'For pity's sake, take off the mask, please.'

But no one took his mask off.

A man with a sharp voice spoke.

'Has anyone harmed you?'

'It's the mask – and I need a bath.'

'I ask again, has anyone physically harmed you?'

'They made me kneel down, they played noises, but mostly it's the mask.' The man was whimpering now.

'Answer the question!'

'No, no . . .'

'Do you acknowledge that you handed over to your superior at the American Embassy the names of the students, Ayala Kaplan, Mustafa Doganay and Ali Keles? And that you accused these young people of being members of the Communist Party? As a result of your information they were arrested, imprisoned and tortured, and to our knowledge Ayala Kaplan was killed.'

'I know nothing about torture.'

'You knew.'

'I did not . . .'

'The girl's own mother could not recognize the bloody mess that was her child.' The prosecutor's voice rose: 'Confess. You are guilty, you are a murderer, a torturer, a spy. You will be shot.'

'No, please, no, please . . .'

The video camera stopped whirring. The man continued to cry out, 'Please, please . . .'

A cassette was removed from the camera – it was placed in an envelope and sealed. A telephone call was made to the American Embassy. Maise Montgomery, who had been recalled to the Embassy just to report on how the family were coping, answered it.

'A video tape has just been placed to the left of the steps that lead up to the entrance to the Blue Mosque. If all our colleagues are not released, and two million dollars is not handed over to us, the sentence on the spy will be carried out.'

CHAPTER THREE

Fae was suffering. Not only was she physically missing Sam, but she was in an agony of fear for him . . . In daylight hours the tightness in her stomach and the continual waiting, the non activity, were the worst things. But at night, in the dark, the phantoms came to keep her company . . .

The room was cold. An uneven stone floor meant lying was uncomfortable, but any movement was hindered by steel cuffs that were linked by short chains to both wrists and ankles. A bowl with water was positioned near enough to be reached only by the mouth, dog-like. But it was the tapes on the eyes, the tapes that couldn't be removed, that held the eyelids closed, shutting out the light, which caused the almost visible terror to swirl in like fog, harrowing the manacled figure.

Someone was screaming, 'God help me, God, God!'

'Fae, Fae, darling – wake up.' Hands soothed and stroked, a warm body comforted. It wasn't cold in the room, it wasn't dark.

'You've had a nightmare, sweetheart. Just a bad nightmare.' A mother's voice was taking away the panic, but even as Fae came out of the blackness she knew that she was dreaming of her father and that he was in a room somewhere, alone, and frightened.

'Oh Mummy, what if they haven't taken the mask off?'

'Of course they would have taken it off, darling.'

'How do you know?'

'I don't know. But I imagine, sensibly, that they would have no need to blindfold him once they had him in the safe house, or whatever they call it.'

Barbara Claremont comforted her daughter as best she could,

then ran her a warm bath. As soon as she had safely installed her daughter, she straightened her white silk dressing-gown, checked her hair and her make-up and went to find Maise Montgomery.

'My daughter is suffering, Miss Montgomery. We are not being told enough. If you can't help us, I shall have to find someone who will.'

'What do you mean?'

'I think we, as a family, should find our own hostage negotiator.'

'I am sure that isn't necessary, Mrs Claremont. William Fairchild arrives today, and frankly he is more capable of dealing with this than anyone you could bring in.'

'That's as maybe, but you people are concerned with the politics. Our person will be concerned with getting my daughter's father home.'

'Why don't you wait and meet Mr Fairchild before you make that kind of decision? He's a good man.'

'I certainly want some sort of action, Miss Montgomery,' Barbara told her.

Maise waited until the white silk body had sashayed through the door, and shut it. Then she telephoned Richard.

'They mustn't bring in an outside negotiator. He'll muddy the waters.'

'Just convince them that William Fairchild is on their side, working for them.' Maise tried to keep the irritation out of her voice. She didn't feel Richard was on top of this case. She'd told Brockwell exactly that just the previous night, after an energetic coupling in the Ambassador's office. Her thighs tightened at the memory . . . the man was a real stud. She'd heard the rumours, now she knew they were true.

Maise smiled to herself, she'd enjoyed it.

Richard was speaking. 'I'll talk to Mrs Claremont myself.'

Maise managed a polite, 'OK.'

She went up the stairs and gently knocked on Fae's door.

'Can I come in?' Her voice was soft. 'It's me, Maise.'

She found Fae sitting on her bed, a little forlorn figure – the real sufferer. Yet Fae Whiteman had never done anything to deserve the kind of pain that she was now experiencing – unless it was believed that perceiving one's father as a hero was wrong.

Maise didn't think so, after all she used to think that of her own father.

She knew Sam quite well, she'd bedded him a few times. They had shared a few bottles, and a few talks. She liked Sam.

'You're scared for him, aren't you?' she said to Fae.

'Yes, I am. Will they hurt him?'

'No, they won't. You see – they need him in good shape because they want to swap him for their friends and money to buy arms. So they aren't going to damage their bargaining point.'

'Are you sure?' Fae was instantly so hopeful, her eyes the huge pools of the supplicant.

Maise avoided looking directly at Fae: she couldn't bear the begging irises. 'I'm sure,' she said quickly. 'Now get dressed, and go and make some waves. That's what you have to do. Just make the bastards uncomfortable – that way they have to move a bit faster.'

Fae quite simply pulled herself together. Maise was right. She would harry 'the bastards'. Suddenly there were things to do. Her face changed, the lines rearranged themselves to give her a sharper, cleaner focus. She dressed in a black skirt and, despite the heat, a light red jacket. She put on high heels. Fae always felt better in high heels. She would go and see the man who called himself a visiting fireman. What was his name? Brockwell, Bob Brockwell. She'd ask Maise how to reach him.

'You don't know who he is?' Maise said.

'He just said he was a visiting fireman, whatever that means.'

'He's the DCI.'

'What's that?'

'Director of the CIA.'

'I imagine that's as good a place as any to start,' Fae said.

She dialled the Consulate herself.

'Good morning. This is Fae Whiteman. May I speak to Bob Brockwell?'

'Good morning, Miss Whiteman. I am so sorry, but Mr Brockwell has already left us. Can I connect you with Richard Marks?'

'No, thank you. I know that Richard is involved with my father's kidnapping, but I need to reassure myself by speaking to someone from the "home base", so to speak.'

'Of course you do, Miss Whiteman. Why don't I arrange for

you to come and see the Ambassador. He is actually in Istanbul at the moment. Would three o'clock this afternoon be convenient? We could offer you some tea.'

'That would be lovely, thank you. But I would be so grateful if you could locate a telephone number where I might reach Mr Brockwell. Perhaps you could let me have it when I come to the Embassy.' The voice was pleasant, but absolutely determined.

Maise wondered what had happened to the lost little girl of but half an hour previously.

As soon as she ended her telephone call from Fae Whiteman, the Ambassador's secretary, an efficient woman who had been with the Company some twenty-two years, made a neat notation in her diary and then picked up the receiver and placed an internal call to Richard Marks.

'Fae Whiteman wants to see Brockwell.'

'Let her.'

'She's coming in to see the Ambassador this afternoon.'

'That's good. Make sure she feels she has a lot of support.'

It was the Ambassador himself who handed Fae a telephone number for the Director. That evening he would be in Cairo and she could reach him there. He would be expecting her call.

'I appreciate this, Mr Ambassador.'

The Ambassador, Dwight Shaw, raised his arm.

'You have the right to reach whoever you want, Miss Whiteman.' Dwight Shaw believed that. The son of an immigrant coal miner, he was part of the American dream. He too had started in the mines, but Shaw went to college, became a lawyer, returned to the mining conglomerate and twenty years later became its President. Faithful support of the current incumbent led to the reward as Ambassador to Turkey.

'Now I'm going to ask William Fairchild, the hostage negotiator, and Richard Marks to join us. And they are going to tell you, and me, exactly how they intend to proceed with this situation.'

William Fairchild was a small, stocky man with a pleasant face. The hand he offered was good and firm. Richard followed him into the office.

'Hello, Fae,' he said. 'How are you feeling?'

'It would help if I was told what was going on.'

'Absolutely.' Fairchild moved next to her and spread some

papers on a low table. 'At the moment the negotiators have only made two contacts with us. The Turks are obviously pursuing their own investigations, we are pushing ours. So far we have come up with several student groups who could be responsible for holding your father. What we have to do now is to personalize the negotiations. We need to talk to them. That's my job, and I'm going to need to spend some time with you to find out some personal data about your father so that when they make contact we can be assured that they're legitimate. Then we'll establish a set of codes and start to build their trust in us.'

'Their trust in you, I don't see . . .'

Fairchild held up a hand, it was small and white, with perfectly manicured nails and a gold wedding ring on the fourth finger of the right hand.

'I have to convince them, Miss Whiteman, that we all want the same thing, the speedy resolution of this case. Let the Turks worry about retribution: right now I want to see your father at home. So I have to make them believe in me. Do you understand?' The man's voice was sharp, it could even have been impatient. Fae felt as if she had been rebuked. Stung, she lowered her eyes.

'Yes, I'm sorry. I didn't think. But how are you going to talk to them? You don't even know who they are, or where they are.'

'We don't know anything yet. But eventually, if they want their people out, and their money, they are going to have to talk to us.'

'That's a bit passive, isn't it?' Fae's voice was sharp now.

Fairchild answered her slowly and deliberately. 'We have to be careful. We don't want to push these people into anything we may regret. This is a painfully slow process, and I appreciate it is hell for you and your family. But we have to build these people's confidence so they trade.'

'I don't understand how they could have made my father say he was a CIA agent. I don't mean to be rude, but he didn't agree with American foreign policy. Libya and Nicaragua, I mean . . .' Fae's voice trailed off, she didn't want to antagonize them. She cleared her throat, crossed her legs.

William Fairchild looked at her carefully. 'Miss Whiteman, I think you ought to be acquainted with all the facts here. Your father does work for the company. He is a spotter.'

'A spotter?'

'Yes. He would locate students who might be helpful and, also, as is the case here, identify groups antagonistic to the cause of democracy.'

'You mean antagonistic to the United States!'

'If you like, but I don't think it's helpful to have a debate about ethics here. The business at hand is to try and get your father back.'

'I can't believe you. My father would never, could never . . . I mean, he just wouldn't.'

'He didn't do anything dramatic, Fae. He's been a company man ever since college.'

'It's impossible. I know him. I know what he believes in.' Fae was shouting, she couldn't help herself, it was all so ludicrous, it was as if the man that she knew didn't really exist.

'It is true, Fae.' Richard Marks was speaking to her.

Fae shook her head, her black hair rippled with the sudden movement.

'No, I'm afraid I don't accept that.'

'Fae. I was your father's control.'

'What?'

'Your father gave his information to me.'

'Oh, my God.'

Fae's heart was actually hurting her. She ran her hands over her face, the edge of her fingers were numb. 'And then you told the Turks and they took my Dad. It's you, you're the one they should be holding, not him.'

'We exchange information with the Turkish authorities. Sam was part of that,' Richard said softly.

The Ambassador got up out of his chair. He went over to Fae, took her hands and looked into her eyes. 'Miss Whiteman, please. I am so sorry for you. If I could change the events I would, but I can't. You have to come to terms with so much, but even that has to be put to one side whilst we get Sam back.'

Fae heard the reason in Ambassador Shaw's voice, and she heard the kindness.

'I'm sorry. I didn't mean to be rude.'

'We all feel you've every right to be rude,' William Fairchild said.

Fae looked up at Fairchild. She half smiled, turned back to the Ambassador and said, 'Thank you for your understanding.'

She could not look at Richard Marks.

'Now, if you can push your anger back a bit, we can get down to the issues here,' continued William Fairchild.

Fae swallowed, she was still aware of her heart pumping in her chest, but she tried to concentrate. 'What about the Turks? What if they won't release their people?' she said.

The Ambassador replied, 'I doubt they will, Fae.'

'And then?'

'It's a very delicate situation. We are prepared to pay for your father, but we can't interfere with Turkish affairs.'

Unconsciously Fae gripped her hands together. Richard saw the movement. 'The Turks want your father back too. We are all working together,' he said gently.

Fae ignored him – she sat back in her chair and allowed William Fairchild to hand her a cup of tea.

His voice was still quiet, but it wasn't deliberate any more. He spoke to her directly, as if she were important. She knew it was a tactic. She took a proffered biscuit, not because she wanted it but because it was something to do.

Whilst Fae supped with the Americans, her stepmother, safe in her father's house, considered her own future. The estate was built high in the hills behind Positano. From the front of the house there was a conventional – albeit beautiful – vista of the blue sea beyond green tree-bedecked hills, but from the back of the house Innessa could look towards sloping olive groves, each divided one from the other by little grey stone walls. She was sitting on a sun-lounger stretching her spine against its turquoise and black cushions, trying to ease the ache in her shoulderblades. Her head thumped, it had not stopped thumping since Sam's kidnapping. She wanted him safe, but she would never go back to live in Turkey . . . nor would she go back to Sam. Their marriage was over, it had been over for a long time, but the final ending had occurred just a few weeks before Fae's arrival.

They had gone to Olu Dag for the weekend. Normally a place to ski, they took Fabrizzi there for good fresh air. It was a place to go as a family, but on that particular weekend Sam was moody and withdrawn. He stayed in the hotel, refusing to venture outside. Fabrizzi was upset.

'Why, Papa? We are here to be together. Come with us, please.'

'No, leave me alone, Fabrizzi. You go with your mother. I have a headache.'

Innessa took Fabrizzi down to the little dining-room for breakfast. And then she returned to their room alone.

'What is it, Sam?' she had asked, tenderly, for he did not look well and she did not like to see him with lines of worry or deep shadows. She had long ceased to be in love with him, but she loved him. He was Fabrizzi's father, he was her husband, and once they had been lovers; all of that allowed for an unfettered care, even when the passion had gone.

'I didn't mean to shout. I have some worries. That's all. Let me mooch around the hotel today and then I'll come with you tomorrow.'

Innessa kissed him on the cheek and put on her walking shoes, took Fabrizzi's with her and left the room.

Sam didn't mean to go to the bar, he didn't mean to get drunk, but he was sure there were men following him. He was frightened in the room. They could get to him there, let themselves in through the door and silently and carefully hurt him. What an irrational fear, he told himself, and went down and had a whisky, then two whiskies, then three whiskies. By the time Innessa and Fabrizzi returned he was in a loud conversation over a set of cards with anyone who would listen. They were all fools, the men he had been playing with, they'd cheated. One of them had pushed him, he had pushed him back. He was no pansy to be shoved around. The man hit him. He struggled to his feet, ready to hit the man back but there was no man in front of him, just his furious wife. So what was the matter with her? A man was entitled to a bit of relaxation, wasn't he? He told her. He could hear his son crying. He didn't like that. He tried to kiss him, but Innessa took the boy away from him. Damn her. Women were not to take his children away from him. Barbara had done that – she'd taken Fae. Well no one was going to take Fabrizzi. He told her. He could hear his son crying again. Why wouldn't she let him hold the boy? He wanted his Daddy. Rough hands pushed him into a room and he fell asleep on a bed, cursing women, cursing Innessa . . . he wanted his children.

In the morning Sam awoke with a dreadful headache and no real memory of the day before – except flashes that bothered him. He would do his best to make it up to Fabrizzi. He would forget those men that seemed to be everywhere. He rationalized that he had to get out of the Agency, the work was pressurizing him. He couldn't do it any more. His heart wasn't in it. He joined the family for breakfast. Fabrizzi was very quiet and Innessa would not speak at all. He ignored the silences and took them high into the mountains. Fabrizzi was happy there, running and shouting, exploring the rocks, finding flowers. Sam was glad to be with his son and even Innessa thawed a little. He was going to tell her not to judge a man for one slip, but then Fabrizzi fell, not far, but far enough. He was stuck in a crevice. Sam leaned over the side of the incline to grab his son, but he made the mistake of looking down. The world spun upside down, around and around, like a kaleidoscope, and he was in it, part of it, unable to get out. The colours of the mountains, the browns, the greens, the pinks and reds and yellows of the flowers all merged into the horrendous spinning top. The sweat came over him, he felt sick.

'Daddy, Daddy,' he heard Fabrizzi. He tried to reach his hand. Damn it, his child was only a little way from him. All he had to do was lean forward and grab his son's hand. But his own hand was wet and sticky. He tried, he swallowed hard, put his hand out, but not far enough. If he just could lean down . . .

'Daddy, Daddy.'

A heel caught his shoulder. Innessa. He spun away from her, lay on his back, looked up at a blessed quiet sky.

'Mummy.'

'It's all right, caro. Give me your hand. I can get you. Now put your foot on that space there. You are a strong boy. You can do anything. No gently, gently, that's it. Now feel my arm. It's as strong as steel, it will never let you go.'

He heard her voice and he hated her strength.

Fabrizzi struggled up the slope for, after all, it was just a little one. Feet pattered towards him, his son spoke to him.

'Daddy, Daddy. I'm OK now. Mummy pulled me up. What's wrong with you?'

'Your father has a headache. It's called a hangover,' Innessa said, and Sam knew she would never forgive him.

That evening Innessa told Sam, 'I will share a bed with you. But I will never trust you with our child again. Soon, when Fabrizzi is ready, I will go back to Italy with him.'

Sam burbled on about men following him. She had laughed at him.

Innessa turned over on her black and turquoise chair. Sam was correct, there were men following him. She felt sad that she had not shared his fear, that she had just dismissed it. But it made no difference . . . she wouldn't live with him any more. Nor would she live with Richard, for that matter. He was a nice man, but he was a symptom of her broken marriage, and that was all. She thought about the night of Sam's kidnapping and how she felt when Fae had burst into her bedroom. She felt no guilt, she just wondered what she was doing with that man in her bed, engaged in some sort of physical release, when really she should have been with Sam's children, sharing the night with them. What was this strange thing that men and women did – an act of passion, an act of release? Perhaps, but to make it worthwhile Innessa needed love, and she didn't feel that for anyone any more. She wondered if she would ever feel it again. She couldn't think about that now, she couldn't think of anything until Sam was released. She was sure he was alive. All his terrors had come up out of his deepest fears, and they were real. Innessa clenched her fists, her nails hurt her soft palms and she prayed for Sam, prayed for him to find his strength.

In a hotel bedroom in Üsküdar, a man lay on a comfortable bed. There was a pitcher of water and a glass on a side table, but the man could not reach it unaided. A black hood covered his head, steel cuffs were clamped on his wrists, his legs were manacled together. He was curled into the foetal position, buried in the blackness of his hood. Someone came in. Someone was pouring some water. Someone lifted the hood above his mouth, someone was putting the glass to his lips, the liquid slurped over his mouth, he drank easily, gratefully.

'Thank you.'

'You don't smell good.' The voice was soft, a woman's.

Sam Whiteman couldn't answer. He hated his filth.

'I'll arrange a bath.'

The woman was gone. A bath, a shaft of light, a hope.

Sam had lost all sense of time. After the trial he had been taken in a car again – he had no idea where. He'd walked up steps into a room, he'd heard a door shut behind him. A man ordered him to walk three paces forward. He stumbled on to a bed. He was ordered to keep his eyes closed. He did as he was told. The blind came off – mercifully off. He told them that if they would just leave the blindfold off, he would keep his eyes shut, he wouldn't open them. But then the hood went over his head and the blackness came back. He cried then, no longer ashamed of his weakness.

As he lay in his black tomb he remembered he'd sensed for some time that he was being followed. He had told Richard, who had laughed at his paranoia.

He had told his friend Ichmet who had warned him to take care. 'The world is full of mad people, my friend, people who don't like the Americans.'

He wanted to tell Ichmet everything, tell him that he worked for the Company. My God, how soft he had become to even consider such a thing. Sam wanted to quit: he'd told Maise Montgomery. Maise had said, 'Give it a few more months.' So he had given it a few more months, and in those few more months he had identified the three students, one of whom now lay in cold, black earth as he lay in his blackness. A just retribution . . . perhaps. Innessa would say so. He brushed the thought of Innessa aside, he did not want to think about her. She knew about him, she knew he was a coward. He would never forgive her for her knowledge. But what did she know? She had never been tested. The fear was the worst part – it tortured and mangled his senses. He had to give in to it. He couldn't fight it, not like Fae, his beloved Fae. She fought. Fae was the brave one. Fae was what he wanted Fabrizzi to be, Fae was what he wanted to be . . . What was she doing now? She was his chance, his brightest chance.

Later, maybe it was an hour, maybe it was just ten minutes – he had no idea – he heard the door of his room open again.

'We are going to give you a bath now,' a voice told Sam Whiteman.

'Oh, thank you, thank you very much.' He was so grateful.

He heard the sound of the key being turned in the chain, heard the chain being released, and then the jingle of steel against steel as the cuffs were slipped off his ankles. He wriggled his toes and would have liked to have massaged his ankles, but his hands were not free. They would do that as soon as he got into the bathroom, they would have to do that, otherwise he could not wash himself. He allowed himself to be stood up. An arm steadied him.

'Come on, old man. You can stand on your own feet.'

'Thank you.' Again the thank you, but he was so pleased. The cap, too, that would come off in the bathroom.

But it did not come off, nor did the handcuffs. Sam was guided into the bathroom and was helped into the bath. He heard the running water, felt the soap and a hard hand rubbing briskly over his back – it was nice – over his arms, around his neck. The cowl was lifted a little, a toothbrush with paste was stuck into his mouth. He tried to take it. His hand was pushed away. He was given water to wash out his mouth.

'You smell better, old man,' someone said, a boy's voice – did he know him? No – it wasn't a voice he'd heard before. But then someone was washing his private parts. Oh no, he could feel himself stirring.

'So you like boys, old man,' the guard said, laughing.

Sam didn't like boys, Sam liked the feel of soap and water – he had always liked it. He was reacting to that. He gritted his teeth, he must not feel, must not give in, must control himself. He tried, he tried, but someone was playing a game, someone was caressing him, he was getting bigger, no – no, he wouldn't. He could feel himself giving in. No, no, he wouldn't.

'Stop that now, you pig.' It was a woman's voice. 'You are no better than scum!'

The hand stopped and Sam could have wept with release.

'When you get him back to his room, leave the mask off.'

'What?'

'Leave it off, we don't want him mad.'

Who was that woman? Sam suddenly loved her, he would do anything for her.

'Thank you,' he heard himself say.

'I will come and talk with you tonight, but before I come in you will have to put on the hood. I can't risk you seeing me.'

'I understand that. It'll be all right, if I can do it.'

'Yes, you can.'

There was a click of the door and the woman was gone. The man did not speak to him any more.

As the door shut behind her, Faroud, the sister of Rashid, smiled to herself. She looked at her watch, she would give the American just two hours, long enough to be grateful . . . But Hayri had better watch himself – Faroud did not like his behaviour.

And Sam Whiteman was grateful. When the voice told him to put the hood back on, he did so. The blackness was not so difficult, knowing that his hands were free, and later he would be able to take it off.

'And now, Mr Whiteman, do you feel better?' The woman's voice had a slight accent, otherwise the English was perfect.

'Yes, I am obliged to you.'

'Well, let's see how obliged you are. How long have you been working for the CIA?'

Whilst Sam considered his interrogator, Fae continued with her efforts on his behalf. After she had finished with the American Ambassador she was taken by an American Embassy car to a meeting with Kamel Batami, a senior official in the Turkish Foreign Ministry.

Richard Marks saw her into the car.

'I hate you,' she said. She was quite calm. 'And if anything happens to Sam I will kill you.'

Fae recognized Kamel Batami immediately. He was the taller of the two Turkish men who had visited her and Innessa on the morning of her father's kidnap. Plumper than she thought, he had a very kind face and a marvellous rich voice, perfect English with a slight American accent. He made her feel very comfortable.

'I cannot tell you how distressed I am that this has happened to your father.'

'Thank you, Mr Batami. I'm afraid I wasn't very gracious when we last met.'

'I think you were extraordinary. I told my wife.'

He smiled at her and came from behind a beautiful black desk embellished with fretwork. In his hand was a file. He placed it on a round black coffee table. 'I don't always like our methods, but they achieve results and in this case I am grateful for whatever information that comes to hand.'

'You are talking about your secret police.'

'Yes I am.'

'You are an honest man.'

Batami glanced over at her.

There was a knock on the door and someone, a young man, entered with a tray on which were two glasses of tea and a plate of small cakes sanded with white sugar.

'Thyme – it's delicious,' Kamel Batami told her as he passed her one of the glasses. 'And now to our work,' he said.

For two hours Fae and Batami talked as he showed her mug shots and documents relating to people who might have been involved in her father's abduction.

'But you aren't sure,' Fae said.

'No, I am not. But I do know one thing. I am sure your father's supposed confession was correct and the kidnapping is to do with the fact that your father gave us information about students. I know it is hurtful for you to face that, but it is a fact. The students mentioned in the video are the key to the people who took your father. We have to find out what group they came from. Which of their friends are still in the University. And believe me, Miss Whiteman, we will.'

At that same moment in another part of the city of Istanbul, a terrified young man stood blindfolded in a basement room below a police station. Several policemen stood around. One – they called him 'the surgeon' – ruffled his hair almost kindly.

'And now you are going to tell us who has taken the American professor, Sam Whiteman. You are scum, communist scum, and by the time I have finished with you, you are going to wish you were dead. But first we are going to have some fun.'

The young man was kicked to the ground, his trousers torn off him. In the name of justice they used their truncheons and their electrodes and their whips to hurt and humiliate him. He said nothing, he had nothing to say – he didn't know who had taken Sam Whiteman. He couldn't have known. He was just a schoolboy of sixteen. His brother was a student at the Bosphorus University, he was staying with him for a week's holiday.

His brother, Hayri, had not been at home when the police had come so they took him instead. He hadn't even been able to leave a note for him.

It was a neighbour who told Hayri that his brother had been taken away. Hayri had returned to the flat to collect a change of clothes and to check that his brother had arrived safely. The arrangements for his holiday had been completed long before the Whiteman kidnapping. Hayri had decided not to cancel anything – it would look suspicious. He just told his brother that he had met a girl – a European girl – and she was leaving Turkey within a few days so he was spending as much time with her as possible. He told other friends the same story – they were sympathetic and arranged to take care of the boy for him. But no one had been there when the police pounced. Hayri sat down on his bed and wept. His brother knew nothing, and his brother would be harmed and there was nothing he could do to stop any of it. After some time, he pulled himself together, grabbed some things and threw them into a backpack. He wouldn't return to the flat. The police were too close – how could they have known of his involvement? He had to tell Rashid.

After Fae Whiteman left Kamel Batami, she returned to the house. Barbara, cool and elegant, made her some English tea and listened to the revelation that her ex-husband worked for the CIA.

'I can't believe it, I still can't believe it,' Fae said.

Barbara tried to help her, even to minimize the importance of his role, but Fae couldn't listen.

'It's as if he has suddenly become someone else, not Sam.'

'Perhaps he always has been someone else,' Barbara ventured cautiously, for she did not want to hurt her daughter.

'For you, maybe, but not for me.'

Barbara nodded her head slowly. 'Fae, he is still your father, and his love for you and yours for him aren't changed by any of this.'

'Of course not.'

'What I mean is that it isn't the issue now . . . whether he works for the CIA. What is important is his release, and then you can talk to him directly.'

'The Ambassador said that.'

'He's right.'

'I know . . .' Fae said the proper words, but that wasn't the way she felt inside. If she turned in on herself and became what she felt, she would have been a great black sea with huge mindless waves billowing and buffeting against themselves. She knew she was becoming irrational. Unconsciously she clenched her fists.

'Weren't you going to speak to Mr Brockwell?' she heard her mother say.

'Yes, yes I was,' Fae replied.

'And I've accepted an invitation from Mr Golabi for dinner. I thought it would do you good, darling.' A cool hand touched her cheek.

'That's good. He knows Sam so well.'

'We all know Sam, but we know him in a different way from you.'

'You mean I hero-worship him, and the image is dented now,' Fae said.

'Yes, darling.'

'What I've always liked about you, Mum, is that you always tell me what you think.'

'I learnt that from Sam,' Barbara said and she laughed. 'Now, I went into that hi-tech kitchen and I made us some fairy cakes. I even iced them. Would you eat one?'

Fae laughed. 'My comfort food. You've always made me fairy cakes when things are bad, but somehow I don't think that little white iced buns go with Mr Brockwell.'

She got up from the chair and walked towards the telephone. 'Afterwards, though, I'll have some with a glass of milk in the bath.'

Just ten minutes before Fae made her telephone call, Robert Brockwell had spoken to his Commander-in-Chief.

'Don't let's have any trouble on this one, Bob. Keep it nice and tight and let's hope we can get him back. I don't want any embarrassment. You had better understand that.'

Mindful of his President's requirements, Bob Brockwell measured his not inconsiderable charisma and spooned it out to Fae.

'Hello, Miss Whiteman. I am sorry I had to leave Turkey so quickly, but I have given instructions that you are to be able to reach me whenever you want. Look, I am going to make a suggestion which I don't think you are going to like. Now that we have a negotiator in place I want you to go back to London.'

'No.'

'There isn't anything you can do for the moment. The best thing for you is to try and continue with your normal life. I know that is impossible, but these things go on and on. It's like water on a stone – drip drip drip – and it's hell. I am not going to tell you anything else. But you have to stay strong, for Sam, for your little brother and most of all for you yourself. I give you my word that if there is any movement whatsoever you will be told. Go back to London, tomorrow. It's the right thing to do, I promise you.'

'I'm not happy about it.'

'I am sure you are not, but will you at least think about it?'

Fae felt herself being swamped by Brockwell's charm; but if she were honest, she would admit she liked Kamel Batami more.

Fae and her mother dined with Ichmet Golabi in his sumptuous home bedecked with rich carpets and burnished woods. She recounted the call with Bob Brockwell.

The old man was slow in his reply, as if to consider every word.

'I think a negotiator is an excellent idea, don't you, Fae?'

'Yes, yes I do,' Fae said.

'And it will allow you to go home with a free heart knowing that someone is here to look after your interests, don't you think?'

'Yes, yes,' Fae said. Sam was here. Inside of her she didn't want to leave.

After a delicate dinner of roast lamb and aubergines served with puréed chick peas, Ichmet offered Turkish coffee on his wood-framed balcony overlooking the Bosphorus. The sounds of the night mingled with the soft slip slap of the water and the rumbling purr of the countless cars crawling to and fro.

Fae sat very still and found herself praying that Sam was safe. She knew her mind had slipped into another place where only he mattered. It was as if reality were around the corner, somewhere else, and she was trapped on her own, wondering, waiting for something – anything. A door bell chimed and Ichmet Golabi excused himself. Idly she wondered who it was.

Rashid Boaz stood in his Rector's hall – he spoke quietly and rapidly.

'Hayri's younger brother has been taken. He is very distressed.'

'I have guests,' his Rector replied. 'Your delightful friend, Fae Whiteman. Join us, won't you, for coffee?'

'I should love to,' Rashid replied smoothly.

Fae was very pleased to see Rashid. She knew it was ridiculous, but for some reason he made her feel better, as if she were nearer to Sam. Perhaps it was because he was one of Sam's students.

After the greetings, the four disparate people talked of this and that. An observer might be forgiven for saying they were sharing their thoughts, but each one, despite the polite chit-chat, was locked into private turmoils. Barbara merely wanted Fae home, safe in England. Fae agonized over Sam. Rashid worried about Hayri and the young brother. Only Ichmet took all the anxieties and intertwined them, understood them, but above all recognized that the boy might admit to anything to stop his torturers.

On the other side of the city in the whitewashed room where there was no night and no day, the young boy sobbed out his pains.

'I'll tell you, I will, I will. Just stop. Please, please stop.'

'What are you going to tell us?'

'Whatever you want.'

'That's not good enough. We need names.'

'But I know no names.'

'I don't believe he does know,' said 'the surgeon'. He put down his instruments and instructed the others to do the same. But the boy felt no relief. He had fainted.

'We'll see the other two students. Find out if the doctor attached to the prison where they are being held thinks they are ready for more interrogation. I don't want to kill them, but I must have the names. We have to get the American back, whatever. In the meantime, round up the rest of the people on the list from the Rector's office. We'll just have to work through each suspect, one by one, until we get what we want.'

* * *

On Ichmet Golabi's balcony the dark night beckoned sleepers, and Fae and her mother bid Ichmet farewell. Rashid escorted them home. In the morning they spent several hours with William Fairchild establishing the family intimacies which would enable him to authenticate Sam Whiteman's kidnappers. Richard Marks obtained their tickets for the flight home.

Meanwhile, Kamel Batami notified his Embassy in London that Fae Whiteman was returning to her own city. He was aware that the Americans would tail her. He would have to do the same, just in case anyone contacted her and she chose not to advise him. He chose Suleyman Gamel, who was not his ideal choice. A former link with a fanatically right-wing group, the Grey Wolves, did not comfort Batami, but that was not his main objection: all the reports on Gamel showed him to be a highly strung individual, capable of an excess of zeal. He spoke English fluently, however, and he was a superb undercover man, capable of finding, as Batami told one of his associates, a needle in a haystack – an appropriately British expression. Suleyman lived alone with his elderly mother. His father had been killed on active service with Mujahedin, as the Cyprus intervention force was known. As such he was regarded kindly by the authorities – they had arranged for him to read politics and philosophy at Ankara University and then arranged a commission in the army.

Batami briefed Suleyman himself. He gave him a photograph of Fae Whiteman.

'Find out everything about her, even who she loves.'

Suleyman gazed at the photograph for a long time. He felt a surge of pleasure. There was something about the girl that interested him – she had black hair just like him.

CHAPTER FOUR

In a nice garden in Ealing the sounds of children's voices floated through the soft air of an English summer evening. Someone on the other side of a fence was barbecuing, and the woody perfume of potatoes cooking in charcoal mingled with the smell of newly mown grass. A television was on . . . the crisp rounded syllables of the newscaster anaesthetizing the day's tragedies, smoothing out the pictures for mass voyeurism. A telephone rang and, as she went to answer it, Nick Newman's wife turned the sound down, thus missing the third item on that evening's programme, Fae's return to England.

'Hello?' She had a lilt in her voice, like a singer making the words lift out of their normal pitch.

'Sally, you are never going to believe who it is. This is Katie Rice, well, I'm Katie Palling now.'

'Katie. Good God. How many years is it, ten? Or more? And how lovely to hear from you. How are you? Of course I've kept track of you. I read your articles. But how did you find me?'

'Extraordinary coincidence. I saw a piece on that clever husband of yours, and who should be standing by his side . . .'

'At the British Academy Awards.'

'Anyway, as soon as I saw you, I had to try and find you. Let's lunch, and then we can catch up. How about Wednesday the 12th, one o'clock? I'm a member of that literary watering hole, Groucho's. How about that?'

'Lovely, it will be good to see you again.'

'If you read my stuff, why didn't you get in touch with me via the newspaper?'

'Well, you know how life is . . .'

'Yes, I do. That's why I decided to call you immediately,

otherwise I wouldn't have done it. Anyway I won't keep you on the blower now, see you at Groucho's.'

'I'm really looking forward to it.'

Sally put the telephone down and went straight to her diary. Wednesday was her turn to ferry the children to swimming. She quickly made a note to change the rota and wrote, 'Groucho's with Katie', in careful letters. She wondered what she should wear.

It was comforting for Fae to be home, but at the same time it was difficult. She felt alienated from everyone – no one could share her experience – it wasn't as if there could be a kindred spirit in suffering . . . How many people could understand what she was going through?

Emily was loving. Emily wrapped her arms around her, and held her tight, using the physical contact to communicate her feelings. They both cried. It was Fae who pulled herself together first.

Hours passed in talk and it was all right, but then Fae went to her room and unpacked her clothes, and she was alone. Emily was using the telephone. She and Jeremy, her boyfriend, were very close now.

'Why didn't Jeremy come this evening?' Fae had asked earlier.

'We both thought he would be intrusive. This is my time with you.'

'I wouldn't have minded at all.'

'Well, I would.'

And Fae realized that Emily was going through the time of change when old friendships were being juggled with new lovers. Fae was glad for her, but nevertheless she turned away from the whispering voice on the other side of the door. A million times, or was it two million, she imagined that Nick wasn't married, that there was no wife to claim her rights.

In the house in Ealing, Nick Newman lay in the dark of his bedroom and dwelt upon Fae, knowing that she was alone in her bed, knowing that she needed him. He felt his wife's fingers glide over his leg, light soft movements. He couldn't touch her, not tonight. Careful not to be unkind, he leaned over and kissed Sally on her forehead.

'Have a good sleep,' he said.

The fingers were removed – too quickly? Perhaps? He couldn't help that.

In the bright grey light of an English morning, Fae prepared herself for work. She took a black suit out of her wardrobe, went into the bathroom, showered, washed her hair and dressed. The telephone rang, her mother, safe in her green and yellow chintz bedroom at her house near Godalming, wanted to know how she was.

'OK.'

'Are you going to work today?'

'Yes.'

'I wish you'd have come home with me, darling. But you'll join us for the weekend, won't you? And in the meantime work as hard as you can, and make lots of arrangements with your friends.'

'Don't worry. I have a list of things to do.'

She glanced at her watch. It was 9.30. Time for her to go to her office in Wardour Street. Strangely, she felt nervous. She wasn't sure how she would be able to cope with her work. Emily had already left, calling out a cheery, 'See you later!'

'Are you in tonight?' Fae heard herself say, wishing immediately that she hadn't.

'Yes. Are you?'

'I think so.'

Emily came into her room. 'Fae, listen to me, I'm around for you. If you need me.'

'I know that,' Fae said. 'I just don't want to be a drag.'

'I'll tell you when you are being boring.'

'Thank God for you,' Fae said at Emily's departing back.

The telephone rang again. This time it was Simon Palling.

'Are you all right, Fae? How about a lunch or a drink? Just to keep in touch.'

'That's kind of you, Simon. But I haven't been to the office yet. I can't really arrange anything until I've seen my diary.'

Fae didn't like Simon Palling very much. It wasn't anything particular – it was just an uneasy feeling. There was no reason for her to feel that way, but she always trusted her instincts. Her mother didn't share her view, her mother liked him.

'I completely understand. So I'll leave and give you a call in a few days then.'

Fae knew he would.

She picked up her briefcase, slipped into her high black shoes, turned her answering machine on and walked out of the flat. She double-locked the door and then clicked her way down the shallow staircase, through the small lobby and out into the street. At the traffic lights she saw a black cab. She raised an arm to hail it, but then she saw it didn't have its light on. Disappointed she dropped her arm, but the cab drove straight towards her.

'Where are you goin', love?' the driver asked. A nice man, iron grey hair, shiny blue eyes, a pink, fresh face.

'Wardour Street.'

'Get in,' he said, opening his door.

'I didn't think you were for hire.'

'I'm actually on me way 'ome. I'm on nights, but I'll take you.' He turned to look at her through his sliding glass door.

'Sorry about your Dad, but he'll be home soon.'

He slid the glass shut, giving Fae privacy.

Fae felt a rush of tears. She was glad to be home, amongst the familiar.

The driver dropped her on the corner of Wardour Street. He wouldn't take the fare.

'Look, I didn't even put the clock on,' he said.

'Thanks a million,' said Fae.

The driver watched her walk into a door between a restaurant and a betting shop.

He reached down for his radio.

'Subject's in her office.'

'King's Cross Station,' snapped a clipped voice underneath a bowler hat, and a manicured hand reached for the silver handle.

'I'm not a bleedin' taxi,' the driver snapped, and drove off, leaving the would-be passenger fuming on the pavement.

To reach British Films Incorporated the visitor would have to walk up close-carpeted stairs of a sickly green colour, round a sharp corner and then bang on a white door emblazoned with the company's name. As Fae made her way into the office, that door was open and Helen, Fae's secretary, was waiting for her with a tray of coffee and her favourite chocolate digestive biscuits. There were hugs and comfort. Fae was beginning to feel much much better. Her office was full of flowers and she knew that Helen had sent the word around that she was coming back.

The mogul, Raymond Grace, arrived shortly after her. Dressed in an immaculate grey suit and matching tie he embraced her courteously.

'How are you? Come in. Bring your coffee and catch me up on what has been happening.'

Fae was surprised at her employer's concern. A film man, he never normally enquired into his employees' lives. A quick smile and a perfunctory comment about the weather, the football or perhaps someone's health were the normal behaviour. But today Fae found herself on the soft chintz settee opposite the huge boardroom table that he normally favoured. He sat next to her, squeezed her hand and settled back to listen.

To her surprise, Fae talked. She talked for an hour, telling the anonymous man for whom she worked as much as she knew about her father's kidnapping.

'And your brother, how is he?'

'Not good, but better now he's in Italy.'

'You must go and see him. And if you need to go back to Turkey, or to America, just use the company travel agents. Don't worry about the fares.'

'Look Raymond, I . . .'

'And in the meantime there are three scripts on your desk. *Dirty Young Girl* is packaged with Jodi Foster and Jack Lemmon. I want a reaction by lunchtime. Oh, and get hold of the new Rushdie.'

'There won't be a movie in that.'

'Just check it out.'

At five o'clock Fae realized she had not looked at her telephone list at all . . . in fact, she had quite forgotten the events in Turkey. Guilt flooded her, she put aside her office work.

First she contacted Colin Pritchard, a film maker who had made a documentary on Turkish Trade Unions. Perhaps he might have some contacts who could help her? A lunch was arranged, Groucho's on Wednesday the 12th.

After she put the telephone down, Fae found herself thinking about Richard Marks again. A thick cloud of anger cloaked her: she was glad, she needed her scapegoat.

She glanced down at the list of names on the paper in front of her. Mostly they were friends, but suddenly she couldn't face the 'how are you?' and the 'what happened?' – the anger gave way to the grey cloak of despair sinking down on to her shoulders, stifling her movements, her thoughts, even her breathing. She wanted to go home, fall into the void of inactivity.

Nick, she wanted Nick. She drew a circle around his name, she sketched little sharp lines from the circle – a hedgehog with its tight prickles protecting itself. Don't touch me? She picked up the receiver and swallowed, tense, not knowing whether she should reach out to him.

Her intercom buzzed, a sharp noise.

'Fae, Bill's called. He wants to know if you want to meet him for a drink,' Helen told her. Bill was a producer, a good friend, she knew he would have rounded up a few good mates.

'Yes, I would,' Fae said. She put the receiver down, glad in a way that she could delay the need of Nick.

But she saw him as she crossed Wardour Street on her way to the pub to meet Bill. He was skirting the jammed cars and the weaving motor cycles. She called out to him. Even in the noise he heard her, and turned towards her. The dust of London stuck to her skin.

'Fae.'

'Hello, Nick.'

'I've been thinking about you.'

'Yes.'

Staccato words, longing fingers. But that was all there could be.

'Look, if you need anything, anything at all, call me.'

'It's OK.'

'I, I'd like to see you.'

'Can you have a drink now?' Oh no, too eager, far too eager, but it couldn't be helped.

'I can't.'

'No, of course not.'

'No, I mean I can't now. I'll call you.'

The same sinking feeling that she had whenever she left him. What was the point? It hurt so much.

Just two days later, on Wednesday 12 August, Fae went to meet Colin Pritchard at the Groucho Club, a meeting place for anxious writers and producers wanting to fall over slightly less anxious publishers, or agents or, heaven be praised, the executive who could actually green-light someone's project. As she pushed through the crowded lobby and signed the members' book she was aware of a blonde woman, well dressed in high fashion cream trousers and a matching cream top, sitting in the corner of the room. The woman was scanning the faces anxiously. Fae smiled at her and then she recognized her. It was Nick's wife. Oh God, don't let her be meeting Nick. But then another woman, one with brown short hair cut in a sleek style with big earrings and bright red lips swept through the revolving doors.

'Sally, it's so good to see you,' the new arrival said, embracing Nick's wife. 'Come on, let's go and have a drink.' Fae watched as the two women walked through the swing doors into the dark blue womb of the Groucho bar.

A voice interrupted her. 'Hello, my love.' It was Colin Pritchard: he put an arm around her shoulder. 'How're you doin'?'

'Could be better.'

'I believe you.'

They sat at a table in the corner of the room. Colin, a huge man with a grainy face and blond hair that hung over his forehead, perched uncomfortably on his little chair. He was not a man made for tidy chairs in pretty restaurants.

'Have you any idea who has your Dad?'

'No.'

'Look, I made a few phone calls. The Turkish exiles here don't know, and this isn't their style anyway, but even so, ring this number.' He handed her a piece of paper. 'Ask to speak to Maurice, not his real name, he's expecting to hear from you.'

'Thanks, Colin.'

'Wish I could do more.' Colin leaned back in his chair as an attractive lady came over to the table with the bottle of Chablis that Fae had ordered. 'But at least I know they will see you.'

They ate fish and Fae attempted to concentrate, and not be distracted by the two ladies who were talking so intimately on the other side of the room – beyond the ceiling fan that caused much havoc to the migraine sufferers.

'So you married the dishy man, had the three lovely children and lived happily ever after,' Katie said as she delicately smoothed creamy yellow butter on to the small piece of French bread that she had chosen from the bread basket.

'Well not quite happily all the time, but most of it.'

'You are a lucky woman.'

'I married the man I wanted.'

'So did I.'

'Are you happy?'

'What's happy?' Katie said, shrugging her shoulders, and quickly steered the conversation the way she wanted. 'See that girl over there, do you know who she is?'

'Yes, yes, my husband knows her.'

Oh, how easy this is going to be, Katie thought to herself, and she couldn't help a small smile.

'She works in the film industry doesn't she?'

Sally glanced over to where Fae sat. She knew exactly who Fae was, she'd known about her for years. She'd hoped, when Fae had stopped working for Nick, that the relationship had ended. But she found Fae's telephone number in a new diary. She'd kept quiet, hoping they would get over each other, burn out the passion. Oh God, how she hated the thought of her husband in bed with another woman. Sometimes she could almost smell her skin on his. Sally could hardly bear to sit in the same restaurant. The girl had even smiled at her just before lunch – how dare she smile? Who was she to smile at anyone?

Katie noticed that Sally hadn't answered her question. She slipped in another, asking innocently, 'How is she coping?'

'Why should I know?'

'Well, I naturally assumed that if she was a friend of Nick's you might have seen her or at least spoken to her.'

'She isn't a friend of mine.'

Katie understood immediately. She took in a sharp breath, she was no bitch – she didn't enjoy trading on other people's miseries.

'Oh, listen, Sally, I'm sorry. I really wouldn't have raised any of this. I had no idea.'

Sally's eyes were unnaturally bright. She was fiddling with the stem of her glass.

'I'd rather not talk about it if you don't mind,' she said, speaking very quietly.

'No, of course I don't mind,' Kate replied. She felt a bit of a shit.

Fae spoke to 'Maurice' as soon as she got back to her office.

'Yes, I knew you would be in touch,' he said.

'May I at least talk to you?'

'In the circumstances, yes. But I must warn you that I don't believe we can help you very much.'

'I'm just grateful you are seeing me.'

'Very well. Seven o'clock this evening.' He gave her an address in Wembley. Fae felt the bite of anticipation. She was doing something, she was actually talking to someone who just might know something about her father. She had an obsessional need to bring his name into every conversation, much as one might speak of a lover. She worried she was boring Helen in the office, but had to relive the events of the kidnapping. It brought Sam close to her, as if he were really with her.

The house in Wembley was in one of those anonymous streets where rows of identical red roofs topped white stucco houses, and roses bordered the front paths. There was a small note saying that the doorbell was out of order. The ribbed glass front door opened the moment Fae knocked.

'Come in.' A young man, maybe twenty-eight, with black hair and sharp black eyes in a pleasant moon-shaped face invited her into the small front room. There were just two other people there. A girl, pretty, with black curly hair and a lovely smile, and another man, smaller, plumper with hair that clung to his scalp and a beard. This was Maurice: he held out his hand. He wore half his uniform – a white shirt, open at the neck, and grey trousers. The tie and the jacket must have been removed and left somewhere – it seemed that 'Maurice' was not a man to be comfortable in formal clothes. The other man wore jeans, the girl was in navy velour trousers and a little top in the same material, heavily embroidered. Fae, dressed in a green sarong-type skirt and a short-sleeved cream blouse, wondered at how the girl stood the heavy material even in an English summer.

'I will get you a tea,' the girl said to her. As she walked past Fae she said, 'I am so sorry for you. To have your father taken away. It's terrible.'

Fae was touched at her kindness. She had to sit down, even without being invited.

'Maurice' sat too . . . the chairs were green, the settee too. The carpet a rust colour, there was a print of some flowers in a vase on the wall behind the settee. The cream tiled mantelpiece was bare, but above it hung a mirror on a bronze chain. It was an anonymous room, but from the kitchen came a distinctive delicious aroma of a slow rich cuisine heavy with spices. The girl in navy returned with tea, without milk, and some biscuits – English ones, shortbread.

'I'm sorry, but I honestly don't know how we can help you. I have made some telephone calls, but none of my contacts know who could have done this. We, of course, know of the young people who have been taken into custody. But they are not affiliated to any of our groups.' He smiled. 'We can only assume that they are political innocents using desperate measures to get their friends out of prison.'

Fae felt her stomach close up. The disappointment was awful.

'So you know nothing?'

'We are not kidnappers, Miss Whiteman. We are trying for social change, not for anarchy. We will try to speak with the young people in custody, but while they are in solitary confinement, it is impossible for our people to contact them, so it does not look hopeful.'

'We are so sorry for you,' the girl in navy said.

Fae tried to stop the deflation. These people seemed to have contacts – she hoped, just a tiny hope, that they might get hold of some sliver of information from someone, somewhere.

'If I give you my telephone number, will you ring me if you hear anything?' she said.

'Of course we will,' 'Maurice' replied.

'I appreciate you seeing me. I'm just sorry I don't know who you are.'

'We prefer, for your safety and ours, that you know nothing about us. And then if anyone asks you – and they could – you can truthfully tell them what you have seen.'

'Yes, I understand.'

Fae drank her tea. It was a little too hot, so she left most of it, hoping the girl would understand. She thanked them for seeing her and left.

She got into her car. She was tired: she wasn't sleeping very well. Her shoulders ached and she ran her fingers over her face and through her hair. Sam was so far away.

'Maurice' and the girl watched her from behind the net curtains.

'Poor woman,' the girl said.

Fae pulled out of the little road and picked up the North Circular. The commuters had long since gone to their homes and it was pleasant to drive in the darkening light. She opened her windows – the air felt good on her arms. She would have put on a tape if Sam had not been kidnapped. After just a few moments, she became aware of a van, its headlights full on, just behind her, immediately behind her. She pulled over to let the van pass, but it didn't pass her, it stayed on her tail. She slowed down, the van slowed down, she speeded up, the van speeded up, always right behind, its headlights blinding her. Fae was suddenly absolutely terrified. She put her foot down and drove as fast as she could, skipping traffic lights, but still the van was with her. She cried out 'Go away', but the big lights blazed into her mirror, huge yellow discs of what had become a tormentor, playing a game with her. Or was it a game? Go past me, drive past me, leave me alone! She saw a turning to her left, the Golders Green Road. Ignoring the sign banning a right turn, she pulled out, waited for a passing car on the other side of the road, and then cut across. But the van was behind her. Oh God, was it going to follow her home? There was traffic ahead: Fae put her foot down, wove in front of another car, and then another – the van was behind her. The traffic lights at the junction of the road leading to Hampstead were orange. She shot forward; she was over before they turned red. She started to relax, drove carefully to the Holloway Road, towards the city and her own home. At Highbury Corner she realized the van was still with her. She started to cry. Where should she go, what should she do? There was a policeman, walking the beat. She drove over to him.

'Please, look, I know you'll think I am mad, but that van has been following me all the way from Wembley.'

The van drove past her, its lights still blazing. The policeman glanced at the van and then back at Fae.

'I know you'll think I'm crazy, but he was on my tail all the time. He frightened me.'

'I'm sure he did, love. They see a pretty girl in a car, if you'll excuse me, and they get cocky. It can cause accidents, things like that, but I'm sure they meant you no harm. Now you go home, safe and sound.'

'I'm sorry . . . I'

'No, you were right to stop and tell me.'

Fae drove off, she was still shaking. When she got to her street, she parked in the road – she wouldn't go into the underground car park. She wound up the windows, gritted her teeth and got out of the car. Heart thumping she locked the door, the key wouldn't move – was it stuck? Oh come on, yes, it was out. She ran to the front door, opened it, up the stairs, there was her own door, just one more turn of a key and then she was in, safe.

'Emily, Emily.' But there was no Emily, just a note – 'Gone to Jeremy's. Love ya.'

Oh no, she would be alone. She heard footsteps, a man's – who was it? What did they want? She heard the doorbell. She wouldn't answer it. She would stay where she was, safe on the other side.

It rang again. 'Fae, Fae, it's me.'

Nick, it was Nick.

Pulling back the bolt and opening the door she said, 'Someone was following me, I know they were. I was frightened.'

'It's all right, I'm here with you. It's all right.'

Hands on skin, anxious to find skin anywhere, mouth to mouth, tongue to tongue, lips on secret places. There in the entrance of her flat, Fae sank to her knees reaching up for Nick.

'Here?' he said.

Her skirt rose high – his fingers, how she loved his long slender fingers – caressed and stroked. She was ready for him, she wanted him. 'Nick, Nick.' Gasping, she felt his mouth on her neck, his hands lifting her hair, he slid into her, a knife in its sheath. She raised herself up, wanting him deeper inside her. The honey flowed from her, for him. The shuddering started, engulfing her, swelling inside her. 'Yes, I love you. I love you.' Whose voice? Her voice, always her voice, he couldn't tell her with words, just her name, over and over. 'Fae, Fae . . .'

After the loving, Nick swept Fae up in his arms and took her to her bedroom. He pulled the duvet down, laid her on the bed, touched her softly, sweetly, and then made her talk about Sam: 'I think one of the most shocking aspects is that I thought I knew my father, but now I discover I don't.'

'That's part of growing up, Fae, discovering that our parents aren't fairy godmothers and godfathers who wave wands and bring happy ever after.'

'Is that my problem, Nick, that I still believe in happy ever after?'

'Yup, because your happy ever after means that other people have to get hurt.'

'That's life is it? Someone is always hurt.'

'I've always told you, Fae, there are no rose gardens out there.'

'And I know that roses have thorns anyway, so you don't have to tell me that. But I still want the smell of the roses – I'll always want that. Life wouldn't be life without the roses.'

Nick looked at Fae. He didn't answer her – for that was the way they talked – never real talk, just in case real things were said, and then real problems would have to be confronted.

Fae leaned over Nick's chest and her black hair trailed over his tanned arm, her breasts against his silk smooth torso. His fingers traced patterns on her face. He reached over to the little shelf beside Fae's bed, picked up his watch.

'I have to go,' he whispered.

'Yes.' She turned over.

He reached out to her with his two hands, he knew how she loved him to cup her breasts, he knew she loved him, he knew it was pointless . . . the pain, the bittersweet pain of wanting her, and then afterwards the blackness of the guilt because of all that hurt. And he would push her away, he had to push her away, out to the perimeters of his mind so he could function as a husband and a father. The hurt of missing her would have to be buried. But that was all for later: now it was just Fae and Nick, and the phantoms of other loves had to step back from his wanting.

He ran his mouth over her, down her taut stomach, over her flowering hips, into the soft crevices of her most private place. He drowned in the feel of her, the taste of her, using his tongue to pleasure her. He felt her shift and moan, she wanted to reach for him, but no, no, this was for her. He pushed her back, tasting her, nipping her, sucking. Her wetness smothered him, and he felt her excitement.

She pushed away his restrictive hand, she wanted to give to him. She shifted so she lay under him and as he kissed her and loved her, she took him in her mouth, ran her tongue up and down him, played games with her lips and her tongue and her teeth. She wanted to be with this man forever . . .

In another room, in another house, the wife of Fae's lover lay alone. She knew he was with Fae, there was little doubt. She felt it in her gut . . . it had to end. She had stood it for as long as she could. She was his wife, she was the mother of his children, she loved him, she would never let him go. She closed her eyes, trying to shut out images of flesh on flesh. No, no, don't do that, don't – you touch me there!

A child cried – had she shouted out loud? Sally slipped out of her bed and went down the corridor to her son James, just five, who was sitting up in his Thomas the Tank Engine bed, arms outstretched for comfort.

'Daddy.'

'I'm sorry, darling, Daddy is out at a meeting. He'll be home soon.' She soothed her child and resolved to end Fae Whiteman's relationship with her husband. When she went back into the bedroom she wrote Katie's name and telephone number on a piece of paper and propped it up on her dressing-table. She would telephone her in the morning.

After Nick left her, Fae bolted her front door and tried not to wonder when she would see him again. He hadn't said anything, he had held her and kissed her, and then waved a hand and shut the door behind him. She went back to her bed, and breathed in his smell. Tomorrow she would change her sheets.

Outside Fae's window there was a fire escape. No one used it normally, as it wasn't very attractive, but she heard a noise, a sort of shuffling sound as if someone were sliding across the iron gratings. She remembered the car behind her on the way back from Wembley. She told herself not to be stupid, there was no one there. But the terror had come back, she couldn't help herself. Fae looked out of the window, she saw nothing, she pulled her white curtains tight. She climbed back into her bed, but she couldn't sleep, she was too frightened. She got up, went back into the hall, and tried to think of the lovemaking. Sitting in a chair by the telephone, she looked at her watch. Two o'clock – it was too late to ring her mother. Would Emily be coming back? No, no, she wouldn't.

Aware that he had made a noise, a man crouched low to avoid the people in the next flat – rowdy partygoers – drunk and happy, but then one of the girls said she was going to be sick and she lurched on to the fire escape, heaving up her night's liquid supper. The man – the young Turk, Suleyman Gamel – turned and ran away.

Fae stayed awake all night. She was exhausted in the morning. Still she showered and washed her hair, and dressed herself and went to her office. What else was there to do?

In the house in Ealing, after Nick had left and Sally had sent the children to school, Sally telephoned Katie at her office and asked to meet her, urgently. They both arrived at the appointed rendezvous, a coffee shop in Marylebone High Street where marzipan animals vied with strawberry tarts and buttery croissants.

'I need your help, as a friend,' Sally said, waiting whilst Katie poured coffee from silver pots. 'That girl, Fae Whiteman, is having an affair with my husband.'

Katie reached out a hand. 'Sally, listen . . .'

'No, you listen. Get one of your friends on those cheaper papers to run the story. I'll give you enough. He won't sue and neither will she.'

On Sunday morning the *News of the World* led with a splash on Fae Whiteman's love affair with Nick Newman. Fae was at her mother and stepfather's house in the country.

Barbara, of course, rang her friend Simon Palling.

'I know, I've seen it,' he told Barbara. 'It's appalling, but you can only do something if it isn't true.'

Katie listened as she peeled her potatoes and felt that justice had been done.

'You'll have to end it with her if you want to stay with us,' Sally told her husband.

'I will end it.'

'Do it now. Write her a letter.'

'No.'

'Then ring her. I want to hear.'

'No, you've had your pound of flesh. Leave us both alone now.'

'I've had my pound of flesh. What the hell are you talking about? It's you, you bastard, you've hurt us.'

'Yes, yes, I did. But it was you who rang Katie Palling. You shouldn't have left her telephone number on the dressing-table. I wondered why you were ringing her – now I know.'

'I had no choice!' Sally screamed to Nick as he left the room. 'I had no choice, you bastard.'

Nick and Fae saw each other that night. He waited for her in the underground car park where she normally put her car.

'Go to Italy, see Fabrizzi,' he said.

'Nick, I didn't mean to hurt anyone.'

'Nor did I, Fae. I'm so sorry.' He stroked her hair, he kissed her, his tears mingled with hers.

'Goodbye, darling,' he said, and he let himself out of her car and walked back to his own. Fae sat still, and wept and wept. Her mind had nowhere to go to escape from the dreadful agony.

Nick Newman drove his car, a black Porsche, out of the car park. He saw the journalists outside Fae's apartment, waiting for her like hounds at the hunt. He ought to go back to her and take her into the flat: he couldn't leave her like that. He stopped the car, got out, and ran down to the entrance. He didn't look at her.

'They are all outside – waiting for the photographs. Let them have them. Come on.'

He took her arm and walked her fast through the jostling hacks. Simon Palling was there, just by the front door.

'I'll take her now,' he said to Nick.

'It's all right, Simon's a friend. You can go now,' Fae said. He couldn't answer her. He walked away quickly, aware of the cameras, but not caring about them.

It was in his car, on his way home, that he screamed.

* * *

In Istanbul, unaware of his daughter's anguish, Sam Whiteman sat in the locked room and waited, but for what? He didn't know. There were three knocks on the door. Obediently he reached for his hood and placed it on his head. He didn't like the blackness any more than he had before, but at least his hands were free.

'Hello, Mr Whiteman.'

It was the girl. She had come back to see him.

'And now it's time to talk.'

'Yes.'

'You agree.'

'It depends what we are going to talk about.'

'We are going to talk about you and the CIA.'

'I have admitted I worked for them.'

'Yes, you have. But now we would like the names of others.'

Faces of dead students came back to fill the blackness with a greater horror. He'd given names, he couldn't give names any more. There would be no more deaths.

'I can't do that.'

'Why not?'

'I just can't. I can tell you about myself. But I cannot implicate others.'

'Come now, Mr Whiteman.' The voice was sharper. 'There was no such moral stance before.'

'I know, and I was wrong. I've been responsible for a terrible wrong. I won't do it again.'

'But you can put your wrong right.'

'No.' There, he had said it. 'No,' he repeated. What would they do? He didn't care. A chair scraped, the girl had stood up, an arm on his shoulder.

'Mr Whiteman, I do understand. But think if you want to do something about my comrades. You could tell us who you betrayed them to, who hurt them, and we can stop those people from doing that to anyone else again. I will leave you to think about it.'

The door swung shut, then came three knocks: he could take off his mask. There was no thinking to do. He had resisted: he would continue to resist.

* * *

'So your methods have not worked,' snapped Hayri harshly.

'Give me time,' Faroud replied. 'At least another five days. He will talk.'

'And if not?'

'Then you can have him.'

CHAPTER FIVE

Richard Marks was irritated by the apparently successful anonymity of the group that had kidnapped Sam Whiteman. The long silence was affecting him. He knew he was not a man who could sit and wait for events to unfurl. He learnt that in Beirut during the early 1980s. Officially at that time he was a young officer in the Marine Corps working at the Embassy, but his actual job was to ferret out information on the Company's key asset, Phalangist militia leader, Bashir Gemayel . . . Gemayel's death just nine days before he was to take office as Lebanon's President affected Richard badly. He had broken all the rules and become personally involved: he adored the man.

For a time he controlled his impulses – he did so well that his boss forgave his emotional responses and promoted him. But then he met Innessa. What happened was extraordinary for, with the exception of his little daughters, Richard had insulated himself against all feeling. And now he had to resolve that love – and in order to do so he had to produce Sam Whiteman, like the master magician pulling the rabbit from the black hat. And how was he to do that with no lead whatsoever? Even the almighty great Turkish Secret Police, fresh from their torture chambers, had nothing much to offer. They were trying to find Hayri Gurbuz – a list they had obtained from the office of the Rector of the Bosphorus University had marked Hayri as a suspect, but no one knew where he was . . . yet.

Richard was determined to break the impasse. He took to loitering around the Bosphorus University, letting students and teachers know what he wanted. For three days there was nothing, and then, in the afternoon of the fourth day, when he was sitting in a tiny coffee house not far from the fish market, he was approached by a young man . . . a student, Memet Safarayon, a good looking boy; broad-faced and sunny. He rowed for the University, streaking through the blue grey waters of the Bosphorus on the day of the Turkish Universities Boat Races – hoping to get to Henley, the boating garden party where the social tit and tat was as important, if not more so, than the muscular young men who slogged out their battles on the muted green of the River Thames.

The boy took out a cigarette and Richard offered him a light. Any prying eye might assume that just a casual exchange was taking place. As Richard snapped his lighter shut Memet said, 'I know who you are. I like Sam Whiteman. I don't like the fact that he has been kidnapped. I might just have an idea who has taken him and I will tell you, but not here, it's too small, too conspicuous. Meet me in the Spice Market, in the new town, at three o'clock.'

Memet drew on his cigarette. 'Thank you.' He was about to turn away from the table. But Richard, ever alert, noticed a young girl, pretty in jeans and a blue sweater, watching from a distance.

'Who is that?'

'My sister . . . who else?'

Memet strode off and met up with the girl. They walked away together and Richard relaxed and settled back to enjoy a coffee. He had no intention of informing anyone of Memet's offer, not until he had his information.

As the time for the rendezvous approached, Richard left the café and took a taxi to the railway station where once the grand tourists of another era had boarded the Orient Express. He paid the driver off and walked towards the Spice Market. He reached the entrance at precisely 2.58 P.M. and saw Memet waiting for him. As he approached him, Richard heard a voice call out, an American voice.

'Is that you, Memet?'

Richard turned immediately and saw a gun – he shouted out, but too late, for the shooting had started. He dived on top of the boy, and took the second direct hit.

The effects of the killings ricocheted like the bullets themselves. The authorities, both American and Turkish, were enraged, and for those who knew Richard Marks, there was sadness. But all the emotions were overshadowed by the need to make alternative plans. William Fairchild spoke with Robert Brockwell: 'For God's sake, Fairchild, why didn't he tell you what was going on? Useless waste of life makes me so angry.'

For the families, there was the grief.

Richard's former wife, Camille, was horrified, and indeed very sad – she shed tears – but she and her new husband resolved to inure the two little girls as best they could against their father's death. Being a sensible woman she consulted a counsellor on how best to deal with the killing. It was in all the papers, and on television: it was agreed that the little girls should attend their father's funeral, a high grade affair with all the paraphernalia of a military event. One child's hand was firmly grasped by their mother, the other's by their Aunty Pat, Richard's older sister – an older woman of forty-one with two children of her own and a husband who worked in the Justice Department. There were, fortunately, no parents to cope with Richard's violent end. His gentle mother had died of cancer when Richard was just twenty-seven. His father, who ran a garage, hadn't lasted much longer after her – just eighteen months.

Memet's parents simply couldn't comprehend their tragedy. Their boy had been the love of their lives, the son, the bright one – how could it happen? His sister understood, but even so, she too was bereft.

As for Innessa, she was entertaining her stepdaughter when she heard the piece of news that would catapult her into the empty abyss of bereavement.

Fae had flown to Rome on the first available flight on the Monday after her exposure in the *News of the World*. Innessa was expecting her – Barbara had forewarned her that Fae was in distress. The plan that Innessa made with her own mother was that she would keep Fae quietly in Rome for perhaps two days. 'Then I will bring her back here.'

Innessa's mother was an elegant bastion of Roman Society. Still beautiful and slim, dressed by Valentino, she was used to turning heads, even at fifty-five. If she had love affairs, she kept them to herself. The Countess Maria Castelloni – the title came from her own father – was happy to let Innessa make any decisions she wished about the young English girl whose indiscretions had made headlines for public consumption. She prepared herself for an afternoon's tennis, bade her grandson a fond farewell and waved to her daughter.

Innessa's father, Roberto, was altogether a different kind of man. A car magnate, his sports' models were often defined as a sexual delight in themselves.

'Give Fae our love. Keep her tranquil, my darling. She has had two terrible shocks. She will need all our help and all our love.'

'I know, Papa.'

The choice of staying in busy Rome for Fae to gather herself was not as unreasonable as might be thought. There was no one in the house, save for the family's housekeeper, whereas the Countess Maria had house guests and both Innessa and Barbara felt that Fae would be in no mood to socialize. However, it didn't take Innessa too many hours to realize that Rome was not a success. Fae was quiet, and Fabrizzi, after the initial excitement of seeing his sister, was very restless. The eternal city was very hot and there was no space for Fabrizzi to play or to run. They did go to the Gardens of the Borghese, but a woman, an English woman, Innessa presumed, was reading Sunday's *News of the World*, so they fled – Fae behind her dark glasses and her huge black hat – back to the cool tranquillity of Innessa's family home.

In the afternoon they drove to Positano.

It was that evening, over the drinks before dinner when, as Innessa observed Fae trying to make an effort with her mother's worldly friends, the news of Richard's death reached them. Barry, the family's English butler, slid on to the crowded terrace and whispered in Roberto's ear.

'Thank you, Barry,' the Italian said. He rose to his feet, a stylish man in white trousers and a navy shirt. 'Innessa, and Fae, will you join me? We have not had a chance to talk yet.'

He walked them down the wide stone staircase before he said anything. He addressed them both, but he looked at Fae.

'The American who was in charge of the investigations into your father's abduction has been shot. He is dead.'

'Oh my God,' Fae said. A sudden, almost shocking image of Richard came into her head. She immediately turned her head to Innessa and unconsciously reached out her hand. 'My God,' she said again. What else was there to say? It seemed that they were in the middle of some sort of dreadful vortex that grew wilder daily, swallowing up its victims one by one.

'How did it happen?' asked Innessa.

'I don't know the details. I understand Mr William Fairchild telephoned. Perhaps it would be best if you spoke to him.'

'No, not yet, if you don't mind,' Fae said, and turned to Innessa.

'When you are ready, we'll call Fairchild, together,' she told Innessa quietly.

Fae looked over to Roberto, and saw the concern, the sudden knowledge in his face.

'Richard Marks was a very close friend of both Sam and Innessa.'

'I see,' Roberto said kindly. He touched his daughter's arm, but no more than that. It was enough, the care was there. Fae could not help but envy Innessa.

Roberto left them together to walk arm-in-arm, in step, the younger, taller girl suddenly the comforter.

'Thank you. It can't be easy for you,' Innessa said.

'I can't get inside your skin. I can only imagine the hell inside you.'

At the doorway of their respective bedrooms, the stepmother and stepdaughter bade each other an affectionate goodnight.

'If you need me,' Fae said.

'I know,' said Innessa.

Innessa did not go into her own room. She could not bear to be alone. Instead she went downstairs and joined the guests for dinner. It was easier to make small talk than to sit and think.

Fae had scarcely sat on her bed when Barry, the butler, brought her a tray – just some toast and tea. He poured the tea himself, and stirred in a lot of sugar.

'I don't take sugar.'

'Perhaps you don't, normally.'

Fae smiled. 'Thanks.' The butler started to leave the room.

'Barry, did you know my father?'

'I most certainly do. He's a great man. Always talks about you, and he loves that little boy. Get him back, Miss Whiteman.'

'Just like that?'

'Just like that.'

'How?'

'Well, you are his daughter. And he's got a way with himself, and if you'll excuse me for being personal, you do too.'

'A way with himself'. Yes, Sam did have a way with himself: he had charm and tenacity. How dreadful that she needed someone to remind her of him. Was he still alive? After all, they'd killed Richard Marks.

And now Fae had to face herself about the American's murder. She truly hated him when she discovered that he was the CIA man to whom Sam reported. It was easy to blame him, but stupid too. Richard just did his job, as Sam apparently did his. Fae put her head in her hands: everything seemed to ache. She wanted it all to stop, wanted to come out of the drama and get back into real life, where the chaos and confusion centred around her, not mad people who made their crusades with guns. She scrunched her toast, making lots of little crumbs on her plate. She was almost scared to search out Sam's fate. Nick came into her mind. She wanted to hold on to him but he wasn't there for her any more. The memory of their love-making haunted her, crawling over her skin with the delicious spikes of remembered passion. She wanted to crawl into the sheets on her bed and hide, and wait to die. Would that be easier? It might be, for some. But Fae knew she couldn't do that. She would grow restless and the hurts would nudge her and nudge her until she did something to make them feel better. Was that what they called being a survivor? Was Sam surviving? Oh God, she hoped so.

Emily, she had to speak to Emily: that would drag her back into a reality – of sorts. Fae hoped she was in.

As soon as the phone was answered, Fae said, 'It's me.'

'What's happened now? It's a drama – I can hear it in your voice.'

'Richard Marks, the American, he's dead.'

'Oh boy.' There was a sigh too, which Fae could hear down the telephone.

'I feel bad, Emily. I've had enough.'

''Course you have, love. It's like a bloody nightmare.'

'Oh, Emily, what are you doing?'

'What? Now?'

'Yeah, now. I need to know what ordinary people are doing.'

'Erm, well – er . . . you know, the usual.'

Was Emily in bed, with Jeremy? Fae wanted to giggle.

'Locker-room stuff then, Ems?'

'Fae.' Yes. She was.

'I'm glad. Have a good time. I love you. Speak to you soon.'

'No, don't get off the phone. Where are you going? What are you going to do now?'

'I'm going to Turkey.'

'Fae, don't go there. It may not be safe.'

'The CIA aren't going to let anything happen to me. I'm important.'

'It seems they let something happen to Richard Marks.'

'Yes, I s'pose they did.'

'Now don't go and make any stupid moves. OK?'

'OK.'

'And ring your Mum. She's worried about you.'

'I will. Did anyone call?'

'He's not going to ring, Fae. He's staying with his wife. Get over him. You must.'

'I wasn't talking about Nick.'

'Yes you were, love.'

Yes. She was.

Fae flew directly to Istanbul. William Fairchild met her at the airport.

'I'm sorry for your troubles, Fae.'

'It got to Turkey, did it?'

'It got to the CIA.'

Fae tried a laugh.

'We'll protect you from all of that now.'

'I'm very tired,' she said.

The car drove directly to the Hilton Hotel.

'Why have you brought me here? I wanted to go home.'

'Your house is pretty well bugged by us, and the Turks. There's a lot of guys there. I thought you would have more privacy in a hotel.'

'Just take me home, please, Mr Fairchild, and get those people out of there, all of them.'

'Someone has to stay with you.'

'It's all right, I understand that, but I have to be in my own home. Maise, let Maise stay.'

William Fairchild looked at her for a moment: she was white with ink black shadows. He squeezed her hand to indicate his acquiescence, and leaned forward to give an instruction to the embassy driver. As the driver promptly turned his car around and drove to the Whiteman house, Fairchild spoke sharply into the phone. 'Miss Whiteman wants to come home. You have five minutes to make sure that place looks like a palace. If I find one beer can, or one cigarette stub . . .'

Fae couldn't help smiling. In her mind she saw the pink and white house awash with crew-cut Americans and gun-slinging Turks, all under the control of whip-cracking Maise, skirt high on her thighs, standing on a step ladder in Innessa's sleek American kitchen, issuing instructions to clean, clean, clean . . .

It wasn't like that at all. The house, well guarded by rather kind Turkish policemen, was just as she had left it, although there were no flowers in the vases. As she climbed the stairs to bed Fae made a mental note to remedy this in the morning.

Whilst Fae curled up to sleep, another of her acquaintances had arrived in the city. Simon Palling checked himself into the Hilton Hotel.

When she woke up, late, Maise was there, filling a pot with coffee, and a jug with orange juice.

'Hi, kid. Not good, huh?'

'No, not good. How are you, Maise?' Fae was glad to see the American woman, she was comforted by her presence. And it was easier to be in Turkey: she didn't have to explain her situation. She was the daughter of Sam Whiteman, an American hostage. There were no distractions from that, no loves to cloud her priorities.

Sam was in his black hole. Strange, he thought to himself, how it is that what we most fear surely comes to plague us. The girl who was his interrogator sat – he assumed she sat – near to him and asked him her questions.

'OK, Sam, now you have had time to think, I'm sure you're happy to give us the information we need.'

Her voice was not as kind as it had been when he was in the bath. He detected an edge. Was it strain? Was it impatience?

'Yes, I have thought everything through: I can't give you any names.'

'Come on, Sam. Enough of that. Give me some names.' A hand stroked his, softly, gently. 'It's hard for you, I know. But wouldn't you like to be back with your family?'

'Oh yes, I would.'

'I can help you. I can persuade them. But I need some names, my friend.'

'Could you really talk to them for me? Ask them if I can go home?'

'Yes, I could try.'

'Names, that's all you need?'

'Yes. Here on the table I have left a sheet of paper and a pen. Write them down, it will be easier for you.'

The shuffle of furniture, the slight shift of air, the woman was gone. The three knocks followed. He took off his hood and his hands shook a little. He blinked against the light and saw the white piece of paper. He felt sorry for the girl, she was so kind; even so, he wasn't going to give her any information.

Fae and William Fairchild arranged to meet for lunch, so that Fae could catch up on the events leading to Richard's death. They met at the Abdullah Efendi Restaurant in Emirgan, where diners can see the Bosphorus from its windows and enjoy the delights of Turkish cuisine, cooked specially for tourists.

She sat with the American whilst he ate his way through hors-d'oeuvres of tarama creamed red caviar, mussels stuffed with rice, pine-nuts and spices, fried calamari and shrimp, and humus and Circassian chicken made from boned chicken covered in a sauce of walnuts and garlic and red pepper. Then there was fish, grilled turbot for Fae whilst Fairchild ate buglama and drank a copious amount of Raki. Between mouthfuls he talked.

'We have some ideas, Fae, but the problem is that we have no clear lead. Richard may have been on to something with the boy, Memet, the one who was shot, but Richard kept whatever he had to himself.' The implication was clear.

'There's been no more contact.'

'No, there hasn't.' William was concentrating on his shrimps, removing the head and the pink shell from the body so that he could eat the white flesh. Fae was suddenly not very hungry. She pushed her turbot away and fiddled with a green salad.

'Fae, you are back, how lovely,' a voice said. It was Rashid, elegant in one of his beautiful silk suits. 'Please don't let me interrupt your lunch, but later I am going to visit Ichmet. Will you join me?'

'I'd love to. But shouldn't we warn him?'

'I will go and telephone now. For the moment, please, eat, and enjoy your food.'

So pleased was Fae to see the young Turk that she didn't notice the cautionary glance from William Fairchild.

'You know that man?' Fairchild asked.

'He knows my father's close friend, Ichmet Golabi.'

'The Rector,' Fairchild said.

'They've both been very kind.'

Just half an hour later, Fae found herself in Ichmet's old Ottoman house in a haven of courtesy and tranquillity. She sat with Rashid opposite Ichmet in the shade of the old man's garden, drinking tea and eating small lemon-flavoured cakes soaked in syrup.

'They are called *kadin gobegi* – the translation is ladies' navels,' Rashid told her – and Fae blushed.

'And now my dear,' Ichmet interrupted, 'what have the Americans told you?'

'Very little, I'm not sure they know very much. There has been no contact from the kidnappers. They keep telling me it's just a waiting game.'

'You know,' Rashid said slowly, 'I am loath to say this to you, but I must. It is possible that this could be an American plot. Perhaps your father was disenchanted with the CIA. Perhaps he wanted to leave, but he knew many secrets. I believe that they kidnapped him themselves. And when Richard Marks discovered the truth, they killed him.'

'But that's impossible,' said Fae.

It was Ichmet's turn to speak: 'At first, I agreed with you, but now I am not so sure. We have heard – from Memet's sister – that an American called out to the boy just before he was shot.'

'But it could have been a Turk. Turks speak with American accents,' Fae commented, but slowly.

'They claim to know so little about your father's abductors,' Rashid pointed out.

'Yes, but that's because they don't know who they are,' said Fae.

'By now they should,' Rashid replied.

'Yes but . . .' Fae countered, but she was confused. The Americans could not have taken Sam, it was impossible.

'Would you like to meet Memet's sister?' Rashid asked.

'I certainly should pay my respects.'

'It is not for that, although it would be a kindness; but it might be interesting for you to hear what she has to say.'

Without waiting for her acceptance Rashid excused himself and went to the telephone. Although Fae could not understand his words, she knew he was making some sort of arrangement.

When he returned to the room he said, 'I can't take you to their home. The parents are in deep shock. But she will meet us – at a bar not far from here. My sister will bring her.'

Memet's sister, now looking very different from the girl who had gazed adoringly at her handsome young brother, was dressed in a black headscarf and a black skirt and jumper. She told Fae that Memet knew the Americans were behind her father's abduction.

'He knew it was not to do with Richard Marks, that is why he contacted him and arranged to meet him. I was behind my brother when they killed him, I heard it all. Someone called him. I saw an American. When my brother turned they shot him. The other man tried to save him, so the American shot him too.'

Whilst Fae listened to the girl, Ichmet Golabi received another visitor, William Fairchild.

'OK, my friend,' the rotund American said in a tone far removed from the deference favoured by Rashid when he spoke to the revered Rector. 'It's time we had a small chat. I'd like to know just what the hell is going on round here.'

The old man sighed. 'Nothing is amiss, Mr Fairchild.' He offered the American tea, but a perceptive eye would see that this was not willing hospitality.

'When are you going to tell us who has Sam Whiteman?'

'When I know where he is,' the Rector replied, his tone sharp and unfriendly.

Ichmet Golabi sat in his garden for a long time after William Fairchild had left him. He didn't like the American at all. He felt his garden had been violated by the man's uninvited arrival.

Fae needed time to herself. She was worried and frightened. Who could she believe? Who could she talk to? She wanted to walk on her own, but Rashid made himself available to her and accompanied her. Irritated by his leech-like behaviour, she made her way to the Grand Bazaar, dodging into the tiny jewellery shops, seeking out those she had known since she was a little girl.

'Fae, why didn't you come before?'

'How are you?'

'Here, drink some coffee, some Raki?'

She wanted to confide in these men and tell them her confusions, but she didn't, nor would she have, even if Rashid had not been with her.

She noticed an English woman, a small blonde woman dressed in a white skirt and a pretty soft green blouse, riffling through carpets. She turned to a handsome white-haired husband. 'Alan, what do you think, darling? This one is wonderful.'

They were familiar, she wanted to go to them, to talk to them – they didn't look as if they were the kind of people who read the *News of the World*. The man glanced at her and smiled.

'Are you here on holiday?' Fae asked, anxious to talk.

'Yes, we've come for four days. Loving every minute of it, too.' He coughed, and Fae knew he'd recognized her. 'We hope you have good news soon.'

'Thank you. It's a bit of a nightmare actually.'

The woman joined them. She put an arm on Fae's arm, for a stupid moment Fae wanted to grab hold of her.

'We feel so much for you – everyone does.' Fae was so grateful for the momentary kindness. She would invite them for tea.

'Evelyn, Alan, come on, we must meet the bus.' A loud booming voice from a small dark woman whisked the English couple into the crowds. So she was left to herself, with Rashid. She didn't see Simon Palling watching her.

Fae turned to Rashid. 'I'm going back to the house now. I'm

tired,' she said. Her voice was crisp. She suddenly knew what to do: she would ring Barbara. Her stepfather would help her too. But then she remembered that the Americans had bugged the house. Oh God, what was she going to do?

'I need to make a phone call.'

'Come to my house, you'll be left alone.'

'No, thank you.' She knew she ought not sound churlish. 'Frankly I want to speak to my mother.'

'Without the Americans listening?'

'Without anyone listening.'

'I understand. Let us go to a hotel. I will organize a room for you, and then, while you make the call, I will wait for you in the lobby.'

'Yes, that's a good idea, but I will organize the room myself.'

The anonymous room in the white block that could be anywhere was no comfort, but at least it was private.

'They say the Americans took Sam.'

'I don't believe it.' Max Claremont's comforting voice came through the crackles of an international telephone call. Why, Fae wondered, when man could get to the moon, could he not improve his telecommunications? Her voice echoed back on herself. How could she have a proper conversation?

'But Max, a lot of it makes sense.'

'Look Fae, it isn't the American way of doing things. They wouldn't kidnap their own man. It's not on. Believe me. Where are you?'

'In a hotel. I couldn't have this conversation from the house, could I? It's bugged.'

'Sensible girl. I'm worried about you being so isolated. That's why you're susceptible to any idea: it's understandable. Would you like me to come out to you?'

'No, thank you. I'll cope.'

'Your mother should be with you.'

'No, Max. I won't stay very long. I'll come home soon. Tell her, when she rings me, not to mention this conversation.'

'Of course I will. Fae, we love you. You're just being confused and I don't like it one little bit. Stay away from those people.'

'Ichmet isn't "those people", he's Sam's friend. He's probably as upset as I am.'

Fae was preparing to leave the room when Rashid arrived at the door. How did he know she had finished her telephone call?

'I asked the telephonist to advise me when the call was terminated, and I have arranged a little refreshment to cheer you before you go home.' The champagne arrived with him.

Fae found herself drinking one glass, and then another. Rashid wasn't leech-like any more. He was funny, and kind.

'It must be hard for you. All of us telling you different things.'

'I don't know where I am.'

She put her glass down on the bedside table and lay back on the bed. Her head was spinning. 'Oh Rashid, it's all a nightmare. And I want to wake up and find Sam still with me – and Nick.'

'Nick?'

'The man.'

'The man you loved?'

'The man I love.'

Rashid was on top of her, rubbing her breasts, trying to kiss her. She twisted her head away from him.

'You like to play, do you? Good, I like that too.' He was holding her arms down, he was strong, she could feel his rock hard penis – it revolted her. Her skirt had ridden up over her thighs exposing her black pants.

'Get off me!' she screamed.

He rolled away from her. Shocked, shaking, she shouted at him, 'Get out of here!'

'I don't understand you. You drink champagne with a man in a bedroom. You lie down on the bed. What do you expect?'

After he had slammed out of the room, Fae picked up the telephone and asked to be connected to the American Embassy, to Maise Montgomery.

'Can you come and get me?'

'Where are you, Fae?'

'At the Ottoman Hotel in Bebec.'

'I'm on my way.'

Rashid walked into the telephone office just as Fae had finished her call.

'She's rung the American woman, Maise Montgomery.'

Rashid nodded. 'She's on her way,' the telephonist continued.

Rashid clicked his fingers angrily. How was he going to explain this to Ichmet? But it was the girl's fault – she had led him on. Even as he comforted himself, Rashid knew that Ichmet would not accept his excuses. He had alienated Fae Whiteman and the old man would be very angry indeed. He had to restore his relationship with Fae without involving Ichmet.

'Do you want to tell me what happened?' Maise asked, once they were in an Embassy car.

'I was stupid. I went to the hotel to ring Max, my stepfather. I didn't want your people eavesdropping.'

'I can understand that.'

'The Turk, Rashid, misunderstood.'

Maise made no comment, and Fae was grateful for that.

Maise took her straight back to the house. She made her coffee, fussed over her. Fae had to admit she was grateful. After Fae had finished her second cup, Maise said, 'Want to eat?'

'Yeah. I am hungry.'

Maise took Fae's hand as if it were her house. 'Come into Aladdin's cave,' she said and took her to the huge freezer where packets of honey-cured crispy bacon and one dozen British sausages were neatly stacked.

'How did you organize this?' Fae said.

'Supplies,' Maise replied with a grin.

'Suddenly I feel better.'

Fae fried eggs and bacon and sausages whilst Maise, under her instruction, brewed tea and made toast.

'And so, as they say, tell me about yourself,' Fae said as she smothered her toast with butter.

'Not much to say. Nice parents, from California – not overjoyed that their daughter is in Turkey. They would've preferred London and a charming British son-in-law, but they've given up on that now. They just enjoy my brother's kids and try to be proud of the unmarried daughter.'

Fae laughed. 'But you've never been married?'

'Nope. It's not that I don't like men, but come on, Fae, they're full of shit. We can see right through them.'

'Do you think that's what we should do: see through them?'

'Yup, that way there's no surprises.'

'But no magic either.'

Maise looked at Fae directly. She reached out, gently touched the huge shadows under Fae's eyes. 'I guess I'm not a girl for the magic. I prefer it real. It's safer that way.'

Fae pushed herself back from the table, extending her arms and legs, trying to ease the thud between her shoulder blades. Maise noticed.

'Hurt?'

'It's like I have a sheet of armour between my ears and my shoulders.'

Maise stood up. She moved behind Fae's shoulders and began a rhythmic deep movement, pressing on just the right places.

'God, that feels good,' Fae said.

'Shitsu massage. Chinese.'

'A lady of many parts. I suppose you picked that up in China.'

'San Francisco's China!'

The massage continued for a few moments, calming Fae, untying knots that she didn't know existed.

'Do you know my dad well?'

'Yeah . . . we've shared some times.'

Fae twisted her head; she looked directly at the American. 'You too?'

'Me too. But it was just fun.'

'Can you do it for fun?'

'What other way is there?'

'Love.'

'Come on, Fae. You're Sam's daughter.'

'What does that mean?'

'He wouldn't expect you to have a romantic view of life.'

'Him! He cultivated it. He's my knight on a white charger.'

'Really? That doesn't fit in with the guy I know.'

'Ah, but I'm his daughter.'

'Figures.' Maise moved away from Fae, and clenched her fingers, unclenched them, relaxing them after her efforts.

'Maise, tell me about him: I need to know. Up to now, he's been Dad, Superman, the man who gets the washing-up done before the dinner is eaten. But I want to know what he is really like.'

'You have to find out what he's like for you.'

'I know that, but I need to know anyway,' Fae insisted.

'Sam Whiteman is a charming guy. Full of bonhomie and chat. He knows a lot about this part of the world, Fae, and he likes the people. But he's old fashioned about his women.'

'What?'

'Sure he lays them, but he doesn't really respect them. That's not the case with you, you're his baby. But what happens when you cross him?'

'I've never done that.'

'It'll be mighty interesting when he gets out of that place – to see just what you make of him. That doesn't mean to say you shouldn't love him. The man deserves that.'

'Do you know your Dad?'

'A bit better than you know yours, my dear.'

As Fae began her friendship with Maise Montgomery, Sam Whiteman heard the three sharp knocks which meant the black hood must go over the head. The door opened and the girl came in.

There was a silence whilst she looked at the paper.

'So you are a stubborn man. Perhaps I can help you see sense. Your big friends at the Embassy, let me tell you about them. Richard Marks, to be precise, the one who was supposed to be a trade attaché. He and your wife have been lovers.'

'Impossible.'

'Oh no, my friend. I will leave you a photograph to look at. And when you have looked at it you should know that he is dead. The Americans killed him. We want to know why. So start writing.'

The shuffle of soft shoes on carpet, the sound of a door clicking shut, the three sharp knocks. Bastards, bastards. Not Richard, not his friend Richard. But there, in front of him, was a photograph – black and white, limbs entangling limbs, the faces of sexual ecstacy. Richard and Innessa. And Richard was dead, shot by the Americans. Why? Who? What for? It made no sense. He couldn't write anything down – his mind was jumping around. His wife and his friend in bed. His friend dead, shot by his countrymen. Sam couldn't make sense of any of it. He needed to talk to someone he could trust. Ichmet. He could trust Ichmet. If only he could speak to his friend.

On the following morning, Maise suggested that Fae 'just get away from the whole goddamn shootin' match. Take the car for a couple of days and go up to Pammukkale.'

'Hey, what a good idea. Can you come?'
'No. I have to see William Fairchild.'
'You don't like him either.'
'Did I say that?'

Fae was glad to get out of the city, to be alone under the rich blue sky. Just her, the car and the road. She drove all day, stopping for drinks and fruit when she felt like it. As night fell she stopped at the first little taverna she found. After she checked in she discovered there was no water after nine o'clock in the evening. She grabbed a shower, ate a small dinner of fish and salad, then fell into a tiny white bed and slept without dreams. She set off early the next morning and reached Pammukkale at around twelve o'clock.

The 'Cotton Castle', as it is called, is a shimmering white cascade formed by limestone-laden hotsprings which over millions of years have fashioned magical fairy tales. Fae stripped off and wandered in the limestone rock pools. She saw a woman behind her, dressed in a headscarf and a raincoat. At first Fae wondered how she could possibly cope in the heat. But then Fae realized that the woman was following her. She started to panic and ran over the pools, through the bubbling water that felt like fizzy champagne beneath her feet. The woman seemed to be gaining on her; Fae stopped herself; maybe the woman had a message. The woman stopped too. She turned to Fae, Fae faced her, expectant, hopeful. The woman spat at her and screamed at her. Fae sank to her knees, the spittle falling off her cheek. She couldn't understand.

'You have embarrassed her. She is a daughter of Islam, you are wearing a bikini,' a voice said, and a hand offered Fae a fluffy white towel to cover herself with. It was Simon Palling.

'What are you doing here?' asked Fae.
'Covering the Whiteman kidnapping.'

She took the towel gratefully, carefully draped it over herself and agreed to let Simon drive her back to Istanbul.

He made all the arrangements, disposing of her car and collecting her one small piece of hand baggage. Within half an hour they were back on the road.

They didn't talk very much, but she did ask him how he got to Pammukkale.

'I followed you,' he said. 'I must say you are a very good driver.'

When night fell and Simon offered an overnight stay somewhere, Fae told him, 'No, just get me back, please . . . I'd like to go home.'

Simon nodded, patted her hand and prepared to drive through the night.

Kamel Batami liked to work at night, burning his lights late at the Ministry. He found it easy to read his agents' reports when there were no interruptions, especially when he intended to think carefully. And indeed he was going to do just that in the case of the Whiteman kidnapping. His agent, Suleyman Gamel, had stopped filing reports after having trailed her to the house in Wembley where she met with members of the Turkish Communist Party. Batami was uneasy. What was Gamel doing? Fortunately Batami was not totally dependent on Gamel's reports, but why hadn't he reported that Fae had flown to Italy? It was a deviation of procedure that Batami did not like. He wrote a highly secret memorandum to his man in London, a junior commercial attaché, instructing him to find Gamel.

He wrote in neat handwriting, but his signature was a flourish. As a little boy he had practised his name for hours, perfecting a scrawl that no one would be able to forge. When he grew up he moderated the style, but never completely altered it.

He put his letter in an envelope and sealed it. His secretary would process it in the morning.

He himself turned to the matter of Hayri Gurbuz . . . he had not been found. His younger brother knew nothing. The interrogators were sure of that. Batami regretted the necessity of torture. He would have liked it stopped. He made a note to himself to enquire after the boy's welfare and to make sure that he was released into his mother's care. If nothing else it might provoke an appearance from Hayri. Batami had obtained the boy's name from Ichmet Golabi himself. And there was a small matter of a photograph that had come into his hands from the Americans. The Rector was, from time to time, helpful to the Americans. When it was necessary Batami reminded him of the necessity of loyalty to Turkey, although he knew that the Rector loved his country. He perused the rest of the names on the list:

suspected Communists and fundamentalists, who had all been rounded up. They knew nothing.

Batami drummed his fingers on the desk. He wanted answers, and he would get them.

CHAPTER SIX

Fear and anger are the black angels of death that pluck the light of hope. The white angels cry, and their tears are the rains that cleanse the wounds and balm the hurts. But if the angels can't cry, there can be no healing. Sally Newman could not cry, and so there was no escape from the black angels.

She did her best for her children, shopping and cooking and cleaning, but the rage held on to her like a desperate lover, gripping her, fuelling a mania, turning her quite simply into a mad woman. She trailed Nick, ringing his office at least four times each day, checking on his every movement, meeting him at the end of his day, making sure that her presence was acknowledged. She was the wife, that was her obsession.

Nick, for his part, had no will to fight Sally. She had to do what she had to do. And he had to survive. His ways were different. He made his little box and put his pain for Fae inside. He embraced his children, he embraced his work . . . all that mattered to him. For the rest – it was beyond the door, over there, behind him.

Nick and Sally were both so involved with the roundabouts made from their colours, with playing their music, that they didn't notice they were being watched by Suleyman Gamel. Suleyman was completely obsessed by Fae. Ever since he had come to England and actually seen her, thoughts of her had constantly filled his head. He stopped filing his reports, none of that interested him any more. He wanted to know everything about Fae, and that meant knowing about Nick Newman.

He had discovered Fae and Nick were lovers on the night he observed them from the fire escape outside Fae's flat. He liked watching them together. Suleyman touched himself, aching with pleasure at the sight of what men did to women.

He wondered if Nick Newman did those things to his wife. He hoped not, he wanted him to do them with Fae. She was the one he wanted to watch. Suleyman followed him to his house and saw him park his black Porsche car. He saw Nick let himself into his house. He saw his figure, tall, slightly hunched, through the windows of his long hall. He saw him go into his bedroom. Suleyman felt his own body quiver – angry, no, don't do it to the thin blonde, not her! Suleyman silently ran across the neat green apron of grass in front of the house. Carefully, he shinned up the drainpipe and swung himself on to a small iron balustrade just outside the bedroom. He crouched low, so he was behind a dressing-table. Raising himself slowly, he stood close to the window, and he could see into the room. The wife lay in her bed, the man, Nick, stood with his back to her. He was taking off his clothes and then he went to the door, said something – perhaps 'Goodnight', turned out the light and shut the door behind him.

Satisfied, Suleyman climbed back over the balcony, slipped down the drainpipe, back across the green apron, over a small road and into his car. He pulled a rug over himself and settled down for a long night.

In the morning, Suleyman saw Nick walk out of his front door, cross over to his garage, open the door and get into his Porsche. Should Suleyman follow the Porsche? The Turkish boy, eating some bread and drinking from a flask of coffee, considered carefully. No, he knew how the man would spend his day. He would follow the wife instead. He shifted in his seat. His mouth felt stale and he needed to relieve himself. He got out of his car, stretched his legs and walked over to a tree, and stood with his back to the house.

'Mummy, what's that man doing?' A child's voice could be heard clearly across the road. It was James, Nick and Sally's five-year-old son.

'He's doing what you do in a toilet,' replied an older voice, Oliver, aged eight.

'I think it's disgusting,' said Elizabeth, the eldest, aged ten, her blonde hair in a pony-tail. 'Eh, look at him. He looks as if he's slept in the car.'

'Maybe he's a spy,' Oliver said. He was interested in that kind of thing.

'Come on,' Sally snapped, ushering her children into her red Volvo. Their chatter was grating on her.

She drove out of their house, looked right and then left, reversed into the little road, and set off on the school round. She picked up other children on the way, doing her turn. Normally she played games with the children, participating in their world, or setting them quizzes, but now she had no interest in their tittle-tattle. She put on the radio and, ignoring their protests, tuned in to Radio 2 and tried to ignore Derek Jameson.

Suleyman drove behind the woman. He noticed her every movement. He was good at surveillance. The last child was dropped at a school gate. That one was kissed and held tight – at five it was still allowed. The woman drove to a big store, where she shopped quickly for her provisions. By the time they reached the home there was someone else there, someone to do her cleaning. He parked his car over the road, but in a different place, and waited again.

It was Mrs Ferring, Sally's cleaning lady, who noticed the car on the other side of the road.

'Who's that man? He's sitting there, staring at your house, Mrs Newman,' she said.

Sally walked over to the window. She recognized the man straight away. 'He was there this morning. He must have followed me.'

'I'm ringing the police.'

'No, don't.' Sally said. 'Maybe he's some sort of journalist . . . the truth about Sally Newman . . . or something like that.'

'Now I won't hear that. You've been through a lot, Mrs Newman. Ring a friend, go out for lunch. Forget him. I'll deal with him.' Mrs Ferring strode out of the back door and over the road. She banged on Suleyman's window.

'Shoo!' she said to the startled Turk, 'Shoo! Away with you. We won't have your sort round here.'

Suleyman looked through the window of his car and saw a moon face, grey eyes under bushy eyebrows, grey curling hair, pink cheeks and a cross mouth . . . a sturdy woman. He had no wish to tangle with her. He turned the key in the ignition and drove off. Mrs Ferring stood, hands on hips, satisfied.

Suleyman stopped his car further down the road. He would wait till the funny grey-haired granny had left.

Mrs Ferring went back into the house. That'll deal with that. Not the kind of woman to worry about how others saw her, she was a stout-hearted, good person, who loved her family and Mrs Newman. She made her employer a cup of tea. She always thought of Sally Newman as a gentle, jolly person, but Sally wasn't now. Still, how could anyone expect anything else? Poor girl, going through all that. Little hussy after her husband. Mrs Ferring thought Sally Newman had behaved impeccably – she'd have given the girl a good hidin'. She poured the tea and walked through the large hall into the cream, blue and yellow drawing-room, an L-shaped room with a double door leading out on to the garden. Sally was sitting on the pale blue settee.

'Drink this, love,' Mrs Ferring said.

'Thank you.'

'Now, who 'yer going to ring?'

'I don't feel like small talk, Mrs Ferring.'

'That's as maybe, but it'd do you good to get out. Have your tea and think about it.'

Sally sipped the scalding liquid. She looked around her room, she always called the drawing-room her room, and she hated it – the blue and cream settees, the carefully draped curtains, the perfectly positioned glass coffee table, Nick's precious abstract on the wall behind her . . . what did it mean anyway, just a swirl of colours and shapes without feelings? She had feelings, she wasn't a thing to be kept in its place and used when it was convenient. She was like the drawing-room, the best room – kept in good condition, but not used regularly. She stood up, turned and smoothed out the cushion where she had been sitting. She would ring Katie Palling and see if she were free for lunch.

The two women met at Groucho's again.

Sally felt no sense of occasion as she went through the swing doors. In fact, she was a few minutes late: Katie was at the bar, her short brown hair as sleek as ever. Slightly hunched over a gin and tonic, she was smoking a cigarette.

'Sorry, I just couldn't get it together,' Sally said.

'Don't worry. How are you, love?' Katie asked.

'I'll have a Bloody Mary, thank you,' she replied.

Katie gave a short laugh and squeezed Sally's hand. 'Bad, is it?'

'We'll get through it.'

"Course you will. Shall we drink here, or shall we water it down with a touch of salad?'

They settled at their table and slipped into easy chat. The 'do you remembers?' and 'have you ever seens?' anaesthetized the angry wound and for that short time Sally forgot the name of Fae Whiteman.

The lunch ended with hugs and promises to meet soon.

'Thanks, Katie, it's been a great boon.'

'Hold on, Sally. You've had a dreadful shock: now let yourself get over it, and get that husband of yours back into your bed. As soon as Simon gets back from his current bash abroad you and Nick must come to dinner.'

'Will he be away long? Why don't you come for Sunday lunch anyway?'

'No, I couldn't.'

'Yes, you could. It would help' – Sally swallowed, it was hard for her to discuss intimacies – 'make everything seem a little more normal.'

Katie Palling was the kind of woman who cherished her privacy and it was not her way to visit those she did not know well. It was obvious, however, that Sally was in great need, and she could not help but feel some responsibility.

'Thank you. That would be a lovely treat.'

'Good. Sunday it is then. One o'clock.' Sally grabbed a piece of paper from the reception desk, wrote down the address and handed it over to Katie. 'Dare I ask where Simon is?' Katie hesitated: it was obviously inopportune to reveal that her husband was in Turkey, possibly at that very moment spending time with Fae Whiteman.

'Oh, er, he's in America somewhere. I'm never too sure of his whereabouts.'

After Katie had left her, Sally stayed uncertainly in the royal blue foyer. She saw the telephone box in the corner: it drew her like a magnet. Her fingers twitched for the ten pence that she needed. She would just say hello to Nick, after all she was round the corner from his office. She could pop in. As she reached the box, a hand sporting a huge amethyst ring grabbed the phone.

Bubbly black hair, creamy skin, perfect make-up, flashed a huge smile whilst a loud voice said, 'I won't be a moment, love.'

Sally turned on her heel and sank into the crowds – if she had looked over her shoulder she would have seen, a few yards behind her, the young Turk following her. But she was concentrating on getting to Nick's office. If he wasn't there she would wait for him, and they could go home together.

In summer when the sun sets in Istanbul, the fiery gold ball sinks into the murky waters of the Bosphorus around eight o'clock in the evening. Fae loved that time of the evening – it was her special time with Sam. That was the hour when they used to walk by the Ortaköy Mosque, just at the edge of the water. By that time the fishermen would have packed away their rods, and the boys who swam in waters that would never lure a tourist would have gone to their homes to eat their mothers' food and then later trail their fathers and their elder brothers to the little cafés where they sat and drank. That little stretch by the water was a special place where somehow the smell of Turkey etched itself more clearly than in any of the mosques or the palaces or even the Grand Bazaar. It was the ships and the fish and the people, all mixing in a spot where the past was alive, as if the real power and lushness that was Turkey still lived, just by the waters of the Bosphorus. It was a special spot to Sam and Fae – where they always talked. It was there that Sam told her that he was going to divorce her mother, there that he told her he was going to marry Innessa. It was there that she would tell him about her little crises. Ever since the kidnapping Fae had deliberately avoided that part of the city. She didn't know if she could bear to go to such a beloved place without Sam.

Her sense of loss was growing each day, and the most painful aspect was that she was beginning to think of Sam in the past tense. 'We used' instead of 'we do'. Deliberately she chose to make the walk on her own, unaware that there were men following her: some for her protection – the Americans and the Turkish police, melting into the stonework; some to check on her movements – young people in anonymous clothes who would report her activities to the men who held her father; and one other who needed to become her friend. But Fae had no interest in any of them. In herself she felt anonymous, she was locked inside her own head, confronting her father.

She realized that she had blocked him out of her conscious thoughts. Nick had banished him, Nick, her beloved Nick – gone too. Both the men she loved were beyond her reach. Both the men she wanted could not be with her. Her loneliness was an intense deep reality. She couldn't fill the cavern of emptiness with actions, they didn't help. Where was her father? Who was her father? Why had all this happened? She tried to trace a map of him in her mind, to understand him, to see him as he really was . . . but the image of the huge man with his comforting arms and his loving filled her up, and she could not see beyond that. She thought of Maise's words: what would Sam be like if she crossed him? She had no idea, it had simply never happened. She had always presumed that he would solve her problems. She went to him for advice and he gave it.

But what if she didn't take that advice, would that love, would that care go? Or would he stand back and support her – come what may? Of course he would. After all, in a sense it was the reverse now, she had discovered something about him that she found unacceptable: the fact that he was CIA. She had no idea . . .

Fae stopped in her tracks. Of course she had no idea. This man, this superman who was Daddy, whose very memory filled her with hurt at his loss and shame at his very public breakdown . . . Oh God, the breakdown. That face on the screen babbling its admission was an aspect of the whole event that had been firmly put into a steel box and locked away. And now the image rose up to haunt her and she had to face her own reactions.

Sam was a physical coward: he was frightened for his own safety. Fae drew in her breath sharply and her stomach contracted as if a knife had drawn itself over her very intestines, lingering on the nerves, a cold blade setting off such trauma that it could almost not be borne. The hero was a coward, the agony of such a realization filled her up. But why? Why? Who was Sam, and what did his actions mean to her? She shied away, a frightened reaction, she didn't want to look at him. She wanted him perfect: it was safer that way. But he wasn't perfect, and she had to come to terms with that. She had always been desperate for approval from an imperfect man, judging herself by his standards of the perfect princess.

She didn't know how to deal with that.

The sound of her own feet clicking over the grey stones bothered her, but the slip slap of the soft waters helped. She stumbled.

A hand shot out, steadied her. 'Are you all right?' It was Simon Palling. What was he doing here? Why was he following her? She was irritated. No, more than that, she was furious. He was spying on her and he was intrusive. She gazed into Palling's flat face, and noticed he had brown eyes and untidy eyebrows, a wide nose . . . too wide, and a soft mouth. If she hadn't been so angry she would have seen it was a pleasant face, but instead she lashed out: 'What are you doing here? You're following me. I don't like it.'

'Yes, yes, I was. No point in lying. I saw you from up there.' He pointed to one of the small tavernas on the other side of the road. At least he had been honest, which Fae appreciated.

'I spoke to your mother this evening.'

'My mother?'

'Yes. I know you think of me as a skunk of a British journalist, but your mother and I have a friendship, and believe me, Fae, I am not trying to hurt you. Yes, I do have a story to write.'

Fae started up, her own personal humiliations whipped her.

'No, not that one. I can't tell you how sorry I was about that. The only story I'm interested in is what is happening to Sam Whiteman, and I would have thought we have parallel interests in that one.' Palling smiled at her, he held out a hand: 'Truce.'

'Truce,' Fae said, sighing.

'Dinner?' Palling asked.

'Dinner,' Fae said.

Fae's discreet attendants watched her walk with the English journalist, made notes in their various books, and reported to their various masters.

In the soft comfort of a local fish restaurant, Palling poured the wine and made no effort to probe Fae Whiteman's life. Instead he talked of the pointless death of Richard Marks.

'I think I've actually shoved it away. I won't think of it, it is so terrible . . . and it makes me very fearful for Dad.'

'Are you going to the funeral?'

'No, I . . .' Fae swallowed, acutely aware that she hadn't really thought about Richard Marks since she arrived in Turkey. A man was dead. 'I actually hadn't thought of attending, but I suppose it would be the right thing to do. I've even lost track of time.'

Palling smiled at her, pursing his lips sympathetically. 'I know. Stress is a dreadful thing, it takes you over, pushes out everything else, doesn't it?' Fae nodded. 'The funeral is in two days' time. Think about it. I don't mean it this way, but it will give you something to do.'

Fae shrugged her shoulders. 'It's the waiting and not being able to do anything . . .'

'I know.'

'Do you know?' She was fiddling with her bread now. 'I don't know anything about Richard. Was he married? Did he have children?'

'Divorced, I understand . . . two little girls.' Palling reached over for the bottle of red wine that he had ordered. He loathed local beers.

Fae looked down at her bread. Two children, a wife, an ex-wife . . . did it matter? They'd made children together. People were in grief, and she with her utter selfishness hadn't really allowed any of it to pierce her own. She was ashamed.

'I will go,' she said. 'One of us must be there, and Innessa can't leave Fabrizzi.'

'Well done,' Simon said.

She looked up at Palling. 'And now you're on the box: question time. Tell me about yourself. Children?'

'No, not yet. We always say we will, but what with Katie's career and . . .' He suddenly looked so sad – as if the curtain that he kept over his own needs had been ripped open and Fae could see in. She realized she was sitting with a very unhappy man. Whatever he did, wherever he went, there was an emptiness within him. The need for children was just part of it, she could see that, and she could see that Palling was making no effort to mask himself. She was drawn to put her hand on his. She began to speak, knowing that was going to be personal and not caring, even if she was breaking the rules.

'You know, Simon, my grandmother – my mother's mother that is – she died, just a few years ago – used to say that we all have a deck of cards dealt us. We may not like what we've got, but at least we know how to deal with our own. Think of my life. My father has been kidnapped, I've discovered he works for the CIA and the man I love has a wife. I'd say I wasn't doing too well.'

'I'd say you are a very plucky lady,' Simon Palling said, filling up her glass with wine again. Fae looked over at him. His eyes were level with hers; the curtains closed again. Had she said too much? She sipped her wine slowly.

Simon noticed that the waiter was bringing the fish. He was glad that he could concentrate on the business of eating.

Just about three miles from where Fae Whiteman ate with Simon Palling, her father Sam sat in his solitary room. His captives had allowed him a Bible and a sheet of paper and one pencil. He was supposed to write down as much as he could about the CIA's activities in Turkey. He was suddenly very tired, and had no wish to tell them anything more. He was an American: they were Turks. Let them fight their wars their way. He wasn't going to give them any more help. He opened the Bible at Genesis and he began to read: 'In the beginning God created the Heaven and the Earth . . .'

He was still reading when the three knocks came. Quietly he put his book down and put his hood on.

There was a familiar smell, he identified the girl.

'Come on, Mr Whiteman, you have written nothing,' she said.

'Go to the people in charge, tell them to use me for whatever they can achieve for themselves, but I have nothing to tell you.'

'I can't protect you if you don't help me.'

'I understand that.'

They moved Sam Whiteman that evening. They took him at night in a car – his legs were tied together, his hands were tied together and his eyes were blindfolded. He was placed on the back seat face down. Someone sat on his legs and there was a sharp object pressing into his back which he guessed to be a gun. They drove for many hours. He was allowed to relieve himself and to drink some water during the journey. Eventually through sheer tiredness he fell asleep. When he woke he was being moved. His legs were untied, he was stood up and encouraged to walk. He couldn't – he slipped out of their hands, down on to the ground.

Different hands picked him up and hurled him over a shoulder. He was taken into a damp place and laid on what felt like a straw pallet covered with sheeting. His blindfold was removed and he could see a small room with rough whitewashed walls and a tiny barred window. The other man wore a hood, with slits for his eyes and his nose and his mouth.

'Well, Mr Whiteman, this is your new home. You will stay in this room during the day; at night you will be allowed outside to feel the air. You will be brought books and newspapers, and we will feed you. We will even allow you a small radio. And here you will stay – for as long as it takes to bargain for the release of our friends. It is just, really, your imprisonment. You will serve as long a term as them.'

After the man left, Sam Whiteman stayed on the small straw pallet that would be his bed. He lay quietly and tried to calm his mind and still his trembling. He wanted to go home, he wanted to be with his family. When would he see them again? Would he see them again? And yet he was still alive, and life meant there was possibility . . . there was always possibility. He felt a sense of peace. He would repose himself and wait with some pleasure for the night to come. He looked forward to feeling the air on his skin.

Throughout the long day, Sam repeatedly looked up at what he could see of the blue sky through the tiny square of window. He started to get impatient for the night. Like a small boy waiting for his treat he kept looking. He had no sense of time, for his watch had been on the bedside table when they had kidnapped him. At last the sky shaded to a pinkish grey. He was brought some dinner – he ate with relish, the baked lamb and salad were excellent. There was fruit, too, rich golden apricots, their plump skins full of juice. He sighed with pleasure. Turning, he saw the sky was black. What time would they come? He heard the key: now, they were coming now. The man in the dark hood pulled him to his feet.

'Can you stand up?'

'Yes, I think I can. I fell down before because I was cramped in one position.'

'Come on, then.'

Sam walked through a larger room where there were other men who kept their backs to him. He understood, and then he was over the threshold, walking freely over dry grass, hearing the croak of the crickets' nightly song, feeling the balm of a breeze on his face, his hair actually lifted slightly.

He turned to his hooded companion: 'I feel as if I have come out of hell.'

'It's a wonderful place. Smell the air, it's sweet.'

'Am I allowed to know where I am?'

'No. I am afraid I cannot tell you that.'

'I am grateful for your kindness.'

'You're a commodity, my friend. We would like to trade you for our friends. You must be in good condition.'

Sam smiled. 'So that's it.'

'That's it.'

Fae was in her father's house in Istanbul when she heard that he had been removed from the city. William Fairchild told her himself. He did his screaming at Kamel Batami, blaming him for Turkish incompetence, after he had spoken to Fae. It was stupid really – the Turks were doing their best – but it made him feel a little better to let off some steam. To his credit, he informed her the moment he received the communication from the kidnappers. This time they simply posted a letter to 'The man in charge of the Whiteman kidnapping'.

Fae sat with William Fairchild in Innessa's sleek kitchen. She brewed him some coffee whilst he told her what he knew.

'Where is he?' were the only words that Fae could say.

'We don't know, but the point is we now know he's alive. We know they're caring for him. It's just a . . .'

'The trade?'

'Yup, the trade.'

'Tell me honestly, do you think the Turkish authorities will release the prisoners in exchange for my father? I don't want you to be kind to me, I need to know some realities.'

'Eventually we will get him out . . .'

'Eventually.'

'Yup.'

'What do I do till then?'

'You get on with your life the best way you can.'

'I'm going to Richard Marks' funeral.'

'I know. I'm glad. Nothing can give death value, but at least the family will know that you mind that he's gone.'

Fae felt again the cutting edge of guilt.

As soon as Fairchild left, Fae telephoned Innessa. She was careful what she said, she had to be.

'I thought one of us should go to Richard Marks' funeral. It had to be me, you have to stay with Fabrizzi. But I know what he meant to you and Sam.'

'Some flowers, Fae, will you organize them?' Innessa's voice was quiet but calm.

'We need to talk properly. Are you all right?'

'Trying to deal with my feelings.'

'Yes. I love you, Innessa.' Fae couldn't stop the words, she meant them.

'And I love you, Fae. Thank you, cara.'

After she put the phone down she wept for Innessa and for Richard. And of course she wept for Nick, for Sam, for her lost loves and for herself. She wanted Emily, but she couldn't ring Emily – it was Sunday, and on Sunday Emily was going to Jeremy's parents, the first meeting for a possible bride. Even through the tears, Fae smiled at the prospect of her friend's very best behaviour. Yes, it was Sunday, Sunday in England, Sunday lunch . . . that was what Nick would be doing. She tortured herself with a vision of the idyll: ruby red claret poured into bowl-shaped glasses, a perfect wife offering bowls of tiny carrots dripping in butter, golden roast potatoes, dark green beans piled high, crisp cabbage, puffy Yorkshire Pudding, dark brown smooth gravy, nice people with good chit-chat spending time with loved children. She longed to have that for herself.

At that very moment, Nick Newman was indeed pouring a ruby red claret into bowl-shaped glasses, the roast and the vegetables were on the table. Sally was making the gravy and Katie Palling was talking to the children. But that was where the idyll faded into the reality. Nick, although tense, was trying to be a good host. Sally chatted too much and Katie Palling was quite swept off her feet by the charm of Nick Newman. It wasn't an unusual occurrence, for she had long ago come to terms with the fact that she was married to her best friend, and that sexual delights were to be had from others. None of them, though, had had the immediate impact of the tall slender man who leant over her shoulder to put the bottle in the centre of the table. She had an extraordinary urge to touch him. Making an effort to control herself, she reminded herself that she was there to assist Sally.

Nick understood why Sally had invited Katie Palling for lunch, but even so he wasn't pleased. She was the woman who had placed the story in the paper. He would have liked to have thrown her out of his house, but form meant he had to be gracious. The presence of the woman made him think of Fae: his mind played hurtful games, throwing her face up at him, her mouth half open, her eyes, her fingers, the feel of her skin . . . he pushed the image away, he couldn't allow it. He turned on his heel, grabbed his daughter, buried his head in her squeaky clean hair.

'Daddy!'

'I'm allowed. I'm the only man who is allowed to do that now.'

'Really,' said a prissy voice, but clinging arms denied the indignation and he held Elizabeth's little body very tight.

'Nick, come on, let's have lunch,' Sally said, her voice a little sharp.

'It looks delicious,' Katie commented.

'Sally's a wonderful cook,' said Nick as he carved the beef and Katie Palling tried to keep her eyes off his hands and her mind away from fantasies that had nothing whatsoever to do with a Sunday lunch.

Outside the house, footsteps sneaked over the gravel drive. A satisfied voyeur returned to his car and the business of watching the Newman household. The Turkish boy, Suleyman, did not like Katie Palling, he did not like the way she looked at Nick Newman. Nick Newman should be with his Fae. He might have to help Fae. He would watch, he would see. He fingered a sharp bladed knife in his pocket. He would just wait . . .

Ichmet Golabi's small garden, overlooking the Bosphorus and shaded by huge cypress trees, provided him with his favourite seating accommodation. From there he could see the blue sea packed with its shipping, and across to Asia. It gave Ichmet a sense of the real Turkey . . . and it was in that small place that he formulated his personal philosophy of the perfect socialist state arising out of the Islamic creed but without the blessing of God. Ichmet wanted a secular state, but one that was essentially Turkish. To that end, being a practical man, he took whatever help he needed from whoever offered it. He worked for many masters, but answered to none. He established separate groups . . . each one self-contained within its own unit, with no contacts outside the group.

Even Rashid did not know of the extent of Ichmet's burrowing into the foundations of Ataturk's protective structure. Ichmet was a discreet man: his friend Sam Whiteman, who thought he knew the secrets of his mind, would certainly have been amazed at his activities.

But there was one man who knew all about Ichmet Golabi. William Fairchild had first met Golabi when he was a professor at Ankara University. Fairchild was Head of Station then. He needed people in the right places. It was luck that led him to Ichmet's door, and a tart. Fairchild's wife had just returned to the United States for a vacation, and he wanted a more rowdy romping than his wife allowed. He found the girl in one of the capital's more attractive brothels. She gave him a good time, and in return he gave her a lot of money. She gossiped a lot, mostly things he knew; but there was one new piece of knowledge . . .

. . . An eminent professor cruised the brothels for young boys. One night he took a virgin to his bed. The boy was frightened, the professor thought it was part of the fun. He tied the boy to the bed and he raped him. The boy vomited. When the professor realized what he had done he was ashamed. He paid the boy well, sent him back to his village and forswore sex . . . to the tart's knowledge he had kept the pledge. When William Fairchild discovered the professor's name, he realized he had a perfect opportunity. The Company knew that Ichmet Golabi was disenchanted with the Westernization of Turkey. He had flirted briefly with the Moslem Brotherhood, and had spent some time in Paris with Khomeini, but it was accepted that he had rejected those views. Instead it was known that he was attracted to a Turkish Marxism. So Fairchild presented himself and made an offer the professor could not refuse: his silence in return for the professor's co-operation in matters that might relate to American security. The professor was to be a sort of double agent.

After his initial disgust Golabi, ever the survivor, marshalled his feelings and turned his activities to his own advantage.

And he tried to protect his own people, being like a father to all of them. He was extremely disturbed when Rashid informed him that Hayri's younger brother had been arrested. He knew that his secretary had compiled a list of possible Communist and Marxist sympathizers for Kamel Batami. It was only after the arrest that he realized Hayri's name had been included. It was an unforgivable slip, but there was little he could do. His secretary always supplied whatever the police required. He told Rashid to keep Hayri out of sight. But when he himself contacted Kamel Batami on the matter of the younger brother he heard worse news. 'The Americans have passed us a photograph implicating Hayri Gurbuz in the murder of the student Memet.'

'Are you sure?'

'We have identified him. But as for the boy, he knows nothing. Any thoughts where we might find Hayri Gurbuz, my friend?'

'None whatsoever.'

'No, of course, you wouldn't. You would let us know if you did. I'm going to release the boy – let him go home to his mother.'

'Good.'

The men bade each other a dignified farewell on the telephone. Ichmet did not pass on the information about the boy's release to anyone. He understood that if Hayri knew that his brother was at home he might be compelled to go and see him, and Ichmet could not permit his availability to the torturers. As for the matter of the other two students, whose original arrest had goaded Faroud Boaz into kidnapping Sam, they had fallen foul of the hell that man can create for his fellow man. They could not give any names, nor would they make up any names – they were not that kind.

If Ichmet Golabi had believed in a God he would have prayed for them.

Fae flew directly to New York from Istanbul, travelling club class. Maise arranged it for her, she even saw her off and bade her a somewhat affectionate farewell that surprised Fae. The free champagne, the nice seats, the kindly staff were indeed a balm. She felt as if she were going home, and in a sense she was. She was going to Sam's country – his family was there, cousins, even an Uncle. Perhaps she might find some answers to why Sam was CIA and who had really kidnapped him. Most important of all, she might be able to find out who Sam really was . . . and then she could begin to find out who she was.

CHAPTER SEVEN

New York in summer was hot, Kennedy airport was crowded and the lines of would-be visitors to the Big Apple waited like all travellers, untidily disconnected from the easy confidence of the native inhabitants. They needed officials to look over their papers, stamp them and open the door to the magic arbour.

Fae, too, stood in line, for Barbara had selected the British nationality, with its embossed, gold-on-blue travel document, and its regal requirement of safe passage on the inside page, as her daughter's passport, rather than the omnipotent eagle of mother America. She noticed the air hostess pointing her out to a slender young man with thick black hair and glasses.

The young man made his way over to her.

'Miss Whiteman. My name is Stanley Schwartz – I've been despatched by the state department to welcome you to the US and to speed your arrival.'

'Thank you.'

'If you would just let me have your passport I'll have it processed for you. I understand you're going directly to Washington, to Richard's funeral service. I'll escort you, if I may.'

'Er . . . yes.'

Fae was flummoxed. The young man was very polite and he whisked her away from the queue, but she would have liked to have asked for some sort of identity or something. She had to admit she was a little nervous.

'Would you like some magazines?' he asked, as he sped her to the Washington plane.

'No, thank you.'

'How's Maise? She's a great gal, isn't she?'

'She's fine,' Fae replied, still cautious. 'Look,' she said summoning up her courage, 'I'm sure you are with the state department, but do you have some sort of identity card, or visiting card, or something?'

'Of course, you must be careful. How stupid of me: I didn't think.' Stanley Schwartz rummaged around in his jacket and triumphantly produced an ID pass. Fae smiled.

They walked down an endless corridor into a tunnel, complete with carpet, that led straight to the mouth of the Washington plane. There was more champagne on board, and smoked salmon or caviar if she wanted it. She didn't.

'Will I be seeing the master magician of all this?'

'Brockwell?'

The 'erum' of confirmation was just about as much as she could manage, for at that moment the plane dipped sharply, leaving her stomach just above her head. When she recovered she managed to say, 'Perhaps that little show was just to let us know that the alpha plusses of this world haven't got it right yet. The gods of nature really have the last word.'

'I don't need any reminders about that, Miss Whiteman,' Stanley Schwartz said, and Fae suddenly rather liked him.

On her arrival in Washington itself, Fae found herself whisked into the glamorous world where no one waits on street corners to hail a cab, where cars glide miraculously to the kerb the moment a foot is placed out of a door, and there is never a need to register like the more common man at the Jefferson hotel in downtown Washington. But even so, as Fae stepped into the car she saw a man watching her – and the finger of fear reached out to her. She pushed it away – it was stupid. She was in America, safe in the arms of the CIA.

For the child of an American citizen, Fae had spent comparatively little time in America. Until Fae was six, the family had spent their Christmases in America with Sam's parents, Mary and Austin Whiteman, but then they had been killed in one of the great blizzards that swept the Mid West. Sam, as their only son, had gone back to America to bury them. That had been the only time, apart from the kidnapping, that Fae had ever seen her father cry. There were other relatives of course. Austin Whiteman had a brother, Franklin, who, despite a dignified age of some eighty-seven years, was still alive. He had written a kindly letter when his nephew had been taken and his son George had telephoned Barbara. He knew her, but they had not made contact with Fae. Now that she was in America, they were anxious to make her welcome and messages awaited her in the hotel. She was looking forward to meeting them, but all that would have to wait – the funeral at Arlington was to take place in just two hours.

Fae thanked Stanley for his company, shook his hand, and gratefully shut the door behind his departing back. It was not that she didn't like him, but he was a stranger and that needed a certain degree of politeness which she found difficult to dredge up from within her. She unpacked, hung her clothes up, placed the paraphernalia for face, cleansing creams and the like, together with her make-up in neat lines in the bathroom. She took off all her clothes – she didn't want to look at her body, it meant nothing to her . . . there was no Nick to give it pleasure – ran herself a tub full of water, poured in some aromatherapy oils that Barbara had given her, and climbed in gratefully. She could easily have fallen asleep, if the telephone hadn't rung. She reached up one soap-swathed arm and answered the connection in the bathroom.

'Fae, it's Robert Brockwell. Have you had a good journey?'

'Yes, thank you,' Fae said. She sat up suddenly and cursed the sound of the water, because Brockwell would know she was in the bath, and she suddenly felt rather embarrassed.

'I was calling to suggest that I accompany you to the funeral. We could then meet later – for a drink, at my office, if that would suit you. Then I could catch you up on all the latest information that we have.'

'That would be good.'

'Fine . . . shall we say I'll collect you in three-quarters of an hour?'

'Yes.'

'Enjoy the rest of your bath.'

Fae heard Brockwell disconnect the call and then she slid carefully and slowly under the water, just so she could hide her blushes from herself.

When she recovered, she reached for the phone herself. Another call to Emily, but Emily wasn't there, so she left a message on the answering machine to let her know where she was. Then she called her mother.

'I'm fine,' she told the distracted Barbara.

'Shall I come?'

'No, I'm quite sure your personal emissary, Mr Simon Palling, will turn up at some point.'

Barbara had the grace to laugh.

Exactly three-quarters of an hour later she emerged from her suite, transformed from the weary traveller into the bandbox fresh mourner. Black suit, small black handbag, high-heeled black shoes . . . well polished, her mother would've been quite satisfied.

Brockwell's car slid up to the entrance as Fae entered the lift. A driver held open his door and Brockwell leapt from the limousine. He was striding into the foyer as Fae came out of the lift. He saw her immediately, offered a hand. 'How are you?' The smile in his eyes was hard to resist. She had to remind herself they were going to a funeral.

Unlike the motley crowd of people who stand around a grave in England, the mourners at American funerals sit on chairs according to their rank and listen to the preacher. Richard's former wife and his two little girls held hands with his sister, much as the counsellor had advised. The Marines sounded the bugle – the flag was folded and offered to the family, the coffin was neatly consigned to the flat earth. A life over, gone, finished, Richard Marks had been conveyed to his last resting place. Fae conveyed her public sympathies, the press took photographs, but inside herself she whispered a silent parting for Innessa; and felt no disloyalty to Sam for doing it.

All the time she was aware of Robert Brockwell. It was not an uncomfortable thing. She watched as he kissed the former Mrs Marks, and the little girls. She had to admire him – he had the touch. He would go far, who knew how far?

'I'm so, so sorry for what has happened,' Fae told the family when it came to her turn.

'Thank you for coming,' Richard's sister murmured.

'I wish there was something I could say,' Fae said, feeling stupid and out of place, and yet knowing that she had to be there. When it was all over she fled with gratitude towards the plush interior of the DCI's limousine.

'Shall we go straight to Langley now?'

Fae nodded her acquiescence, preparing herself for her small sneak into the citadel of power.

'I'm very sorry about Richard,' she said.

'Yes, it's not right for little girls to grow up without their father.'

Fae glanced over at Brockwell, his tone was very personal, and then, suddenly awkward, she turned away.

Robert Brockwell had studied her father's file quite carefully on his way to the funeral. Whiteman had been recruited when he had been at college. He had at first been eager to work for the Company, taking his job as a 'recruiter' very seriously, but it had been noted that his zeal had considerably decreased in the last few years. His relationship with Ichmet Golabi had provided interesting reading. A careful watch had been kept on their friendship. Brockwell also noted with some interest that Sam Whiteman shared his own taste for 'a good time'. But the man clearly adored his daughter, and that had to put her into a different category for Brockwell. Despite the fact that his own 'companions' were sometimes even five years younger than Fae, he was determined to view her quite differently. She was a daughter, not a prospective lay.

He noticed that Fae Whiteman was sitting carefully, her nice legs placed side by side. She was very attractive, gazing out of the window as the car sped out towards the sprawling complex known as Langley, home of the CIA.

'I know that you want to find out as much as you can about your father's situation, and we're going to be as forthcoming as we can, but I also hope you will enjoy yourself in this strange little village of ours,' Robert Brockwell said. He had a beautiful speaking voice, low modulated tones, and a familiar accent that made Fae feel very comfortable. She realized again how attractive he was, with his open smile. His piercing eyes were very appealing too. But it was the quintessential power of the man that was so devastating.

Fae was disappointed by Langley, a flat building with more concrete than windows set in flat, partially wooded countryside. A sign identifying the next turn as the Central Intelligence Agency/Intelligence Community/Federal Highway Administration destroyed any sense of the romantic. They drove directly into the car park, and took a lift which was operated by a key directly to the seventh floor. Fae was disappointed – she would have liked to have seen the entrance. She was ushered into a small sitting-room and offered some refreshment whilst Brockwell conferred with an aide. After a few moments he came into the room.

'And now you and I are going to spend a private hour or so talking about your father, but mostly I want to talk about you, and I want to hear how you are really coping.'

And Fae, delighted by such dazzling charm, told him. She forgot who he was and what he represented, and she talked of the nightmare of Sam's abduction, of her disbelief that he had worked for the Agency, of her confusions and her distrusts.

'Who's on my side? Who has got Sam? Are those such difficult questions to answer? Some of my Turkish contacts say you've got him.'

'I'm not going to tell you anything tonight except for the fact that, whatever you may think, none of us is the kind of person who would deliberately kidnap an American citizen, deprive him of his family, and his family of him, because he was disenchanted with the CIA. We'd kick him out. We might play political games in countries where we need to . . . and you can debate that with me, but we're not a totalitarian state, for God's sake – we're accountable. And thank God for that.'

'I want to believe you.'

'Reserve your judgement until after you've had your briefings. OK?'

'OK.'

Fae shifted, she glanced at her watch. The time had passed. She was sure she was expected to go.

But no, Brockwell was settling back in his chair, easing his back as if he were unwinding himself. He picked up his drink and drank long and slow. She wondered what it was. She supposed because it was in a glass and colourless that it was gin and tonic.

As if he read her mind he said, 'There's nothing quite like a glass of water.'

'Water?'

'Yeah. That's what I drink. An all-American boy.'

'With respect, Mr Brockwell, there is nothing of the boy in you.'

'You'd be surprised, Fae.' He paused. 'Have you heard from him?'

'No.' She averted her eyes quickly. She didn't want to discuss Nick, she didn't want to feel the hurt. 'And I won't,' she continued. 'Nick has made his choice.'

She looked down sharply and her hair fell over her face, obscuring the curve of her cheek. Brockwell was suddenly rather moved by her.

He pulled himself together. Sex was his protection. If he were not careful he would have to seduce Fae Whiteman, for Robert Brockwell used sex to harden himself against any emotion – emotion was uncomfortable.

'Would you like to eat something?' he found himself asking her.

'I'd love to, but I'm actually on my knees.'

'Of course you are.' Immediately solicitous, he stood up and used the phone to summon the car to sweep her back to her anonymous hotel suite.

'Will I see you again?' she asked him.

'We still haven't talked about your Dad. Not properly. Unfortunately I am stuck with a political dinner tomorrow night – a Washington ritual.' He smiled apologetically. 'But it may be interesting for you. Would you like to come? I can arrange for Stanley to bring you.'

'I'd obviously be very interested.'

'Good. Then I'll see you tomorrow night.'

'Thank you.'

Fae sank back into the upholstery and tried not to fall asleep until she was safely in the soft clean sheets of her comfortable hotel bed.

Brockwell climbed into his own car, whose bullet-proof windows never rolled down. He pulled the partition between himself and his CIA security guard and driver firmly shut, and picked up his telephone. He dialled a number where he knew he would be welcome. After a quick whispered conversation he instructed his driver to go straight to an address in Georgetown. He wasted no time when he got there. His hostess, a good friend, sensed his mood and offered no chit-chat. She conducted him into her bedroom, carefully and invitingly opened her blouse. The DCI slipped his hands inside, touched soft, milk-coloured flesh and thought of Fae Whiteman.

Whilst Fae Whiteman slept and Robert Brockwell took his pleasures, Simon Palling wearily climbed out of a cab and checked himself into the Jefferson Hotel. The same liveried bell boy whisked him up to the sixth floor – he'd specially requested that he be installed near his friend Fae Whiteman. A cautious reservations clerk had made a quick telephone call to Langley. He returned to his desk, his face sheathed in smiles: 'That'll be just fine, Mr Palling.'

'Thank you,' replied the rather disgruntled journalist. The Company had obviously given him clearance – there would have been trouble if they hadn't. He just wished Fae could stop her gallivanting around, as he called it. Of course, she had to go to the funeral – he himself had advised it – but now he wanted to go home. He needed to make sure that the builders had installed the new windows properly. Katie just wasn't reliable enough in those areas. And anyway she sounded a bit off when he telephoned from the airport: tired, he supposed. She'd gone for a Sunday lunch at Nick Newman's. She hadn't enjoyed it, he could tell that. He knew Katie.

Katie Palling had been in the bath when her husband rang. She'd just installed herself with a cup of tea by her side when she'd heard the phone ringing. She knew it would have to be Simon, heaved herself out of the bath, grabbed a towel and padded into the bedroom. She'd picked up the receiver and automatically lit herself a cigarette.

'Where are you?' she asked, not hiding her exasperation at such a late call.

Whilst she listened to his explanations of where he was and what he was doing, she smoked her cigarette and thought of Nick Newman. She wanted him and he obviously wasn't happy with Sally. Perhaps she and Nick might snatch just enough uncompromised pleasure from each other to enable them to deal with their respective marriages. She'd ring him the next day, and do an interview. That would be the best way, and then she could do her best to encourage him.

* * *

Fae and Simon encountered each other over breakfast.

'Surprised?' he said jovially as he sat down at her table.

'No. But I'm curious to know if it's my mother who has you trailing around after me, or your newspaper.'

Simon laughed. 'It's not your mother! Seriously, Fae, I think we should do some stuff on you looking for your father's roots.'

'I don't.'

'You've got to make sure your Dad is in the public eye. Keep the pressure up. Let's just do one interview and then we'll both go home.'

Fae sighed: she supposed that Simon was right, but after what had happened to her and Nick, she dreaded any publicity.

'What do you want?' she asked.

'Pictures of you at evocative places . . . you know the kind of thing.'

'No, I couldn't cope with the intrusion. Sorry, Simon, but I will give you an interview.'

'All right.'

'When do you want to do it?'

'As soon as you can.'

'I'm going to Langley today, to find out what's going on, so maybe tomorrow.'

'Whenever. Now, what are you going to have for breakfast? I'm going to indulge in something very fattening, and full of cholesterol,' Simon said grinning with absolute delight. 'There's got to be some consolations in trailing around after you.'

It was Fae's turn to smile. And she continued to do so whilst Simon ordered waffles with whipped cream and blueberries. But when she sipped her coffee and orange juice she tried not to look at the huge globules of white cream that clung briefly to the edge of his mouth.

She was not sorry when a different liveried bell boy hovered respectfully and told her that her car was here.

'See you soon,' she said and delivered herself up into the jowls of the monolith that was the Central Intelligence Agency.

Once again she was conducted into the same sitting-room. But this time there were other people there: William Fairchild and, to her great pleasure, Maise Montgomery, whom she hugged almost joyously. There were also two other men, introduced as

Michael Darwin from the Analytical Directorate and Barry Gower from the Operations Directorate.

Fairchild explained that Sam was employed by Operations and as such Mr Gower was there to explain her father's job and what was actually happening to get him back. Mr Darwin would highlight the various groupings inside Turkey and make what they all hoped were accurate predictions.

'And Maise?'

'I've been doing a bit of snooping and we thought it would be helpful if you knew what we are actually up to.'

'So you weren't just my bodyguard.'

'That too.'

During the next five hours, with just a few breaks for coffee and a delicious lunch that she couldn't digest, Fae tried to absorb the politics of the different factions within the Turkish political arena. She learnt the political nature of the Kurds, she was taught the philosophical difference between the Sunni Muslims who make up the majority of the world's followers of Mohammed and the Shiite Muslims who revere a different descendant of Mohammed. She was shown the geographical importance of Turkey to the West. She was talked through the specific ramifications for Turkey of good relations with Iran. The Iranian–Turkish border was an uncomfortable reality and the rise of Fundamentalism in Turkey was a dangerous reminder of that Iranian proximity. But even so the popularity of the Islamic code was not too far from the very seat of Government itself. Her father was a pawn in the game of power. His role had been to identify possible agents for the United States. He also alerted the Embassy to those sympathetic to the Kurds or the Fundamentalists. One such group pounced on him.

'I have something to show you,' Maise said. 'It's a photograph which we have had for some time. It gives us a lead.'

'A lead?'

'Yes, it tells us who killed the boy Memet. Unfortunately we can't find him now, and we don't know who else is involved, but we will find him,' she continued.

She handed Fae the photograph. It had been taken at the moment that the boy Memet was shot, and it showed the gun pointing in his direction, held by a man whose face was encircled in red.

'His name is Hayri Gurbuz. He's a student at the Bosphorus University.'

'How did you get this?'

'An informer, on the Turkish side, gave us Hayri's name. We put a tail on him. That's how we got the photograph,' answered Maise, smoking rapidly. Fae watched her grind out a cigarette butt, and immediately light up the new small white tunnel to cancer.

'But if you knew this boy was killing Memet, why didn't you stop him?' she asked, and then – for a horrible truth was lurking, waiting to be recognized – she said, 'You could have saved Richard, you could have saved your own man.'

'We had no choice, Fae. Richard went out on a limb, he didn't tell us what he was doing. We had no time to warn him. No one wanted him dead, he just got in the way. It was horrific for the agent who took the photographs. But we did not dare blow cover. If we'd gone for Hayri, we'd never get close to Sam and, who knows, they may well have killed him.'

'Oh my God, this is absolutely awful.'

Someone, Fae didn't know who, was offering her a glass of water. She didn't want it. She felt absolutely sick. This was no game, no shoot-out on the silver screen of make-believe, where moving images took risks, and fired guns, and the good guy never lay in the gutter – only the black hat spilt his blood. In the real world there was no right to life for anyone. Fae didn't know how to deal with herself: she was shaking her head from side to side as if she were some sort of demented creature trying to escape from the inescapable into her own fantastic world.

'Oh God,' she said again.

'Fae, come on. Hold it together, breathe deeply, you're OK.' It was Maise with the water and the cool voice. Was Maise the agent who had taken the photographs of men dying?

'Was it you?' she asked. She had to ask.

'Does it help to know who it was?'

'No, no, it doesn't. I just wondered.'

'There is no "just wondered" in our business, Fae.'

Fae crouched over in her chair, ran her hands over her face, through her long black hair.

'Look, I'm not sure I can take much more today. I know I should, but I just can't.'

They were solicitous and instantly kind. Maise would take her back to the Jefferson. She could rest until the dinner.

'Dinner?'

'Yes.' The Director had specifically requested an invitation for her to attend his party in honour of the new Chairman of the Foreign Affairs Committee, Senator Jack Abbott.

'Oh no, I couldn't attend a dinner after this. I need time.'

'You'll have time,' Maise said. 'Stanley Schwartz is going to take you.' There was something in her voice that made Fae react. Not a threat, not even a nasty tone, but it was an instruction and Fae was not sure she liked it. She started to protest.

'I don't have to go anywhere if I don't want to.'

'Of course you don't, Fae. Let's go back to the hotel, have a rest and we'll talk some more and you'll see how you feel.' Maise helped her up, held her arm, ushered her into a high-speed lift that seemed to take her directly to the car. The low-level black Company limousine swung into the traffic and purred towards the Jefferson Hotel. Fae wouldn't speak: she couldn't speak. Maise took her straight to her suite, so that she didn't even notice a quizzical look on Simon Palling's face as he entered the hotel at the same time. After Maise had helped her on to the bed, removed her shoes and promised to return in 'just a few hours and then we'll talk some more', she retired to the bar and to Simon Palling. There was a vodka waiting for her.

'How are you, Maise?' Simon said as she sat down next to him.

Fae slept fitfully. She dreamt she was a child again, swinging in her father's arms, except she was not a child – she was a grown woman, and the man was not her father, he was Richard Marks. And whilst he swung her high above his head someone fired a bullet which lodged like a third eye in his forehead. As he sank to his knees Fae screamed, 'Daddy, Daddy, Daddy,' but the words did not come out as Daddy, instead it was 'Brockwell, Robert Brockwell, Robert Brockwell.'

The Director of the CIA cut an elegant figure in his black tuxedo and his snow white shirt and his silk bow tie. His wife, an extremely beautiful blonde woman in her early forties, wore a jade green satin dress, cleverly draped over one hip with a heart-shaped neckline and long tight sleeves. She greeted Fae very kindly: 'My dear, how lovely that you've joined us. I do hope you can forget your pain for just a short while and enjoy your evening.'

Fae, pale in a strapless royal blue silk sheath, slit to the knee, completely unaware that she'd never looked more beautiful, thanked her hostess. Brockwell held her hand for just a moment too long.

'I hear you've had a very rough day. I'm just grateful you've joined us.' He turned to a big, square-faced man with silver hair and silver glasses on his right: 'Senator, this is Fae Whiteman.'

'We'll get your father out, Miss Whiteman, whatever it takes. Don't you worry about that.'

'I believe you,' Fae answered quietly, and let Stanley propel her towards the influential and the powerful who made up the guest list for the Director's dinner.

The party was being held at one of those discreet and highly exclusive clubs that serve as backdrops to every administration's political manoeuvring. Waitresses in black dresses and white aprons flitted backwards and forwards with their trays of drinks as the pre-dinner conversation peaked. Stanley explained that everyone knew where to sit, having been given cards with a small table plan and the number of their table clearly marked by their name.

'We're rather privileged. We're actually at the DCI's table.'

Fae didn't care where she was sitting. She was haunted by Richard Marks' death, and couldn't understand these people who just didn't seem to care. She felt as if she were about to explode, like some huge balloon that had been filled with too much helium; as if she were floating above the people in the smart room, who by now were making their way through a door into a smart dining-room with tasteful tables decorated with tasteful flowers and tasteful candles.

'Come on, Fae, hold on to my arm, tight, then you won't fall down.' It was Brockwell himself, ignoring the small plump wife of the Chairman of the Foreign Affairs Committee.

'Shouldn't you?' Fae pointed to a kindly woman who was looking at her with soft eyes.

'Mrs Abbott was the one who suggested that you might need my company for a few moments. Actually I was grateful to her:

I was trying to work out how I could get over to you without appearing to be rude.'

Fae stopped walking, and stood firmly on her royal blue high heels and looked up directly into surprisingly gentle grey eyes. 'Look, I didn't want to come here this evening,' she said.

'I know you didn't. But I'm glad. I should have told you everything myself.'

'Would that have made it more kosher?'

'No, it wouldn't. There's no way you can clean up a death. But I ask you to remember one thing. We didn't want Richard to die. He lost his judgement, but he was as much a victim of those men as Sam, and we want to keep Sam alive and bring him home.'

Fae averted her eyes quickly. She was in danger of crying.

'Now, just for this evening, watch Washington at play with itself.'

'Maise said it would be a social slight if I didn't come.'

'I know what she said. I told her to say it.'

'Why?'

'I think I really like you.'

'You think?'

'It's not a situation I allow myself too often, Fae.'

It was later, when they danced, that Fae realized that Robert Brockwell wanted her. She shifted back from him, she couldn't deal with it.

Katie Palling telephoned Nick Newman at just five minutes past ten on Monday morning. She wanted to be sure to reach him before his day began. She explained to his secretary that she had had lunch with him at his home the day before. He'd mentioned his new film. She'd like to do an interview before he got too bogged down in pre-production.

Nick groaned when the message was relayed to him.

'Come on, Nick, she's getting quite a reputation – you can't afford to alienate her. What harm is there in a quick drink?'

What harm indeed when the quickened blood heightens desire, and long red nails caress an unwilling knee, and eyes heavy with lust spell out the come hither message?

'Do you want to go on to dinner?' Katie asked, in a slow voice, when the formalities of her interview were over.

'No, thank you. I have to get home. Sally will worry. Unless you'd like to come with me? She knew you were doing the interview, so I'm sure she'd be delighted.'

'Thank you, but I won't intrude on the happy family.' The voice was normal, but the nails dug in and scratched long and hard, leaving a red mark even through trousers.

Suleyman watched from a seat at the bar. He saw the fingers working on the man, he saw the man get up and leave the pub. He told himself that the woman, Katie Palling, had better not try to see Nick Newman again. It would be bad for her if she did.

Fae was very tired when Stanley finally dropped her off at the hotel. She declined his offer to accompany her to her suite.

'I'm fine,' she said.

She smiled at another liveried bell boy and let him open the lift gates and take her to her floor.

Robert Brockwell was waiting by her door. 'How did you get here?'

'When you've got my job you can get away from anyone – except your bodyguard.'

'Is he here?'

'Downstairs.'

Fae put her key in the door: 'I'm sorry but I really can't cope with anything more this evening.'

'I know that,' Brockwell said.

Fae opened the door and turned to bid the man goodnight, but there were soft fingers on her shoulders, down her back, playing wondrous games with her skin. There were hands through her hair. Nick, Nick, but no, it wasn't Nick, she couldn't have Nick any more. This man, this man was different. No, she wanted Nick. Not him, not Brockwell. But a gentle palm comforted her breasts and treacherous nipples hardened through the silk of her dress.

'Oh Fae,' he whispered, and a cool mouth and deep kisses did things they should not do.

'No, no,' she whispered, meaning it.

But he'd picked her up and carried her to a welcoming bed, and the cushions felt good under her head. She felt his hands at the back of her dress releasing the zip, and the dress slipped down and his mouth nuzzled at her breast. What was he doing? – but her spine arched and she needed the loving. 'Oh, but you're beautiful,' he whispered, as he took away her dress and parted her legs and as she felt him fill her up she wept at her compliance, but still she moved with him.

Afterwards she said, 'Why did we do this? It's wrong.'

'We couldn't help it. Neither of us.' He sketched her face with his fingers. 'I want to stay with you, and I can't. But before I go I have to tell you something. I've had a lot of women and I have a lot of women. Just once in my life I fell in love. I lost her and I swore I would never allow myself to feel again. Tonight, with you, I felt. Thank you, my beautiful Fae. I'll never hurt you.'

He got up from the bed, kissed her, dressed and left her. When the door was shut behind him, Fae realized that she had not looked at his body.

When she woke the following morning, Fae telephoned Maise and told her that yesterday had been simply too much.

'I can't take much more revelation. I'm going to visit my father's uncle in Oklahoma. I need some time to myself.'

She contacted her father's cousin and he was delighted to hear from her. The warmth in his voice was good to her ears. She arranged the time of the flight with him and then made her travel arrangements with the hotel. She started to pack. There was a knock on the door. Unwillingly she went to open it. She did not want to see Robert Brockwell – she did not want to think about him. Why had she slept with him? She didn't love him . . . and yet there was something. There was another rap, louder. She would have to answer it. She opened the door just a little and found herself staring at Maise. She let the American woman in.

'It was me. I was there. I wanted you to know.'

'Why?'

'I haven't had too good a time since it all happened.'

'I'm the confessional.'

'In a way. So you're beating a retreat. You don't have to pack everything: this suite is reserved for you throughout your time in the US. Oh, and your flight booking has been upgraded to first. The car's waiting for you.'

'The Company knows everything.'

'Everything,' Maise replied and pointedly looked at Fae's untidy bed.

'I don't know what to say about Richard, Maise.'

'I don't expect you to, Fae. We all have to live with ourselves.' Maise's face was taut and white, her eyes unnaturally bright, and Fae realized she was in real grief; but even so, Fae could not find it within herself to console her.

Oklahoma City was clean and bright. There were kin at the airport, and no limousines to fetch and carry. But by now Fae was wise to the world and she glanced around the airport, looking for the man or woman assigned to her. She picked her out, it was a her, she wore a red suit and carried a case. She was reading a newspaper, but she was sitting just by a mirror and every so often she glanced in it to check that Fae was still there. Fae shrugged, she didn't care any more, this was her pilgrimage into Sam's life. And no one was going to take that away from her.

She saw Franklin Whiteman within two hours of her arrival. He was installed in one of those old people's homes that don't look like a home; where on the surface there is independence, a little apartment, even a kitchen, but not one big enough to cook a real meal. Those are taken in a big dining-room, and the recreation facilities provide better opportunities than the small bright sitting-room.

'He was a gutsy little tucker. Loved to fish. I remember one time he went with your Grand Daddy and he got stung by a big wasp. But your Grand Daddy was nursing a catch and the little boy, couldna been more than five, never said a word. His arm was as big as a ball, but he just kept his mouth shut and waited till your Grand Daddy had finished his business.'

Franklin Whiteman was an old man with the cruelly gnarled hands of the arthritic. He sat straight in his chair, his fingers curled over, but his gaze was level and his voice clear. He was pleased to see Fae, and said he remembered her when she was a little girl.

'I want to find out as much as I can about him. This CIA business – I had no idea, and it's as if my father isn't who I thought he was. I need to know about him.'

'But he's still the same man, honey,' her great uncle told her. 'Your father's a patriot, that's something.'

'You see him that way?'

'That's what he is, isn't he? A man who fights for his country. I'm mighty proud of him.'

'But he broke down, he . . .'

'That blabbering probably saved his life. So I'm grateful he did, aren't you?'

Fae smiled at the old man. He was so direct, so clear in his views. Her Dad was a patriot. He was no coward, he 'blabbered' to save his life. All her problems and her doubts had been solved. Or had they? At that moment she didn't care. She'd come into Sam's world and she could feel her father for the first time since the kidnapping. It was wonderful.

She didn't stop to wonder whether she liked her cousins. They were kind, they were family. She felt welcome.

'What do you think will happen?' her cousin – or rather her father's cousin – George asked her.

'I've no idea. I spent the day at Langley, listening to their analysts, but they haven't yet told me what to expect. I know that the Turks won't trade their prisoners for Dad.'

'Nor should they: we should send in the Marines.'

Fae smiled. 'George, we don't know where he is.'

She was sitting in a comfortable drawing-room, furnished in an American style: Hepplewhite furniture, good paintings, bowls of flowers. Patty, George's daughter, who was three years younger than Fae but already married to Glenn with a daughter of her own, was sitting with them. She was a nice looking girl with short brown curly hair and a fresh open face. Her mother, Hope, was in the kitchen, preparing what seemed to Fae to be a feast.

'Oh, it's just pot roast and potatoes, a few beets with sour cream and corn fritters and some snow peas. Not very much.'

But before the pot roast there was a wonderful chicken soup with corn muffins and lashings of butter.

'If I lived here, I would be the size of a house,' said Fae as she devoured her second feather-light muffin.

'Are they bein' good to you – the Agency I mean?' asked Glenn, the son-in-law, a small man with wispy blond hair and pale blue eyes.

'Yes, they've been extraordinarily kind.'

'Gosh, I'd like to meet Bob Brockwell. He's so handsome,' Patty remarked.

Fae choked on the rest of the muffin in her mouth.

'He's very nice,' she managed, and could see the hero worship in Patty's eyes. She quickly averted her own and turned the conversation back to her father.

'I'd like to go to his school. I want to find out as much about Sam as I can,' she said.

Plans were organized. Fae was to go to the school the following morning, but that night – late, at around 11.30 P.M. – she received a telephone call from her mother that summoned her back to Europe, to Italy, to Fabrizzi . . .

CHAPTER EIGHT

Innessa had taken Fabrizzi to Rome for two days. She had needed to escape the routine of her parents' summer activities. She was suffering with headaches – she knew it was stress. Her mind raced in and out of her longings and her fears, and her guilts. She was missing Sam, and worrying about him, and she wasn't sleeping. The memories of their good times, the essential reliability of the man, his humour – slowly those good things were seeping into her consciousness, balancing out the disappointments and the failures. And there was Richard, too, whose death preyed heavily: she thought about him a lot. At times she regretted the infidelity, it cheapened their friendship – at other times she relished all that loving and she mourned its passing.

It was the evening of the first day and she decided to have a dinner at Otello, a favourite place, just by the Spanish steps. Fabrizzi ate chicken and chips, she ordered an osso bucco. She drank wine and laughed with some Swiss tourists, two men who had come to see the Sistine Chapel. They played a game of the vanishing coin with her son. Fabrizzi pointed out two boys who seemed to be staring at them. Innessa glanced over: they were standing in the courtyard openly flaunting themselves at Innessa. They were young, maybe eighteen or so. The proprietor ordered them off: his restaurant was for eating, not for gawping.

Finally Innessa called for the bill. The evening had cheered her – the soft air of Rome, the bonhomie, Fabrizzi's happy face and an appreciation in the eyes of the older Swiss man all contributed to her pleasures. She and Fabrizzi linked arms and walked up the cobbled stone street. They were about to cross into the square when they both heard the roar of a motor bike. Fabrizzi turned first, she felt him twist away from her, and then she saw the bike, its lights blazing. It blinded her – it was coming straight at her. She grabbed Fabrizzi and screamed, but still the bike came. At the last moment it swerved, missing her, but its handlebars hit Fabrizzi, hurling him up into the air. She saw him, her baby, thrown across the road. The bike crashed into the plate glass window of a shop. The sound of the splintering glass, the screech of agonized brakes and the terrified shouts of petrified youths were terrible. One of them smashed his head and his blood shot out, staining the pristine merchandise behind the shattered glass, while the other lay moaning by his machine. Innessa ran to her child who lay still and white by the fountain. The kids who a moment before had been sitting and drinking and talking on the Spanish steps crowded around, appalled, wanting to help, not knowing what to do. The police were there. Someone said he was a doctor.

'Don't touch him,' he told Innessa.

'I'm his mother!' Innessa screamed. But she knew enough not to move Fabrizzi. She stroked his still face and whispered, 'Fabrizzi, Fabrizzi. My boy. My son.'

They took him in an ambulance to the nearest hospital. Innessa sat with him, holding a limp, but still warm hand.

A nurse asked, 'Is there someone we can call? Your husband?' 'My husband has been kidnapped – he's somewhere in Turkey.'

'Your husband is the American? Whiteman, yes – that's the name. You poor woman, now this. Your parents perhaps? We could contact them.'

'Yes, and my stepdaughter. Fabrizzi's sister. Fae. I want Fae.'

The fastest way for Fae to get to Rome was to fly back to New York. But there was no flight that night, she would have to wait until the morning, until 9.30. There would be just a one hour stopover at Kennedy, and then on to Leonardo da Vinci. She had no sense of time or place. She just had to get to Rome, to the hospital – to Fabrizzi, to Innessa. Barbara had told her as much as there was to know.

Fabrizzi was in a coma and it was too soon to measure the extent of the damage.

She packed her one case, and sat all night in her clothes, waiting for the dawn. There was no question of sleep.

George drove her to the airport, waited whilst she telephoned

Langley. Brockwell was not available, she left a message with his secretary.

Then she telephoned Emily. She heard the familiar ringing tone . . . oh God, let her be there!

'Hello.' Emily's voice was bright.

'It's me. Fabrizzi's been knocked down by a motor bike. He's in a coma.'

'Fae!'

'I'm on my way to Rome – I've had enough, Emily, I've really had enough.'

The flights were interminable. Fae found that she sat on the edge of her seat – as if she were ready to leave the flight before it had even taken off. On the Oklahoma–Kennedy connection she held on to her case, looking at her watch every few moments, refusing even a coffee – as if it would hinder her making a fast exit. She was slightly better on the flight to Leonardo da Vinci – she couldn't eat, but at least she didn't keep her case on her lap. Immediately she was able to disembark, Fae rushed through passport control, past customs and into one of the waiting taxis. The Rome traffic crawled its way into the city through one of the worst storms the city had ever seen. The ink black sky was lit up with sharp slices of lightning. The modern city rose up against the storm, as if it were challenging the gods, whilst old Rome shivered in its ruins, a proof of mortality.

By the time Fae reached the hospital she was exhausted and over-emotional. She looked up at the slate grey sky. She shook her fist.

'Enough . . . it's enough now, I want change.' The slam of the thunder turned her brave cry into a hopeless whimper.

She asked at the desk for Fabrizzi by name. A kindly nurse took her to the door of his room and pushed it open for her. She saw her little brother, his body so still, his face so quiet. She saw the tubes and the drips.

Innessa was sitting in a chair by his side, so like him – so little too, but her hair was combed, her make-up was on and her mouth was firm. It was just that in the harsh light of the hospital, Fae could see that her eyes were red with crying. Fae sat on the edge of the bed between the mother and the child. She put one arm around Innessa and with the other she touched Fabrizzi's arm, gently stroking the warm flesh.

'Oh my God, what is happening to us?' Fae said.

Innessa shook her head. 'Just talk to your brother. Wake him up: tell him we want to go home.'

Fae continued to stroke Fabrizzi's arm, talking of things that would interest him – Arsenal, Michael Jackson.

'I'll get a cassette player as soon as I can. We should play his favourite tapes, and if we could set up a television and a VCR, we could run those Arsenal matches for him . . . I've read that that's what you do when people are in coma.'

'My father will organize all of that for us,' Innessa said.

'Don't you want to go swimming, Fabrizzi?' Fae continued quietly. 'He always swam with Sam,' Innessa said.

Fae looked up sharply, there was such nostalgia in Innessa's tone. Their eyes held together.

'I went to Oklahoma,' Fae said, 'to see Dad's uncle. He said Dad was a patriot, and he'd blubbered to save his life. He said it was the right thing to do, that he was proud of him. And Innessa, I wanted to be proud of him too. I just don't understand any of this, why he worked for the CIA, why he . . .'

'Why he isn't perfect,' Innessa finished quietly.

'I s'pose so. You know he was always superman to me, he never let me down, he was the one really reliable person in my life. Mum was late for things, school things, you know. If Sam said he'd be somewhere, he'd never not be there. And suddenly, through all these horrible things, it's as if I've been robbed of that man. It's as if he wasn't who I thought he was.'

'No, that's not true. He's still all those things, but my God, he's human and he has his frailties. Are you perfect?'

'No.'

'So why should Sam be? He's a weak man, maybe a little too proud of himself, bombastic perhaps. But so what? He's still the man who never let you down.'

Fae spoke very softly, near to tears herself: 'You're missing him too.'

'Very much,' Innessa replied. 'And Fabrizzi. He needs his Daddy, he needs Sam. Especially now.'

'If they could see us now,' Fae said smiling. She put a hand on Innessa's face, noticing the smudged black pencil line around her eyes, the little rivulet of a black tear down the highly blushed cheek. 'They'd say your make-up needs fixing.'

Innessa laughed.

She walked over to the basin and automatically smoothed out the damage. Fae sat watching her. She was so grateful for the shared emotion. At least they'd grieved together.

She turned back to Fabrizzi. 'Come on, kid, wake up,' she said.

From the mirror, Innessa took the measure of her stepdaughter. Fae was tired, a deep-rooted fatigue that had little to do with jet-lag.

'Fae, go back to the apartment. Pamona, our housekeeper, is there. She'll give you some tea and then you go to sleep. I'll come in to you when I get back. Then you do the morning shift, and I'll do the afternoon . . . and so on.'

Just three little words, little words that held such terror: how long was 'and so on'?

Fae stood outside the hospital and waited for yet another cab. She liked the feel of the air on her face, she liked the solitude of the waiting. In Washington there had been no such moments, the oiled cogs of the facilities worked smoothly and effortlessly. She wondered how Brockwell could bear it, the constant movement of his life, always people to fetch and carry for him. The thought of him jarred her, she hadn't allowed him into her mind till that moment. She realized she didn't want to think about him.

Fae did not stay with Innessa after all. Her stepmother's parents had decided to move back to Rome to be near their daughter and their grandson. Of course their hospitality was offered to Fae, but she needed to be comfortable and could not tolerate the idea of having to observe any kind of form. Politely she excused herself from being their guest, but she did agree on dinner that evening. She wondered how Innessa would feel. Innessa's mother, so like her daughter in style but not in manner, was on the telephone summoning doctors from every point in the globe. Her father, courteous and kind, as ever, was concerned about Fae staying at a hotel.

'But, if you insist, I will organize a suite for you at the Hôtel de la Ville. It isn't far from us.'

'Thank you.'

It seemed to Fae that the Hôtel de la Ville, with its marble entrance hall and its carefully arranged, plush, but slightly faded furniture in its salon, was more like a grand palazzo than an actual hotel. It didn't have an anonymous feel about it, and it was as if the guests ought to know each other. Indeed a few of them did, for as a rather weary Fae was led towards her room she passed a couple sitting at a corner table, talking in an intimate fashion – the woman was leaning forward, her eyes shining with sexual excitement. The man was sitting back on his chair, his eyes smiling in a lazy come hither way. Fae knew that smile of Nick's very well.

Lead filled her veins, nailing her to the floor, preventing movement, robbing her of speech. In that moment the woman looked up, the sexual flush froze for a moment, the eyes clouded over. Nick, seeing her face, changed, turned to follow her gaze.

'Fae, Fae.' He was up out of his chair, coming over to her.

'What are you doing here?' she managed to say, searching his face, the eyes that crinkled at the side, the wide cheek bones, the soft mouth, even the texture of a skin that she knew as well as she knew her own.

'I'm doing a recce for my new picture and, er . . .' He turned to his companion. 'This lady is a journalist who is doing a piece on me, so she came along too. Fae, meet Katie Palling.' His arm was gripping Fae's, forcing the blood back into her limbs.

Simon Palling's wife. What was she doing here? Why was she looking at Nick that way? How did she know Nick?

'I know your husband,' she heard herself say. 'Everywhere I go he is sure to follow. And now I get to Rome, and instead of him I find you.' She hadn't meant to be rude, it just slipped out.

'I can assure you, Miss Whiteman, that I'm not on your story. It's Nick that interests me.' Fae saw the slight tilt of the head, the pink tongue between the lips, the eyes that lingered just too long. Oh, God, how much pain could she take?

'I can see that. Excuse me.' She shifted her arm away from Nick, walked away from him towards the lift where the porter stood patiently.

In the quiet of the pretty bedroom, Fae sat still, victim to a dreadful sexual jealousy that whipped her back and forth, as if her body were gripped by its horrible tentacles, and she, too weak to escape from its lashing, took its punishment, almost as if she were one of the early martyrs, dying not for a faith of pure love that in itself brought a blessed peace, but for a passion that was hell.

He was with that woman and he'd slept with her. She knew the look. Let him have her – she had Brockwell. Yes, she had Brockwell. He wasn't Nick, but in time . . .

She picked up the telephone and dialled the operator, all the time searching in her overnight bag for the black book of numbers. 'B' for Brockwell.

'Pronto.'

'Yes, I'd like to make a call to the United States, a personal call to Mr Robert Brockwell. His number is . . .'

She heard a knocking as she finished the figures. She replaced the receiver. She got off the bed, and straightened her hair. She knew it was Nick and she was glad, she just wanted him to put his arms around her.

He came into the room, his anger tangible, his face white and set, his eyes hard.

'What kind of performance was that downstairs?'

'What?'

'You sweep into the hall, glare at me, are incredibly rude to an important journalist and then just walk off.'

'You're sleeping with her. It hurt.'

'What are you talking about?'

'Well, are you?'

'Am I what?'

'Sleeping with her?'

'That's none of your business.'

'Isn't it?' Nick, Nick. I love you, hold me, touch me.

'No, it isn't. What's between us is ours, special, no one can touch it, no one can take it away. But that doesn't mean to say I can't do what I like with other people. They have their own value to me.'

Nick, tell me there is no one else, just tell me. 'Are you saying you can sleep with who you like?'

'In essence.'

'In fact.'

The temper was raised off the flat mat of good behaviour. The voice was hot and sharp. 'In fact, I can do what I judge to be correct.'

The telephone rang: a shrill sharp sound, butting its way in, having its say. Fae picked it up.

'Yes?'

'Fae, how are you? I was going to call you. What news of Fabrizzi? I know they're holding the guys who did it. It's just too much for you to take. I'm so concerned about you.'

A soft warm caring voice, so different from the hard cold eyes that stared into her.

'Oh Robert, it's good to hear you. Listen, I'm just in the middle of something. Can I call you back, or are you going to be doing something important?'

'I have to go to the White House for a briefing. What's the time your end now?'

Fae looked at her watch. 'Six o'clock.'

'OK. I'll call you at midnight, before you go to sleep.'

'That would be nice.'

She replaced the receiver carefully.

A voice cut across her, clean sharp incisions drawing blood.

'Who's Robert?'

'That must be my business.'

'Of course it is.'

Oh Nick, love me. She turned her back on him, feeling tears.

'Well, then.' Was the voice softer? Was it gentler? Stay with me, stay with me. 'Have a good night, whatever you're going to do.'

She turned quickly and looked at him, her eyes wide – she was pleading. 'Yes, and you.'

'Right, catch up with you, then, some time. Take care of yourself. I hope you have good news about your father.'

He started out of the room. 'Nick?'

'Yes?'

'I . . .'

'Yes?'

She almost said it 'I love you', but the voice was polite, the eyes controlled, and so she retreated into the side of the bed, sunk on to it. 'Wish you luck.'

'Thank you.'

He was gone, on the other side of the door, and she wept.

As Nick walked down the corridor he tried to hold on to his cold rage at Fae. If he didn't keep his temper firmly in place he might weaken and turn back to her. And what point would there be in that? He felt the sadness creeping over him. He pushed it away, quickened his step and went to his rendezvous with Katie Palling. He hadn't wanted her to come to Rome, but God she had been persistent, finally contacting the studio which was funding his picture, promising a big profile. So they'd insisted. Take the lady to Rome, give her all the assistance she needs. His agent, Duncan Wood, told him to sleep with her if necessary. 'By the looks of her it won't be too much punishment, might be just what you need.'

It wasn't what he needed. What he needed was the clean pressure of doing good work – it was the one place he could go to get away from the whole mess of his life.

He and Katie ate in a small restaurant behind the Via Veneta where simple pasta dressed with cream and small pieces of lemon was served. Nick tried to be charming. He listened to her anecdotes, poured her wine and his own and drank two glasses to her one, and when her fingers reached for him he did not move away.

Fae dragged herself to her appointment with Innessa and her parents. She was dreading the dinner, but she found herself comforted by the communal caring. They went to the hospital to collect Innessa. No one was anxious to leave the small boy, a hand – that of Innessa's mother – smoothed a sheet. Her father fidgeted with the drip, whilst Innessa straightened the little body. Fae just held his hand and talked and talked. She had no idea what the actual words were, but they meant 'Wake up, wake up'.

When it was time for food they went to a simple white restaurant near the hospital where they were offered small artichokes dressed in oil and garlic and vitello tonnato – the smooth rich tunny fish sauce and the cold slices of veal an unexpected feast of flavours.

Whilst Fae enjoyed her meal, a small, lithe Turkish youth fidgeted with the lock on her bedroom door, but he could not break in. So when the chambermaid opened the door to make the bed, he slipped in behind her and hid in the bathroom until she left the room. Suleyman had taken the same flight to Rome as Nick Newman and Katie Palling. His obsession with their behaviour would not have allowed him to stay in London. When he saw the object of his passion, Fae Whiteman, arrive at the hotel, he was overjoyed. He had to go into her room, he had to touch her things. He opened her bottles, smelt her perfume and looked over her make-up – taking a lip gloss out of its case he smoothed it over his own lips, his unsteady hand denying him a clean outline. He used her mascara. There was some peach eye shadow – he put that on, all over his lids. He used her blusher over his cheeks. Did he look like her? He had dark hair too. He smoothed it with his finger and then with her long handled comb he fluffed it out, turning his hair this way and that till he was satisfied. Going back into the bedroom, he opened the wardrobe, fingered her clothes. She had a white silk nightdress. He liked it, buried his nose in its softness. He tried to put it on, but it was too small. He lay on the bed, wrapped the silk nightdress around his arms, imagined that he was Fae, wearing the soft silk nightdress.

Fae did not stay out late, she was tired. Innessa walked her to the hotel.

'Shall I come up?' she asked.

'No, you're tired, and so am I,' said Fae.

'I'll see you tomorrow – I'll get to the hospital at around nine o'clock.'

'OK. You know your mother said she would come?'

'Yes.'

'She's a nice woman.'

'Yes, she is.' Innessa squeezed Fae's shoulder. 'I'm glad you're here with me, but I'm worried about you, Fae. You're not happy.'

'How can I be at this time?'

'No. I s'pose that was a stupid comment. Put it down to fatigue.'

Fae collected her key from the concierge and made her way to her room. She opened the door and was surprised to find the light on. She assumed the chambermaid had left it on, so she half turned and closed the door behind her. Then she saw it – a grotesque parody, half man, half woman – on her bed, cuddling her night gown. She screamed and screamed and screamed. Paralysed, unable to move, the sound from inside her kept coming and coming.

Suleyman leapt up from the bed. It was her, she was there, standing in front of him. She was frightened, he had to calm her, he was part of her, he loved her, he wouldn't hurt her. He went over to Fae, tried to put his hand on her arm, to tell her he meant her no harm. She backed away from him and grabbed the big light from the dressing-table. She was trying to hit him with it. She mustn't do that: she would hurt herself. He had to take it away from her, he had to stop the crying. He hit her, feeling her cheek under his hand. Oh, her cheek, her beautiful cheek. Someone was banging on the door behind them, they had to go away, they had to shut up, they were adding to her fears. He didn't like that. He took his gun out, he fired just once, to make them be quiet.

There was a crash of glass, someone had jumped into the room. They would hurt Fae: he had to stop them. He turned and pointed his gun. He would have to fire, but didn't want to.

'No-o-o!' He turned back to Fae, just to tell her not to worry, but the man was on top of him, throwing him to the floor, twisting his arms behind his back, he was hurting him . . .

'Awwwww!'

'Miss Whiteman, please, I don't want to let him go – can you open the door?' The voice was American, calm and sensible. Shaking, but no longer shouting, Fae managed to open the door. The Italian police swarmed into the room. An Inspector, she supposed it was an Inspector, took her hand and kindly put her in a chair. The others took the man, who was looking at her. He was revolting.

The American spoke again. 'The Embassy are sending someone to take care of you.'

Fae bent her head into her hands, she didn't want someone from the Embassy, she wanted Nick.

In a room, some two floors up, Nick Newman lay on a bed and felt a woman's mouth on him, blessed wonderful relief. Her hands lingered over his skin, her hair brushed his chest, she was light and gentle. He reached down to her, raised her face to his, his tongue met hers, he put his arms around her, he felt her small firm breasts against him, her long legs. In the distance he could hear a woman's scream and he sat up. It was Fae. No, it couldn't be Fae – he mustn't think of Fae. He turned back to the woman, gave in to her lips.

The person from the Embassy turned out to be William Fairchild. Fabrizzi's accident had not gone unnoticed and the Americans were anxious to find out just who the two young motorcyclists were. It turned out they were just show-offs who would never show off again.

William Fairchild arrived at the hotel just as the Italian Police were leading Suleyman out into a waiting police car.

'Can I have him?' Fairchild asked the Inspector.

'You can't have him, but you can talk to him,' the Inspector replied.

'Good. I'll be over to the police station later, but first I must spend time with Miss Whiteman.'

'I've called a doctor.'

'Thanks.'

Fae was sobbing. She simply couldn't stop. Her heart felt as if it were broken into tiny pieces, some parts labelled Sam, others Fabrizzi, a big part was called Nick Newman, a little part Robert Brockwell. None of it had her name on it, for who was she? She was merely the victim.

'Fae, it's William Fairchild. I'm here because of your brother's accident. I just wanted to check out that it had nothing to do with Sam's kidnapping. I was at the Embassy when the call came through. I'm so sorry for you, you really have had enough now. What with your brother and all.'

The telephone rang: it was Brockwell. He had said he would call. William Fairchild spoke to him, and recounted the incident.

'Get him to talk.'

'You can believe I will.'

'Can I speak with Fae?'

Fairchild held out the phone. Fae shook her head. 'I want Nick,' she whispered.

'She's beat, Robert. Leave her be for this evening.'

'OK, tell her . . . tell her, I'll call her in the morning.'

'I'm sure she'll be glad of that.'

Fairchild replaced the receiver. 'The DCI will call you in the morning, Fae. I've left a man on the door. He won't go away. I have business with the Turk.'

Fae nodded, but after Fairchild left she could not rest. She got up, she had to open the door and check on her guardian. He smiled at her, a young guy, dark hair and nice brown eyes.

'Go to sleep, Miss Whiteman, I'm right here.'

Fae nodded and shut the door, but she couldn't go to bed. She was so restless that she paced, literally paced, up and down and up and down. Her mind was in a turmoil: she didn't know where to go to escape from whirling thoughts that had no shape or meaning. It was the physical sight of the man, so firmly implanted on her mind that it was a photograph in front of her, always there taunting her, that was so horrible. It made her feel dirty. She took a shower and washed her hair. By now it was one o'clock. Even so she could not sleep. Nick was there too, in her mind, but just beyond her reach. She could almost smell him, touch him, but he was in profile, his face turned away from her. She wanted to reach up and turn his face back to her so that she could see him, but she couldn't. She had to get out of the room; she couldn't stand it; she felt as if she were going mad. She opened the door and spoke to the American.

'Listen,' she said, 'if I wanted to go to the hospital . . . to see my brother, would you come with me?'

'Sure thing.'

'Thanks.'

Fae slipped into some jeans and some sneakers, pulled a T-shirt over her head, and she and her bodyguard made their way to the hospital.

Fabrizzi lay much as he had lain all day. The American, a courteous young man, stayed outside the room whilst Fae drew up a chair and held Fabrizzi's hand and began to talk.

'You're my brother and I love you. And you have to wake up 'cause I'm in the shit and I hurt, and I need you. And if that's selfish it's too bad. Fabrizzi, listen to me.'

She leaned over him, she took his shoulders, she shook him. 'Listen to me. Can you hear me?' She was shouting, she knew she was shouting but she had to make him hear her.

He fidgeted, he moved. 'Fabrizzi, Fabrizzi,' she shouted again. Her eyes huge, her heart thumping – was she imagining it?

'Don't shout at me, Fae.' A voice, a little voice. Fabrizzi's voice. Eyes flickered, eyes opened.

'Nurse, get someone, my brother – he's awake,' she shouted.

'Where am I? What's happened to me? Fae, why am I in this place? I want Mama.'

Fae grabbed Fabrizzi and she cried.

'Don't Fae, don't! Where's Mama?' Fabrizzi asked again, holding on to his sister's hand.

Medical staff came from everywhere. The nice American immediately telephoned Innessa. She arrived with her parents, still in her nightgown, and thanked God for the miracle of her son.

'It's going to be all right now, Fae. It's a sign,' she told her.

'Now Sam will come home, you'll see. I truly believe it.'

Fae wanted to believe too, she really did.

At the police station, William Fairchild found himself face to face with Suleyman. The make-up was still smeared on the boy's face and it made him feel a bit sick. But his voice was quiet and almost kind: 'And now, Suleyman, you're going to tell me who you are, and what you have to do with Fae Whiteman, and who took her father.'

Suleyman shook his head.

'Oh yes you are, my friend.' Fairchild took off his coat. 'Because I'm a very angry man. You see, you frightened a young lady tonight and I don't like that.'

Fae got back to the hotel at around six o'clock in the morning. Her bodyguard took her into the lift. It went past her floor, someone else had obviously called it.

'Shit,' the bodyguard said and hit the emergency button. The lift shuddered to a halt, just one floor above. The guard pressed the appropriate button and the lift descended, taking them to Fae's floor.

'Thanks,' Fae said. 'I wouldn't have done that and then I'd have had to look at some all-night partier and it would have been very embarrassing.'

The all-night partier was just two floors above. Nick Newman, in his trousers and his shirt, and carrying his shoes, waited for the lift, watched the comings and goings on the little green floor indicator and wondered who was playing around with the buttons. He just wanted to get into it, and go to his floor, to his room, and to bed. In a few hours he would have to face what he'd just done.

At that very moment an extremely cross British journalist was checking into the hotel. A journey to Oklahoma had been a pointless exercise, for after allowing himself a rather pleasant night with some good Oklahoman folk he'd met in a bar, Simon Palling had emerged from his bed to discover that Fae had flown back to Italy. Then he'd found out in someone's else's paper that the boy, Fabrizzi, had been run over. His news editor was breathing blood. Palling himself made another call, to another place of employment, and screamed his own fury down the phone to a hapless clerk whose boss was away for a few days.

By the time he'd gone by New York to Rome, he'd lost a whole day, and he was very fed up.

'Mr Palling, will you be joining Mrs Palling?'

'My wife?'

'Mrs Katie Palling.'

'Good God. I'd no idea she was here. She didn't tell me. Look, just let me have her address, here's mine, just in case it's not her.'

Once his wife's presence in the hotel was confirmed, a delighted Simon Palling waited for the same lift that Nick Newman had just taken.

CHAPTER NINE

William Fairchild considered himself a typical American, a man with the right values who would, if it were required, kill to protect his own. A Company man since his army days, he had a wife and two children – his son was at West Point and his daughter was at medical school. He had long ago established respect for his fellow spies, men and women who did an honest job for their country, using whatever methods were necessary – but creatures like Suleyman Gamel were a different matter. The little Turk sat hunched over, the make-up smeared to a dirty streak. The thought of that dirty little man feeling his way through Fae Whiteman's clothes brought about such a revulsion within William Fairchild that he had physically to grip the table or else he would have lost his balance and quite possibly might have killed him.

Fairchild leant back in his chair, took in a breath, filled his square cheeks, his stocky chest, and blew out softly, feeling the whistle of air between his teeth. He glanced at his watch. The Italian Inspector had given him an hour. He needed longer than that, or did he? He glanced at the notes the police had shown him. Gamel claimed he was a student. He'd come to Italy on holiday. He'd seen Fae Whiteman – she was beautiful and he'd followed her.

'Are you some kind of pervert, or something?' Fairchild said.

'Excuse me?' Suleyman said.

So the man spoke English.

'Pervert . . . you know the word. Someone who makes good things nasty.'

'I don't know what you're talking about.' The Turk had a light voice, almost girlish.

'Really? Why are you wearing Fae Whiteman's make-up? What were you doing lying on her bed, wrapped in her nightdress?'

'Who are you? Why are you here? You are an American policeman. I don't have to speak to you.'

Fairchild's eyes narrowed. Clever little bastard. He kept his voice even and merely said, 'Miss Whiteman's father is an American.'

'But she's English – she lives in London.'

'How do you know that, Mr Gamel?' Whip-like, the words were fast. Don't give him time to think. 'Come on now, give me an answer . . . how did you know that?'

'I . . . I, I saw her passport . . .'

'Her passport was with reception.'

'I saw it, I saw it, it was in the drawer.'

'I don't think so.'

'It was when I opened the drawer. It was there, I'm sure it was there.'

'OK, Gamel. You want the gloves off, we'll take them off. I'm an American policeman and I'm trying to find out who kidnapped Miss Whiteman's father, and I've a pretty good nose for the smell of you. You've got the rotten smell of a man who's implicated up to his dirty armpits.'

'I don't have to talk to you. I'm a Turkish policeman. I was trailing Miss Whiteman in the course of my duties. You may ring Kamel Batami. He will tell you.'

Fairchild did not look at Gamel again. He let himself out of the interrogation room and walked quickly down the corridor into the Inspector's office.

'A nasty piece of work,' the Inspector said quietly as Fairchild strode into his office. 'You saw that we found a knife.'

Fairchild nodded. He watched the Italian pour him a large brandy.

'He claims he works for the Turkish police, for Kamel Batami. Can I use your telephone?'

Fairchild had a short conversation with Batami.

Suleyman's status was confirmed, but the Turk was appalled and disgusted at the behaviour of his agent.

'Send him back to me, I'll deal with him,' Batami said.

'What's happening at your end, Batami? We want our man back.'

'So do we,' Batami snapped.

He put the phone down on Fairchild. He was a very angry man. Something had to be done to release Whiteman, and quickly. Hayri Gurbuz had to be found.

Thus as Fae Whiteman turned over in her bed in the Hôtel de la Ville and contemplated another day, the pressure on the men who were looking for her father was building. She knew none of that. Her mind whirled its own films like an old movie camera, showing her rapid quickfire pictures – even in black and white – Fabrizzi in his coma, Fabrizzi lying still and quiet and the obscene Turk lying on her bed, swathed in her clothes. Above them all superimposed on the screen of her mind was the face of Nick angled towards a different woman, listening to her intimacies. Fae turned over in her bed, shaking her head, trying to rid herself of the image, trying to think only of Fabrizzi's magnificent return to life, trying to banish Nick Newman from her thoughts. She knew she was gripped by a black nightmare of obsession. Her longing was like some dreadful poisoned tarantula whose little black furry legs brushed against her, caressed, and then gripped at her, turning her insides over to her twisted mind, ripping her open, leaving her raw, red and bleeding, spelling out the name of Nick. And there was nowhere to go with her pain. Obsession is a lonely, dreadful thing, unattractive to others, especially to the love object. But how to be rid of such a dreadful part of oneself? For obsession is indeed buried in the flesh and in the soul, a parasite licking and devouring at healthy flesh, turning it rotten and hungry, for it can never be satisfied.

She wanted her father, and she saw his face big – even huge, filling up the screen of her mind, but he was gone, taken from her, the fantasy of perfection taken from her too, leaving her only Sam Whiteman – a real man, who was no hero – perhaps a liar, even a cheat. Even so, she wanted him. That at least was a comfort.

The intrusive sound of the telephone stopped her picture show. Was she glad? She didn't know.

'Fae, it's Robert Brockwell – how are you?'

'Fabrizzi is better, a miracle really.'

'I'm so glad, I've been worried about you.' The voice was

warm, it was near, it was strong. 'How're you feeling?' The emphasis on the *you* was very nice.

'Not good.'

'Your visitor?'

'Yes.'

'Come back to me. Be here, at least I'll know you're safe.'

It took one second for Fae to make the decision, to run from hurt into the arms of an almighty power that was on her side.

She took a shower, relishing the feel of the water on her skin, lathering the soap to a rich creamy white foam, she washed her hair, cleaning herself diligently of the grime and hurt.

'Miss Whiteman, you in there? You all right?' Her little Marine, except he wasn't so little.

'I'm fine.'

'There's a Mr Newman here to see you.'

No, a voice said inside her head, I'm not fine, I don't know what to do. What shall I do?

'Fae, are you OK? What's happened?' Nick's voice.

'Shall I let him in, Miss Whiteman?'

'Yes, yes, thank you.'

Wait for the sound of the door to shut. Wait for the click. She heard it. She picked up a towel, tried to wrap herself in it . . . where was her dressing-gown?

Nick, Nick. The feel of his mouth, of his hands, of his lips, just where she loved to feel him, she reached up to him, arched her back, offering her breasts to him, her mouth open . . .

'Miss Whiteman, you in there? You all right?'

Eyes open, no one, no Nick, just an empty aching nothing. Oh God, where was he?

Nick Newman sat on the bed in his own room at the Hôtel de la Ville. He was angry with himself for his behaviour the previous night. He had had no intention of sleeping with Katie Palling. It had happened because Fae had behaved so stupidly – she could never hide her feelings, she would have compromised them both. But even as the thought played inside his head he knew it wasn't correct. He remembered when he was younger a friend had said, 'You're a charmer, Nick, but a terrible messer with women.'

He never meant to hurt anyone – he liked the flirtations, he always had, but that was when he was young, before he was married. Now he was past the lure of the soft look and the tantalizing fingers – or so he had thought, but his unhappiness had trapped him in the soft teeth of sexual release. In daylight those teeth snapped shut and ground the guilt into a vice that gripped his insides and played havoc with the required behaviour of his mind. He wanted Fae, he just wanted to hold her. He picked up the receiver. He dialled the number for the operator.

'Miss Whiteman, please,' he said when she answered.

'Just a moment, Mr Newman.'

Fae heard the telephone – she stood in her shower, she couldn't move. She heard her little Marine call out.

'Hey, Miss Whiteman, you want me to get that?'

'Yes, please.'

'Hello?'

When the flat nasal tones greeted Nick he put the receiver down, picked it up again and dialled reception.

'Yes, Mr Newman?'

'I'm checking out this morning. Get me on the first flight you can to London, please.' The recce was abandoned, he had to get back to London where he could rely on his good behaviour.

Fae packed her luggage, tried to pay her bill and discovered that the Americans had taken care of all those inconveniences.

A shiny black limousine was waiting to take her to the hospital to say her farewells to Innessa and Fabrizzi, and then on to the airport. She was back in the world of privilege and at that moment she was glad.

It was when she was sitting in the car that she saw Nick come out of the hotel. He was carrying his case and was alone. She leaned forward to ask the driver to stop to offer him a lift. But then she saw Katie Palling coming out after him. She turned her head – she didn't want to see any more.

'Nick, Nick, how are you today?'

'Oh, hello.'

He turned to face her, he saw her eyes sweep over him, take in his suitcase. He wasn't pleased to see her; he hated scenes.

'You didn't have to leave. You can imagine the shock I got when Simon walked into the bedroom. I'm sorry.'

'Simon?'

'Yes, my husband. I assumed you knew and that's why . . .'

'No,' he interrupted gently. 'That's not why I'm leaving. Although of course, it illustrates exactly why I must.' He touched her cheek, kindly. 'I'm not going to let that happen again. You're a nice lady, you know my wife. You've got a husband.'

'Yes, but we can help each other. That's what I told you, uncomplicated stuff.'

'It's never uncomplicated.' He turned on his heel and got into a waiting cab. 'Take care of yourself, Katie. Goodbye.'

Katie Palling watched Nick Newman's cab turn around on the widest part of the road, just above the Spanish Steps. Her mouth was set in a straight line. 'You may think you aren't going to see me again, my friend, but you are – you most certainly are.'

They told Suleyman Gamel that they were taking him to Turkey . . . he didn't care, he was glad. He saw that Fae Whiteman was at the airport checking in for the American flight as they marched him, handcuffed like a criminal, along the concourse – a man with a gun in front of him, a man with a gun behind him and two men either side of him.

Inside the mind of Suleyman Gamel the image of Fae Whiteman had risen up and become him. He wanted to be her . . . she was so beautiful. He would grow his hair, wear it long, like hers . . . then they would be twins. He had dark eyes like her, he would wear black trousers and a black T-shirt, just as she wore black trousers and a black T-shirt when he had first seen her in Turkey. What a pair they would be, walking together – arm in arm. People would stare at them, want to be with them, but they, the beautiful twins, would only want each other. Until at night, when Fae would be with her lover and Suleyman would sit quietly and watch them, taking Fae's pleasure as his own. He thought about that, about how he had seen her with the Englishman, Nick Newman . . . how much he had liked that. But those other women – the wife, and the short haired woman – he hated short hair on a woman – they were claiming Nick Newman. He would kill them, yes, that's what he would do, he would kill them both – for Fae; and she would be so grateful she would love him forever – her friend, her twin, her sister . . .

* * *

As soon as Fae checked in her baggage she was taken into a small but beautifully furnished blue and silver room with tasteful prints and low comfortable settees. There was a telephone at her disposal, a drinks trolley, excellent coffee and the most gorgeous bouquet of white lilies. A small card was attached to the cellophane. She smiled to herself, thinking that Robert Brockwell really was the most appreciative of men. The lilies weren't from Brockwell at all, however, they were from the airline company. She laughed. Then her mood changed. It was a sudden thing: the nasty edge of panic cracked through her, much like an electric shock. She sat down carefully, folded her hands in her lap, and tried to deal with the very real fear that seemed as much a part of her as arms and legs.

She picked up the telephone. Emily. She'd try Emily. She rang home but the answering machine was on, so she dialled the office. Emily wasn't in yet, did she want to leave a message? 'Yes, just say I've rung. Fabrizzi's OK. I'm going back to America, she knows the hotel. Tell her I'm all right.'

But she wasn't all right. Should she ring her mother? Would Barbara be able to help her?

'Darling,' the clear voice rang through the receiver. 'Innessa's father phoned. I'm so glad that Fabrizzi is recovering.'

'Yes.'

'You must be so relieved.'

'Yes.'

'And you, how are you?'

'I'm going back to America.'

'Why, darling? Come home, please.'

'I have to see Brockwell.'

'If you think it will help. Your film mogul rang. He was very nice.'

'Oh God, I've forgotten about work.'

'He said to tell you he's bought an option on the new Rushdie book, the one you wanted him to buy. And who do you think should write the screenplay?'

'I didn't want him to pick that up. It's unfilmable!'

'Well why don't you ring him and tell him?'

'No, not yet. When I can . . .'

'Fae, the sooner you get back to real life, the better.'

'But this *is* real life, Mum. Sam's been kidnapped. I can't change it, and make everything like it was before.'

'I know that, my darling girl. I know that.'

'I just wonder what he is doing right now.'

At that very moment Sam Whiteman was sitting in the shade of a giant tree, enjoying sweet tea and a particularly challenging game of chess with the nameless confidante who guarded him, cared for him and talked with him.

Life, for Sam, had assumed a pleasant regularity. There were no stresses any more. There were courtesy, good food, books for him to read and regular walks in the dry air.

He was unaware that he was being watched by two newcomers.

'He looks happy,' the girl said.

'Why shouldn't he be? He has a place to sleep, adequate food and good company,' her brother replied. 'But now it's time for Mr Whiteman to know that his son, the boy Fabrizzi, has been involved in a motor bike accident orchestrated by the CIA.'

'I'll tell him, Rashid,' Faroud said.

She adjusted the look in her eyes, assuming a quiet concern, smoothed her combat jacket, lifting the collar just slightly, she checked her belt, pulled a hat with a low brim on to her head and put on her dark glasses. Then she walked out of the little stone house down the grass towards Sam Whiteman.

As the American listened to the young Turkish woman, the dreadful make-up artist of time wielded her brush and old age claimed him.

'My son, my boy, is he . . .?' Sam Whiteman could not say the word.

'No, no. He's not dead, my friend. But the news is not good. According to the newspaper that I have here he is in a coma. I cut it out for you.'

A front page from the London *Times* was shown to Sam, the headline 'Hostage's son victim of Motor Bike Accident' was ringed in red . . . If Sam had been in a mind to notice such things he would have seen that the date of the newspaper had been clipped out, but he devoured what he could of the words in front of him, until the mist of horror obscured the rest of the facts.

He was helped back to his bed. They were kind to him.

'Let me go to him, please, please, just let me go to him.'

'I will ask them, I will try for you,' the Turkish girl said. He gripped her shoulder, not to hurt her, but to try to convey how important it was that he be with Fabrizzi. He was unaware that his bony fingers dug into her collar bone, he had no idea that he caused her pain – how could he? He was in too much agony himself. He turned on his side, away from the sound of voices.

He heard again the sound of Fabrizzi's screams.

'Don't hurt my Daddy, my Daddy, my Daddy,' mixed in with his own cries, 'My son, my son.'

Faroud strode out to Rashid as he sat waiting in the car. She rubbed her shoulder.

'The American really pinched me.'

'You just told him about his boy.'

'Yes, it worked well, I think. Tomorrow, we'll tell him that it was the CIA.'

Rashid stared at his sister: her eyes were calm, untroubled. She was changing out of her combat clothes into the uniform of the devout Moslem girl, the long black pleated skirt was pulled over her head before the baggy trousers were removed, the neat blouse was underneath the combat jacket. It was obvious that the man's grief had not touched her. Rashid was shocked. 'You're hard, Faroud,' he told his sister.

'I have no choice, brother. We are at war.'

On the plane back to Turkey, Suleyman thought about his situation. In his position a wise man might have pleaded for himself, but not the young Turk. His own arrogance gave him a certain blindness – he was the best undercover agent that Kamel Batami had, and Kamel Batami wanted to find Sam Whiteman. So did Suleyman, for then the wonderful Fae would know that he was the hero who had brought her father back to her. It could all work beautifully. He just had to convince Batami.

He was taken to see him as soon as the plane landed.

'Your behaviour has brought disgrace upon the Turkish nation, upon our service, yourself and upon your family,' Batami told him.

Suleyman did not reply. There was nothing to say – he knew that he would be berated by people who did not understand how he felt about his beloved. 'You will be held in custody, and tried under the criminal code.'

'You still don't know where Mr Whiteman is, do you?'

'No, we don't.'

'I can find out – I will find out for Miss Whiteman.'

'Are you trying to make a deal with me?'

'You are the one who needs the help.'

Batami leaned back in the chair and appraised the man who stood in front of him. He really was scum. He had a sudden urge to smash the smug, almost pretty, face . . . it shocked him, he was not a violent man. But even so he had no access to those who had taken Whiteman. It was extraordinary. He sighed, what had he got to lose if he let Suleyman into the hunt? His integrity? That had gone long ago when he had taken on his job.

'You are right, Gamel, I do need help. You have twenty-four hours to find me the men or women who have Sam Whiteman. If you don't deliver, I will find you, and I personally will deliver you to the Secret Police.'

Gamel smiled. He had no fears.

'Need a car,' he said, 'and money.'

He drove directly to the University. There was a basketball game in progress in the centre of the campus. The benches overlooking the Bosphorus were full of studying students. Some loitered, gossiping; others jogged. Batami went straight to the cafeteria. He bought himself a coke and stood around, much as Richard Marks had done. He found a girl, she was pretty, but nothing like his Fae.

'Who's taking Sam Whiteman's classes?' he asked her.

'At the moment, the Rector. But if you want to know more, ask Rashid Boaz. He's over there.' The girl pointed to the slim, handsome young man.

'Why would I want to talk to him?'

'He knows Sam Whiteman well. He looked after the daughter when they came back to Istanbul.'

Stiff sharp needles of jealousy . . . the man had been with his Fae.

Suleyman walked over to where Rashid stood surrounded by a group of enquiring students. He pushed his way through quite rudely. 'You know Sam Whiteman?'

There was a sharp flicker in the blue eyes, a momentary blink that someone less observant than Suleyman would have surely missed.

'Why do you want to know?' Rashid asked.

'I'm a journalist,' Suleyman replied. 'I'm looking for a story.'

'I'm afraid there is nothing I can tell you. We just want Professor Whiteman to come back to us. Now, if you'll excuse me.' Rashid slid his way past Suleyman. Too quickly, yes, too quickly. Suleyman smelt the edge of tension; like an animal searching for its food he sniffed the air. He had found his quarry, he was sure of it. And so he began to track Rashid. He watched him at the University, dazzling his fellow students with graceful smiles and kind manners. He took lunch at a small café, some chicken and some fried potatoes. He was with two men and two girls. After about half an hour, Suleyman saw him excuse himself. He went to the Rector's office, he didn't stay long, just a few moments, but when he emerged the Rector was with him. It seemed to Suleyman that the two men knew each other very well. Rashid drove the Rector to his house. He did not go in, he merely helped Ichmet Golabi out of his car and helped him to his gate and then he drove off again. Suleyman was behind him. He drove west on the sea road past the Dolmabahçe Palace, over the Galata Bridge, into Kennedy Caddesi and past the Topkapi Palace. On one side of him the sea, on the other the squalid leather factories with their cracked panes of glass and smoking chimneys. He stopped his car just behind another car. The occupant of the first vehicle got out and went to sit with Rashid. Rashid handed him an envelope. The newcomer took it, they talked a while and Suleyman took photographs. When they had finished their conversation they separated and drove off in opposite directions.

Suleyman went straight to Batami. He waited in his office whilst the photographs were developed. The second man was easily identified – he was Hayri Gurbuz. He had ignored Ichmet's instruction that he stay under cover when Rashid told him that he had a letter for him, from his brother . . .

A watch was immediately put on Rashid Boaz and William Fairchild flew back to Turkey.

All of this was relayed to Fae by Robert Brockwell himself as he lay in bed with her, as he coaxed pleasure from her.

'The bastard, he knew . . . all the time he was seeing me, he knew where my father was.'

'So it would appear. But save your temper, Fae, until we're sure.'

'I feel sick, Robert. I've been used by everyone.'

'Not by me.'

'No?'

The lips stopped their game-playing. 'Fae, listen to me. I care about you, I care too much. But I'm a married man and I'm an ambitious man. The combination stinks. It means I'll dabble in other waters but I'll never let those waters sink me. Do you understand?'

'Yes, I understand.' At least this time there was no false hope, no false dreams, for that is the stuff that turns happiness into nightmares. But what was there?

Fae Whiteman sat up in the huge bed of the Jefferson Hotel in Washington and made herself realize that she was in bed with a man she didn't love, who was married to someone else, whilst the man she wanted was sleeping with two other women, one of whom was his wife.

What the hell was she doing? Pretty power was not pretty when it was naked.

She got out of bed and went and sat in a small chair by the window. She looked across at the smooth faced man who but a moment before had lain with her, skin to skin. She shivered.

'Why are you doing this with me?'

'Because we both want to.'

'Do we?'

'Yes.'

'You may, I don't. Get out of here.'

'Fae!'

'No, go. I don't want you. I don't. I'm sorry. You are married. Please, respect my wishes. And no hard feelings, OK?'

Brockwell nodded. He slipped out of the bed and began to get back into his clothes.

'At least will you pour me some coffee?' he said.

'Yes, yes, of course.'

Fae put on a dressing-gown, belted it tightly, and walked into the sitting-room – an anonymous pink and cream room dominated by a huge mirror – poured black coffee into a white china cup and set it on the low coffee table.

Brockwell came into the room behind her. 'Thank you,' the American said.

'I . . .' He sat down, Fae was surprised to see that he was not comfortable. 'I only said all that to you because for the first time in a very long time I could care too much. And I don't want to hurt you. A long time ago I had to make choices. I met someone . . . an actress.' Brockwell swallowed, Fae could see it was difficult for him to talk. She didn't stop him. 'It started out as an affair, but then . . .' – he half smiled, twirled his coffee spoon over the brown crystals of sugar – 'like all good love stories we fell in love. She believed we would live happily ever after. So did I, for a while. But then I realized I'd lose my kids, and my best friend – my wife.' He smiled apologetically. 'Madeleine took it very badly. I changed my number. I didn't call her. Right was on my side, I was the married guy! She had to cope . . . but she didn't cope. She killed herself.'

'Oh, my God.'

'I can give you all the platitudes – you know the lines, she was unstable, she had no right to do what she did. But she was beautiful, fresh . . .'

'Did you love her?'

'Yes.'

'You mustn't blame yourself.'

'You don't mean that.' Brockwell's voice was kind.

'I wish I did.'

For a moment neither of them spoke, each locked into their own thoughts. Fae was thinking about Madeleine, the young woman who had loved a married man, thinking about herself loving Nick. Robert was remembering, he didn't like that, he was a man who preferred partying. He broke the silence. 'So you see . . . I can't love again. Not anybody.'

'I'm sorry for you,' Fae said quietly. She got up from her chair and went over to him, she put her hands on his arms and gently kissed his cheek.

'Will you go home now?' he asked her.

'I don't know,' she said. And she didn't. She had no idea. At twenty-eight years of age she had no place to go.

But then Fae received a telephone call from Emily, from home, from what was real.

'Oh darling, I'm getting married and I want you with me. I want you to be my chief bridesmaid. You owe me that.'

And so Fae left the world of make-believe power, and the world of horror and loneliness and she went to an English country wedding in a stone church where men and women had worshipped for centuries. Wild flowers grew in the graveyard, and roses curled around the arched wicket gate that led into the place of worship.

Dressed in peach, Fae shed a tear and wished Emily so much happiness, trying not to mind that such an ending could not be hers and Nick's. Two men in dark glasses carrying walkie-talkies eyed the gathered friends and watched Fae. She minded their presence but Brockwell had insisted.

It was late September and the sun shone, but the air was tinged with the scent of the coming autumn. Sam had been gone for four months, how much longer would he spend away from them?

'So you're Emily's friend. How dreadful for you, all that awful suffering, my dear.' A nameless woman pressed a glass of champagne in her hand. 'Drink up, it'll help,' she said, her neat blonde hair hidden under a huge blue hat that topped a blue dress and blue shoes and a blue bag.

Emily, lovely Emily, her friend, gone to a new life, whilst she was left without the old one.

But even so she was glad to be home. England was home. The heat of Turkey, the exotic glorious life it offered, the sensuous passions, they were right for Sam, but not for her. And America with its honesty and its kindness was a welcoming place, but home was home, and the polite structure of a good-mannered society was finally Fae's natural habitat.

The swirling chiffons and the patterned suits and the morning coats and top hats were all so comfortable. The pale pink of the late salmon, its creamy mayonnaise, the waxy potatoes, the green peas, frozen, were a joyful feast. And when the time came for the speeches, Fae settled back for the rituals.

It was Jeremy who talked about her.

'And to our beautiful bridesmaid, to Fae: you're home now, and we're going to take care of you, all of us.'

Oh England, this England, this safe haven from the mad of

this world who think that God is on their side when they offend man.

Whilst Fae Whiteman participated in the marriage of her friend, William Fairchild paid another visit to Ichmet Golabi. His visit was briefer than usual.

'Rashid Boaz is in this up to his neck. We know all about him, Ichmet. It's only a matter of time before we get him, my friend.'

After William Fairchild left, Golabi mused on this unpleasant information and then sent a message to Rashid summoning him to a meeting.

None of that was of any concern to Sally Newman, who welcomed her husband back from Italy and then discovered that he had slept with her friend Katie Palling and that he was going to leave her.

'And the children?'

'I'm not leaving the children.'

'You are, you bastard.'

'No, I'm leaving you.'

'Well, was it good? How did it compare to your whore?'

Nick refused to answer. He packed his cases and kissed his children and tried to ignore the crying and the pain.

'Why? . . . Why?'

'I slept with her because I missed Fae,' he told his screaming wife.

'Daddy, don't go.' Little fingers held on to his legs, little knives of steel that dug into him and left marks that would never go away.

'I love you,' he told his babies, for they were his babies and he took their fingers off his legs and told them he would ring them that evening.

He put his cases in his Porsche and drove his car out of his drive and on to the road. When he was out of sight of his house he stopped the car and put his head in his hands and he cried.

On another empty road to London Fae Whiteman kept her foot on her accelerator, listened to her music, and dreaded the lonely night.

CHAPTER TEN

Fae Whiteman's own well of loneliness was sucking her down into darkness, robbing her of the will even to claw at the sides and look for a handhold to help her clamber out of the slime of despair. She just lay on her couch and drowned.

She didn't want to see the Americans, she wanted Nick. Was she ever going to rid herself of the longing? It burnt into her, playing the cruel game of memory and tantalizing her with the soft touch of past happiness. Was it worse because Sam was not there to cool the pains? The father who, it always seemed, had protected her from hurt. But it wasn't like that, none of it. Sam was no hero, no big man . . . she realized with a shock that he was just five foot eight, a little man, but he was her father, and he did love her. Even so it was not enough to enable her to reach the handhold and get off her couch.

In the small house in the Northern part of Turkey, an old man sat and blinked in the unnatural glare of a television light and a video camera.

'I've just been informed of the terrible accident that has overtaken my son, Fabrizzi. I have examined the options presented to me . . . and reluctantly I have to agree with my Turkish friends that the action against my son was carried out by the CIA to warn me against revealing the extent of their activities in Turkey. It has served no purpose. I now see that the CIA is an evil organization that must be revealed to public scrutiny.'

He cleared his throat, looked down at some papers, like a newscaster scanning a script.

'The activities in Turkey were controlled by Richard Marks,

who was recently killed in an incident at the Blue Mosque. The senior covert agent is Maise Montgomery.' He droned on about CIA assets in Turkey, implying that they were senior military personnel, government ministers, industrialists, journalists. He talked of the companies that were run by American agents, but he gave no names. On and on went the information, reams of non-essential material . . . because that's all Sam Whiteman knew.

The broadcast still created its ripples.

For one thing, Maise Montgomery had to bid farewell to her posting and prepare to go back to the routine of Langley. Maise was particularly annoyed, she liked her life.

Brockwell himself was sympathetic.

'It's the "Stockholm Syndrome" . . . he's dependent on his captors, and has grown to like them and to mistrust us. So when they plant ideas, he grabs them . . . they make sense to him.'

Fae worried about her father. She no longer cared whether he appeared to be a hero or not, it was obvious that he believed that Fabrizzi was near to death. Her own unhappiness was despatched back into the pending file and she was able to reach up out of her well of despair.

She took a shower, tidied her flat and pondered carefully about who she should contact – the Americans, the Turks, the British . . . She rejected all of them and turned to the media.

Simon Palling was sitting at his desk when the call came through from Fae Whiteman.

'Simon, have you seen my father's interview?'

'Yes, I have, Fae.'

'He looks terrible, he obviously believes that Fabrizzi is in a bad way. What can I do?'

'Very little, they obviously control what he reads, but I'll do some thinking and see what I can come up with. Let's meet for a drink – later today . . . around six o'clock?'

'Great . . . where?'

'There's a pub opposite the Old Bailey – it's called the . . . Bunch of Grapes. You can't miss it – it's a black building with gold lettering.'

Simon replaced the receiver, dialled a number himself and was connected to the Whitehall mandarin, Martin Godfrey.

'Our friend Fae's telephoned. Worried about her father.'

'I don't think there's too much cause for concern now. I would imagine they will let him go, don't you? They must realize that actually he doesn't know very much. Presumably they don't know the cousins are on to them . . . they think they'll get the money. All of this should suit them very well.'

'As long as they don't shoot him.'

'They have nothing to gain by his death – a pointless exercise in all, I would have thought, as they have no doubt discovered.'

In Turkey, a furious Rashid – unaware that all his movements, if not his words, were now being monitored by Kamel Batami's men – paced the floor and fumed over his miscalculations.

'I thought if we could not get the two boys out of prison, he would at least have information we could highlight to get at the government, and the Americans. Instead he talks of things you can read in spy books. Let's kill him now . . . he's no use to us alive.'

Meanwhile, Suleyman Gamel went to the Turkish Airlines office in Taksim and booked himself on the first available flight to London.

The agent that Batami had instructed to watch Gamel reported the booking to his superior, who reported it to Batami.

'Stop him,' came the order. But the order came too late. Suleyman was already on the way to London.

'Damn,' Batami shouted. Reluctantly he telephoned Brockwell's office and relayed the information that Gamel had departed for London. He told Brockwell's incredulous aide, 'He is obviously after the Whiteman girl.'

But Suleyman was not 'after' Fae. His business lay with Nick Newman, for through him he would be able to find Katie Palling, and then he could kill her.

A friend of Nick's – a producer who had made the big jump over the water and was now making his first picture at Warners – had loaned him his house, a flat-fronted terraced house where rich carpets and delicate furniture soothed harried nerves but did nothing to encourage children to play.

'It's very nice, Daddy,' Elizabeth said when she came to stay. Sally had decided that James was too young, and Oliver ought to stay with his brother. Nick had been furious, but grateful all the same for Elizabeth's presence. Maybe if he could explain to his daughter, if she could understand, then it would make it easier with the boys.

He tried desperately to remember favourite foods, a trip to the supermarket on the King's Road meant cartloads full of flavoured yoghurts and chocolate fingers and Bounty's. Sally had a magic cupboard, crammed with goodies the children liked to eat. Nick wrestled with casserole dishes and put them away in other places, clearing a space for the bars of chocolate, and the crisps and oh, Jaffa cakes, she loved Jaffa cakes. Another quick run to the supermarket for the Jaffa cakes, and whilst he was there he grabbed two more bottles of Coke and a lot of lemonade. Thus laden he returned to the smart house whose cupboards, he felt, virtually shivered in disgust at the invasion.

'Come and see your room,' Nick said, holding his hand out to his daughter. Her long blonde hair gleamed in the muted light of the sitting-room. She was wearing a blue skirt, which was new, and a T-shirt. Some brightly coloured elastic bands adorned her wrist. He knew better than to make any comment. He picked up her case and together, holding hands, each as nervous as the other, they mounted the stairs to the bedroom he had chosen for her. By her bed he had put a single pink rose with a note.

She ignored the room, went straight to the flower, read the little card that said, 'Welcome, Elizabeth – I love you, Daddy.' She turned on her heel and ran into his arms.

'Oh Daddy, I love you too.' And then she sobbed so much he thought his heart would break, and all he could do was hold her very, very tight.

Later, over Jaffa cakes and lemonade, she talked.

'Mum is horrible, she shouts all the time. James misses you and Oliver is trying to be the man.'

'Elizabeth,' he tried to say, to justify, to do something.

'No, Daddy, don't say anything. There isn't anything you can say. I know you aren't happy with Mummy . . . I know it's not us. But it hurts, you see. Children want their parents to be together.'

'And parents want to be together, most of the time . . . it's just that Elizabeth – I really like your mother, I think she is a strong, good woman – but we just can't live together. She wants more of me than I can give. My work, it's very important.'

'More important than us?'

'No, but we are all made up of different things that make us into whole people. I love you, I love my work, I like Mummy, and everything fits into some sort of pattern of my needs. I suppose that makes me selfish, but people have to be selfish.'

'You're always telling us that we should share.'

'Yes, and so you should, and so should I. It's difficult, but in order to be able to share you have to be at peace inside yourself.'

'And you're not, Daddy.'

'No, no, I'm not. I miss you all so much I hurt.'

'Even Mummy.'

'Even Mummy.'

'But not Mummy enough to come home.'

'I suppose that's right.'

Elizabeth put her sixth Jaffa cake down on the plate. Sally would never have allowed such extravagances. The biscuit crumbs stuck to her mouth.

'Can you at least find a home that's better for us?'

Nick grabbed his daughter. He loved her so much he hurt. 'Oh darling, we'll go and find somewhere that's better for you all tomorrow.'

The weekend passed too quickly, in a whirl of home-cooked food and too many videos. There was no question of a solitary sleep in a prim white bed for a little girl who loved her Daddy. They curled up together in Nick's bed and talked long and late into the night. In the morning they had breakfast in bed, and went out to find a house. Elizabeth was quite the little madam striding around other people's homes. Amused, Nick realized that his little girl suddenly saw herself as the woman in his life. He would have to deal with that, but not yet . . . it was all too raw. He was missing the boys, the next weekend he wanted them too.

He informed Sally when he returned Elizabeth.

'I'm not sure they want to come,' his unhappy wife told him.

'They will, Mummy, it's important for us to see Daddy. I know it isn't nice for you, and I'm sorry because I love you so much, I love you both.'

Tears pricked Nick's throat, he touched Sally's arm, but quickly, before she could respond, he spun on his heel – just like a ballet dancer. He started down the garden towards his car, twisting his head so he could wave goodbye. He saw his wife and his daughter standing together, their arms around each other in the doorway of his house – he wanted to turn around and run back through the door, to go to them, but he knew that he couldn't. He wasn't part of their lives any more. He drove away, trying to deal with himself.

When he got back into the house he ran himself a bath, poured himself a glass of milk and set about tidying the house so the lady who came in to clean the following morning would have nothing to hinder her activities.

He had just relaxed into a tub full of green bubbles when the telephone rang. Irritated, he pulled himself out of the water and, without a towel, slip-slopped over a white carpeted floor to the master bedroom. He picked up the receiver.

'Yes?'

'Nick, it's Katie.'

'Katie?'

'Yes, Katie, nice surprise?'

'It's certainly a surprise. How did you get this number?'

'Ways and means, my dear.' She didn't say that Sally had rung her, and hurled her hurts down the phone.

Nick cleared his throat. He wasn't worried about this lady, she was tough enough to take care of herself, and as for the consequences, he no longer cared. The only thing that interested him apart from his children was the quality of his work and, after a soak in his bath, he was going to turn his mind to that. There was no room, let alone any inclination, for Katie Palling.

'I'm sorry, Katie, but I don't want you to call me. I meant what I said in Rome. It was nice for the night, but that was all.'

Nick was unaware that Katie Palling was phoning from her sports car just at the top of his road, attired for the night of love that she was sure was going to be her just reward. She put the phone down, buried her head in her hands, trying to still the burning shame. She had never been rejected before. She didn't like it. So stunned was she that she didn't notice a dark figure creep silently to her car, she didn't see the man raise his arm and thump something hard and sharp against the side of the window, but as the glass shattered, she turned. Shocked and frightened, she saw a man reach into the car, his face white. His skin seemed to have lifted away from his bones giving him a mask-like appearance, and thick globules of sweat glistened on his cheeks and his chin. Mesmerized, Katie sat there and watched his hands come into the car. She wanted to cry out, to do something, but it was as if she were completely immobilized. The hands were red, covered in blood – the glass had cut them.

'Come here, you bitch,' he said as he reached into the car. The voice wasn't rough, these were the obvious rich rounded tones of the British upper class.

'What the hell do you think you're doing?' another voice said and two more hands grabbed at her attacker.

'Come on, sir, nice and quiet like.' Katie saw it was the police, the flashing blue light from their car bounced off her overhead mirror.

The attacker twisted and turned, trying to get away, but the man held him firmly, he couldn't escape. He was wrestled away from her car. Someone held her driver's door open and helped Katie out. It was then that a fierce pain in her chest overtook her, and she lost rational perception.

'Come on, love, you're all right now. It's a dreadful experience, but give us a number and we'll call a friend to take you home, or else we'll take you ourselves. Get a nice cup of tea down you and a bit of good chat and you'll be right as rain.'

'But who would do that? Why?'

'That's what we'd like to know too, love,' one of the policemen said.

There was someone else who was equally curious about Katie Palling's attacker. Suleyman Gamel had watched the entire event from the corner of the road. He'd seen Katie Palling park her car, use her telephone, he'd seen the man watching her, and then he saw the man attack her. He wondered what Katie Palling had done to that man.

Unaware that she was attracting further interest, Katie walked around a bit, taking deep breaths, trying to pull herself together.

'Can we call someone for you, love?' one of the policemen asked.

'No, it's OK. My husband's on a story. I'll be all right.'

'We'll drive you home.'

'Absolutely not. I'm perfectly all right. Just give me a few minutes and then I'll be fine.'

The older policeman – a kindly man in his late forties – knew better.

'Listen, love, you've had a shock. We're going to run you home.'

'What about my car?'

'Well you can't drive it with all that broken glass anyway.'

'No, I suppose not,' Katie said, and suddenly to her horror she began to cry. 'You could try my husband, if you like. His name is Simon Palling, you can get him on 272-5012, it's a direct line.'

'Right, love, you stay right there.'

In the yap-yap of a crowded smoke-filled pub where the smell of alcohol-free beer vied with the scent of Caleche, Simon and Fae sat in a corner and discussed serious matters.

'I've called a contact of mine, he's pretty confident that your father will be released soon. That interview he gave on the CIA. It was so obvious, this man said, that your Dad was not involved in anything important there is no point in them keeping him.'

Fae cleared her throat. She was wearing a coral-coloured dress in a clinging jersey material cut on the hip, swirling into a full skirt, not her usual style at all, but nevertheless quite lovely. 'Would they kill him?'

'No, they won't.'

'Aren't you being kind?'

'I'm not a kind man, Fae. Oh, easy on the charm, but that's not hard.'

Fae laughed, she suddenly realized that she did like Simon Palling.

'Another?' he said, pointing to a glass of red wine.

'Why not?' Fae said.

She watched Palling ease his way out of the table and go over to the bar. He was a stocky man, almost square shaped, nice hair that curled into his collar. He was wearing a pink check shirt and grey cords. A grey tweed sports jacket lay crumpled on the bench beside him. She relaxed, realizing how nice it was to be with a man who was a friend, there was no anxiety of longing to cloud their talk.

* * *

'I'm sorry, Mrs Palling, but your husband isn't there. Apparently he's on a story, with a Miss Whiteman.'

Katie threw back her head and laughed and laughed. The sound was not pretty. There was no tinkling of bells: it was a harsh, difficult sound. The policeman noticed.

'How about calling someone else?'

'Yes, how about that?' Katie said, and strode off down the neat little street where the residents parked their cars in residential parking bays, and went away for the weekends.

She rang Nick's doorbell.

The plop-plop sound of effervescent headache pills in a glass, white bubbles snapping open and shut in the water, until there was just a fizzy drink that Katie drank carefully, screwing up her nose and her eyes against the taste. A cup of tea brewed in a pot, milk poured into a cup followed by the rich brown liquid, and then two spoonfuls of sugar.

'Here, drink this,' Nick said.

'Thank you,' said Katie.

'Now relax here for a moment. I'll get dressed, and then I can run you home.'

He'd opened the door in his bathrobe, his feet were wet. She wanted to touch him, to run her fingers over his skin, to open his bathrobe, to sink down, lips on lips . . .

Instead, there was surprise and a degree of cold formality. She told him what had happened, he saw the blood on her collar, the madman had got that close. He was immediately concerned and she was glad. Would he hold her? But no, he simply guided her to a chair, ministered to her in a kindly manner and now he'd left her to get dressed. She started to cry again. Was it shock, or was it because he didn't want her? She knew that now. She pulled herself together, drank her tea, tried to fix her make-up.

Nick arranged for the police to take care of her car. He would drive her home. It wasn't far, just to Islington.

Suleyman Gamel watched carefully as Nick Newman ushered Katie Palling into his car. He must not lose them, he had to follow them. A taxi was passing – its yellow 'FOR HIRE' sign gleamed brightly against the London night.

'Follow the car there, please.'

'The Porsche?'

'Yes.'

London by night can be beautiful, but the travellers noticed neither the stately grandeur of the sculptured squares nor even the fairy lights of Harrods – the gold-plated department store – nor the sweep of Hyde Park under the watchful eye of Boudicca on her chariot. Shaftesbury Avenue and the hard throb of its theatres and clubs were not even registered, the car and the taxi sped on. None of the occupants spoke: the driver of the cab did his job, Suleyman kept watch, Nick Newman drove and Katie Palling tried not to want the man sitting next to her.

The Porsche turned north up Tottenham Court Road; the cab turned north. Chic London, fun London, dirty London slid by and, to the left of King's Cross, the London of the Londoners took over. Nick drove down Liverpool Road, turned left into Barnsbury Street.

'Eighty-one, please,' Katie said.

Suleyman paid off the cab at the end of the road. He ran silently down on the other side to Nick Newman's car.

Nick helped Katie out of the car, he stood by her as she opened the door.

She turned the inside light on.

'I don't suppose you'll come in?'

'No, but I'll wait till the door is safely shut.' He bent down and offered a kind kiss on too eager lips, and then Suleyman jumped, his precious knife in his hand. He caught Nick's hand and pushed him out of the way, sending him sprawling on to the ground. He grabbed Katie by the throat, his knife silver bright in the lamplight. Nick was up off the floor, on his back, throwing him to one side, kneeing him in the groin, hitting him, smashing his head against the grey granite pavement.

'Don't, Mr Newman,' Suleyman screamed. 'I can't hurt you, for Fae, I can't hurt you. You belong to Fae.'

Fae, Fae . . . the words splintered Nick's rage. He held Suleyman on the ground, his fist over his face, ready to grind it in if necessary. Katie was screaming, she couldn't stop. It was at that moment that Simon Palling arrived home.

The police took Suleyman Gamel away. Simon Palling, before examining the mess in his own life, made a telephone call to Martin Godfrey and advised him of the intervention of one Suleyman Gamel into his own domestic affairs.

'I think he's the nutter who's fixated on Fae Whiteman. It may be interesting for you to have a go at him,' he told his boss.

'Thanks, Simon.'

Martin Godfrey left his nice plump wife and drove his own car to his office in Whitehall. He collected a buff-coloured file and then went down to the entrance, where another car was waiting. A police officer greeted him.

'Gamel is being held at Hackney. All the arrangements have been made to give you a little privacy.'

'I'm most grateful.'

On Godfrey's arrival he was conducted to an interview room. The Turk sat in a straight-backed chair, surly and unwilling to talk. A policewoman sat in the corner ready to take down any statement. The station's Inspector, CID, a rough man, had his jacket off, he'd settled down for a long night. He was not pleased when the urbane and unsmiling Martin Godfrey kicked him off the job . . .

'I don't have to speak to you,' Gamel said.

Godfrey ignored him, and instead he addressed the British policeman: 'I won't be long, Inspector, just need to know a few things.' He smiled at the policewoman and she left the room.

Godfrey grabbed Suleyman's hair – he dragged his head so far down by the force of the pull that the Turk was bent back double over the chair.

Suleyman was terrified, he recognized Godfrey's cruelty, and he knew there were no sensual pleasures to be obtained here, just pain.

The Turk blabbed, the Turk sobbed, he spoke of his love for Fae Whiteman, of Katie Palling's affair with the man Fae loved . . .

A tawdry story, and one that did not interest Martin Godfrey one little bit. There were no coups to be scored here. He let the Turk's hair go and meticulously rubbed his hand on the wall. He could smell the hair grease – it really was most unpleasant. He banged on the door to let the Inspector in – and the policewoman.

'And now Mr Gamel, you're going to tell my friends exactly what you told me and then I'm sure they are going to put you in prison for quite a long time. You can't go around trying to kill people. We don't like it, we don't like it at all.'

'My country, my country won't like it.'

'I don't think they will.'

'They will take me home.'

'I doubt it. You're a common criminal, Mr Gamel.'

Martin Godfrey swept out of the police station and into his car. His driver turned the car around and drove south, back to his plump wife. On the way, Godfrey telephoned Robert Brockwell.

'Any news?' he asked.

'None, but we imagine he'll be let out, or killed, very soon.'

'We caught your Turk trying to kill one of our brighter women journalists – appears she was having an affair with Fae Whiteman's married boyfriend, and he thought the boyfriend should stay with Fae.'

Robert Brockwell replaced the receiver. His wife was waiting for him, they were going to one of Washington's tennis parties. This one was being given by the Danish chargé d'affaires, a handsome man who was quite a catch with the ladies. Brockwell didn't want to go, suddenly the social dalliances of Washington bored him. Fae, pretty Fae, how was she?

His wife shouted up the stairs, her voice crisp and clear: 'Robert, come on! We'll be late. And I've scheduled you to play with the First Lady.' He never failed to be dazzled by her resourcefulness. He picked up his tennis racket, and glanced at himself in the mirror. He knew he was a handsome man, he spoke well, he had a lot to offer. He wanted high office, and by God he was going to get it. He'd paid the price in personal happiness. Still he wanted to see Fae, he wanted to see her very much.

Simon Palling sat in his lemon kitchen, which he had designed himself, and contemplated his wife's infidelity. What a ridiculous word, so full of pomposity and propriety! What would Katie do, if he acquired another passion? He smiled to himself, he knew exactly what would happen. She would kill him. Her passions were very simple. What was hers was hers. And him, what did he feel? A more placid person, he knew he loved his wife, very deeply. They'd met when they were both just twenty-one, cub reporters for a news agency in Fleet Street. Katie had been in love with an older journalist, a sports columnist on the *Daily*

Record. Simon had bided his time, courting her, but not too much, until, jilted by the sports writer, she had turned to him.

She never knew about the private side of his life, his relationship with the mandarins of Whitehall who used his cover as a journalist and sent him into sensitive areas to keep a watch for them, and sometimes to be more active. He certainly didn't do it for the money, nor indeed for patriotism, although he loved his country. He did all that for the thrill, the edge, for knowing you were there, and mostly for knowing the truth. But all that truth wasn't much good now. He had to contemplate the wreck of his marriage and refloat it and put it back to sea. Because that's what he wanted. He wouldn't contemplate a life without Katie.

He heard her coming down the stairs. She'd had a bath. Wrapped in a housecoat she lost her burnished brightness, and her hardness. He got up, made her a pot of tea, lit her a cigarette. She took both from him, and said, 'Sorry, Simon. It was a bit of madness, I'll get over it.'

He nodded.

'Want to eat something?' he asked. 'How about some fish and chips? I'll nip down the road to Bell's.'

'Will they still be open?'

'If not I'll ring on the doorbell,' he said, and he was gone.

Katie sat on one of the pine kitchen chairs. That was Simon. He could always produce the goods from somewhere. People liked him. She liked him. She wished she loved him, but like was better than nothing, and Katie couldn't face nothing. She needed Simon, she knew that. She really cared about him. Her mother always told her, her only child, that a good man is better than all that passion, and she should know – she married her best friend. At that moment, Katie tried to agree with her.

Nick Newman began to drive back to the King's Road. The whole Katie Palling incident left him with a feeling of distaste. He regretted having slept with her, he wanted Fae. Suddenly he turned his car towards the Barbican. He had to see her. It was stupid, staying away from the woman he loved. He drove fast, even jumped some lights. He parked his car in the place where he always used to park his car. He saw Fae coming down the street, she was carrying two white plastic carrier bags full of food, she'd been shopping at the all-night delicatessen. He was really very nervous.

Fae knew he was there even before she saw him. It was the burn in her heart, the blood that stung her veins, the sudden inexpressible joy that warmed her skin and brought back happiness.

There was no need for talk, it was simply a homecoming. The loving was glorious, the fitting together of a man and woman who wanted to pleasure each other, who knew each other, who understood each other. Mouth to mouth, lips to lips, hands that moved like blind people's, remembering, rediscovering.

Fae lay in Nick's arms and wondered at the miracle – Nick was back, and Nick would stay. She knew that, she sensed it. She looked at him, his head against her breast, his mouth playing wondrous games. She loved him.

The words came later, the sorry's, the forgivenesses, the forever and forevers.

'Fae, listen.' His hand was tracing marvellous patterns on her skin. 'When you accused me of sleeping with Katie Palling . . .'

'You didn't, I know,' she whispered, her head bent, her mouth on his leg. She loved to kiss him in surprising places.

'I did.'

'What?' She stopped what she was doing. Cold air hit her face.

'That night . . . I did.'

'I see.'

'It doesn't matter to us . . . It's nothing to do with us.'

Fae sat up. Before, she would have said, 'No, no, of course it doesn't matter', glad to agree with him, glad just to be with him. But now she said, 'It does matter . . . I needed you then, and you weren't there for me. But still . . . I slept with Robert Brockwell.'

There was a slight shift in the bed. 'Did you?'

'You said it doesn't matter.'

'Of course it doesn't. We were estranged then.'

'We weren't estranged, as you call it. You had stopped seeing me!'

Nick tried to laugh 'That's estranged,' he said, moving over to touch her – covering her breasts with his hands, moving his fingers over her nipples, teasing them into life. He felt her soften, twisting into him. He bent his mouth to her, wanting to bite her, to mark her as his . . .

The next day, Fae received a telephone call. It was William Fairchild. 'There is news of your father. You have to come back to Turkey.'

CHAPTER ELEVEN

Since he had been told of Fabrizzi's accident, Sam had been unable to function in the same manner as before. He no longer played chess, he didn't walk over the dry grass. He asked, every day, for news, and he was told, every day, that there was none. He stayed in his little room – and he read his Bible. He no longer entered into conversation, nor did he prolong any dialogue addressed to him. He was polite, but he had nothing to say to anyone. He was locked in his own inner world where he talked with Fabrizzi as if he were sitting by his bed instead of so many thousands of miles away from him. He told him how he loved him, of his hopes for him, of his own childhood. He concentrated on the image of his son and sent his thoughts to him.

In Italy Fabrizzi thought about his father. By now he'd left the hospital and spent his days being spoilt and indulged in his grandfather's villa.

'Papa is on my mind,' he would tell anyone who would listen. Innessa understood and they spent many hours talking about Sam. The mother and son had become very close to each other. His grandmother would try to distract him. 'God knows what has happened to Sam. It's better that Fabrizzi does not think about him,' she told her husband. She could not say that to Innessa, her daughter wouldn't listen to such talk. Even her husband reacted differently. He encouraged Fabrizzi to articulate his feelings.

'He's thinking about me,' the boy told his grandfather. They were walking together on the beach near the family villa. Fabrizzi, his leg still bandaged from the accident, wore a navy striped T-shirt over a swimming costume, and a navy baseball hat, back to front, on his head.

'I'm sure he thinks of you all the time.'

'No, it's more, it's like he's telling me to get better.'

'He knows you are unwell, the kidnappers told him.'

'How do you know?'

'They released a video of him. They told him the Americans were responsible.'

'But they weren't.'

'Exactly.'

'Poor Papa . . . I hope he knows I'm better now.' Fabrizzi was kicking sand with his feet, it was obvious that the boy was experiencing a reaction to the positive proof that his father was alive, that his father was communicating with him. He looked up at his grandfather, his eyes challenging. 'Have you seen the video?'

His grandfather looked back at him. 'I have.'

'Why haven't I? He's my father. I have to see it now.'

'I have to be honest with you, Fabrizzi: it may make you sad.'

'Is he hurt?'

'No, but he looks very unhappy.'

'That doesn't matter. I have to see it.'

'I don't know how your mother will feel.'

'How would you feel, Grandpapa, if it were your father?'

'I would react the same way as you.'

'Well, then . . .'

'But sometimes it is better for children to be protected from things that are painful.'

'I know you're trying to protect me, but I'm going to Mama now to discuss it with her.'

Fabrizzi turned and walked away from his grandfather, his little body striding determinedly across the sand.

He found his mother sunbathing in her favourite chair.

'There's a video of Papa. I want to see it.'

'Your grandfather told you,' she said carefully.

'Yes, and I'm very angry that you did not show it to me.'

'Fabrizzi, come here.' Innessa held out her arms but her son sat perched on the side of her chair in a determined stance. He was not going to let go of his anger, even for her. 'It was a difficult decision. Your father looks very ill in the video . . . he has obviously been told of your accident, but not that you're better.'

'I know, grandfather told me.'

'Can you be strong?'

'Yes, I can.' Her son's eyes, a perfect match for her own, stared into her.

Innessa, always a graceful woman, rose from her chair and took Fabrizzi's hand. Together they walked into the library, so called because it contained the bookshelves, and a desk. But it was really the room in which they watched television.

Innessa sat next to Fabrizzi as her son carefully watched the grainy flickering image of his father.

When the tape had finished the boy re-ran it, silently examining every nuance, every look, as if he were older than his years.

'How long have you had it?' he asked when he had finally finished.

'Just one day.'

'You should have told me,' he said again.

'Perhaps – but I thought it best that I protected you.'

'I don't need protection, I'm with you – it's Daddy who needs help.'

Innessa observed her son – his face was set, he gave her no access to his feelings, she had no way of knowing how he felt. For the first time since she had become a mother she understood that parenting did not give any automatic rights – even though he was only eight, she had to respect his privacy.

'I love you,' she said softly.

'And I love you,' he said, 'but what are we going to do about Daddy?'

'The terrible part of all this, my darling, is that there is nothing we can do.'

Fabrizzi cried then, and Innessa's heart burnt.

The telephone was ringing, but she took no notice of it. After a few moments, the butler answered it. She heard Barry's voice, and then the click-click of his polished shoes on the marble floor. He rapped hard on the door, an insistent knock.

'What is it?' she said.

'News, Mrs Whiteman – it's William Fairchild, he says it's urgent.'

Innessa shifted slightly on the sofa, reached behind her and picked up the receiver.

'Yes, Mr Fairchild?' Fabrizzi had climbed on to her lap.

'We've been alerted by the Turkish authorities that the kidnappers have announced that the decision on Sam's future will be made at four o'clock this afternoon, Turkish time. That's two o'clock your time.'

'What does that mean?' Fabrizzi stopped crying – he sensed that Innessa had tensed, like a piece of string suddenly jerked tight.

'If they're going to let him go – or if they're going to kill him.'

'I will come.'

'Why don't you wait – until we know what the situation is?'

'But when will you know?'

'As I said, they say they will let us know by four o'clock their time. I will call you the moment I have news.'

'Fae, Fae, she should be there. Fabrizzi and I will wait,' Innessa said and replaced the receiver. She was overcome with numb, cold fear – the kind that squeezes the gut. She glanced at her watch – 9.30. Four and a half hours to wait. What could she do till then, to fill the hours, to deal with the anguishing electric stress within her? She looked at Fabrizzi – his little face looked up at her – his eyes were full, and frightened.

She and Fabrizzi sat together, even holding hands, and yet they were separate in their needs. For Fabrizzi it was a simple thing.

'My Daddy could be coming home.'

Innessa had censored the content of the phone call – she merely told him that the kidnappers were deciding whether to let Sam go free. There was no mention of death in the script for Fabrizzi.

For her there were different problems . . . by nightfall she would know whether Sam would be alive or dead – whether she had a husband or not. Widowed, the very word conjured up a black veil over her mind. And yet life would offer Innessa terrifying choices, whether to be Mrs Sam Whiteman, or not to be Mrs Sam Whiteman. Should she stay Mrs Whiteman for a little longer, to help Sam through the trauma of his return, to cushion them all and perhaps, if she were honest, to find out what she wanted.

Since Richard's death she had lived in a sort of vacuum, not knowing her own needs. She functioned, she missed Sam . . . but she missed Richard too. At first the grief was too painful and there was guilt. He'd died trying to sort out the mess of Sam's kidnapping. His death wasn't just. He had so much to give. He loved her, and he knew that she had withdrawn from him. She couldn't have changed that, but she felt very, very sad. If Sam hadn't been kidnapped would she have married Richard? Innessa knew that plans are made, and then the gods laugh, for with one small click of their fingers the future tumbles down like a house of cards.

Innessa could feel the house closing in on her, as if the books were falling off their shelves, piling up around her, giving her no air. The walls seemed to move in on her like part of some horrific set that could be moved at will by an unheard puppet master who laughed at his own jokes and never shared with anyone.

'Let's get out of here – just for a few hours, darling,' Innessa said to Fabrizzi.

They took her car, a convertible, and they drove inland – feeling the wind on the backs of their necks, and the hot sun reaching into their shoulders, wrapping them both in shawls of heat. They played music on the cassette machine, alternating the tapes, Michael Jackson and Prince for Fabrizzi, the thumping passion of Bizet's *Carmen* for Innessa. It helped: the solitude of the road, the balm of music, the rush of air, all of it encased them in their own womb – secure, safe, away from those realities that must await their return.

The hours ticked on.

In Turkey, at four o'clock, Sam Whiteman was roused from his bed.

'Any news?' he asked. He always asked.

'None.'

'None you wish to give me.'

'None we can give you.'

He was led out into the harsh bright sunlight. A car stood with its door open. Men, masked in black, stood with guns. Was this the end, a final sinking into the oblivion of peace? He did not want that: his children, they needed him – both of them.

A blindfold was slipped over his eyes. He didn't care about that, as long as there was no death.

He was pushed, it seemed by a hundred hands. 'No-o-o!' he shouted, and stumbled. Life, yes, life – that was his right. He had to know about Fabrizzi.

He was being helped to his feet, pushed again, his head was being pushed down, he bent his knees.

'Get in,' someone told him.

Get in what?

He banged his knee against something sharp – the car, of course, it was the car.

He managed to manipulate himself into the appropriate place – a seat, soft, ah, good. His hands were tied, and his feet; his mouth was taped shut.

Oh God, no, not death!

Fae flew into Istanbul airport at exactly the same time as her father was being blindfolded. Her heart was constrained, as if an elastic band had been snapped around it, making the business of breathing difficult.

William Fairchild was waiting for her. They travelled from the airport together. It was a difficult journey. The rush hour had already started. The Embassy limousine moved slowly, bumper to bumper in what seemed to be an endless stream of traffic. They passed a legion of workmen carving a new road out of red dust. Fae sat in her air-conditioned luxury and avoided the stuff that rose up out of the earth, but there was no escape from the clogged arteries into Istanbul. She tried to stay calm, but her mouth was dry, even her lips were numb.

At four o'clock there was no announcement.

'Bastards,' Fae said.

'Oh God,' Innessa said.

'Poor Daddy,' Fabrizzi said.

Sam sat quietly in the back of the speeding car. He was as finely tuned as a prized musical intrument, aware of any variations in the noises of the engine. He listened for a long time, hours and hours it seemed, but then the car stopped, his feet were untied, he was pushed out of the back, made to stand up.

'Piss if you want to,' he was told. He did not know the voice. But where? And his hands were still tied, his mouth too.

As if they had read his mind his hands were unbound, he was turned around and was walked ten paces.

'You are in some bushes.' There was the sound of feet walking away from him.

But was he in some bushes?

He stumbled forward another five paces, felt some sort of foliage, performed his business, turned on his heel, and then walked back the ten, no fifteen paces.

He stood still, an ear cocked for sound, any sound . . .

Nothing.

Then the noise of a car going – leaving him, alone, frightened. Were they going to kill him now? He sank down to the ground, waiting.

Silence, just silence.

He reached up, took the tape off his mouth.

'I'm going to take off my mask,' he shouted.

No sound, no reply.

'The mask is coming off,' he shouted again. Still no answer.

Quickly he pulled at the blindfold.

Shiny sharp light – crisp green leaves, a dusty dirty road. An empty silent world. He was free, but was he? Were there men and women waiting with shiny black emissaries of death? He didn't want to receive any of them. He ran, hard, fast, panting – but a man out of step with his body cannot run far, and so when a small and old vegetable van choked its way down the road the driver found him – face down – in the road. He was just ten kilometres from where he had been kidnapped.

The driver took Sam, skirting around the tourist traffic, bleating his horn angrily, to the hospital in Izmir. The admitting sister recognized him, she telephoned the police. Just ten minutes before, the kidnappers, using the specific codes to identify themselves, had announced that Sam Whiteman had been released on the road to Kuşadasi . . .

It was Ichmet Golabi who had made the decision when he had learnt that Rashid was under surveillance. He had met with him at the University, in his rich wood-panelled office.

'Sam Whiteman is to be released,' he told a blatantly truculent

Rashid. 'Killing him will not help us at all. This was your exercise, you were sure it would achieve the release of those in custody. A coup for your cell. And then you assured me that it would achieve some sort of coup against the CIA. It has failed, and I no longer wish to leave you in control. I understand that you have been linked to the kidnapping, so you are dangerous to us now. Unlike our poor friends in custody who do not know your identity, you know everything and could implicate us all. You will step down from this operation.'

In his hospital room Sam spoke only once.
'How is my son?' he asked.
No one knew, but a kindly nurse made it her business to find out. She told him Fabrizzi was well.
Sam just nodded.

A small military plane flew Fae to Izmir. William Fairchild was with her, she didn't like that – she wanted it to be a private time. She was nervous enough . . . she couldn't cope with an audience. A white police car drove them to the hospital. The grey-green policemen roamed around everywhere. Four stood at the entrance, guns cocked.
Fairchild stopped, held back.
'I'll wait,' he said.
Fae didn't thank him – it was her right to be alone with her father.
At the door to his room Fae paused, suddenly shocked into immobility. After the months of worry, she was unsure what to do. Sam, Sam, beloved Sam, still her father, so loved, so wanted – and yet he was not the Sam she had known, or thought she had known. They were changed, both of them, by the single event – the kidnapping – so that what 'was', was now past, gone, only to be recovered in memory, never to be touched again.
And yet she could touch the new man, the real father. But would she be able to do that, now that he was not who she thought he was? She drew in her stomach muscles, as if to give herself strength, and pushed open the door.
Sam was sitting by the window. He'd had a shower – his black hair was wet – his face, matted with exhaustion, seemed

older. He was somehow much smaller, huddled inside the hospital dressing gown . . .

'Daddy.' She'd meant to say 'Dad'. 'Daddy,' she repeated.

He turned his head towards her, he looked up and reached his hand out to her face, stroked her skin – there were no wild embraces.

'Hi, honey,' he said.

'You're back.' The edge of a tear wormed its way up into her eyes. 'I never thought I would see you again. I thought you'd be gone forever. I missed you.' She put her arms around him. His shoulders felt thinner. 'How are you?' She crouched down by his chair, looking up into his face, searching for the remembered past.

Sam smiled.

'Beautiful Fae, strong Fae. What have you all been through? But first I must know about Fabrizzi. Here' – he gestured with his finger towards the corridor – 'they told me that he's OK.'

'He is. The kidnappers didn't tell you the truth.'

'No. But who does, Fae?'

'It was two boys on motor bikes. He was in a coma for about twenty-four hours, but he's fine now. He just wants to see you, and be with you. He and Innessa were waiting for definite news before coming, in case . . .'

Sam interrupted Fae: 'In case I was dead.'

Fae nodded. 'Yup.'

Sam sighed and stood up.

'No – they didn't hurt me.'

'Oh, Daddy,' Fae said softly.

Sam sucked in his cheeks. He saw his daughter in front of him – her eyes anxious, caring, but different, somehow. He searched her face for signs of the old Fae, but they were gone, the adulation was not there, there was anxiety and uncertainty.

Sam closed his eyes. He didn't want to look at her: she was the reality. In her he could see his own failures confronting him, the terror, the cowardliness, the betrayals. He wanted to be away from the reminders – yes, from Fae too – now that he knew Fabrizzi was well. He wanted to be back in the little house, up in the hills, with his chess-playing guard. He'd been happy there.

Fae saw the sudden retreat – as if a curtain had come down

and cut Sam off from her. She didn't want that, she wanted him to respond to her.

'Dad, Fabrizzi and Innessa are coming tonight – and then you could go to Italy with them.'

'No, no, I don't want to leave Turkey. I will go to Ichmet, I need Ichmet. I don't want to see anyone else.'

'Of course you do. You want to see Fabrizzi. And there are other people you have to see.' Fae got up and turned away from him. She wished she had a cigarette, wished she had something to hold, something to do. 'William Fairchild is here.' She turned back to him and saw a childish set to his lips, even a pout. It was a shock.

'You know that Richard Marks is dead.'

'I won't talk about him. He slept with Innessa – I saw photographs of them.'

'And you've slept with God knows how many women!' Fae snapped. She didn't mean to lose her temper, but her father was so petulant. Then, as soon as she said the words, she regretted them. He'd been through so much, she must be careful, she couldn't impose the same rules on him that were in place for everyone else.

'I'm sorry, I shouldn't have said that – but you have to see William Fairchild. The Company have to talk to you.'

'What do you know about that?'

'Dad, I know everything. It's better that way.' She held out a hand – would he take it? 'We can begin again, please?'

Briefly hand touched hand, but that was all – he turned his face away from her.

Fae hurt, a deep inside hurt. She bent down, kissed him briefly on the cheek.

'I'll see you later,' she said, trying to mend a bridge.

'Yes,' he said, but he offered nothing else, no repairs from his side.

Unable to hide her feelings, Fae slipped out of the room.

She tried to get out of the corridor without anyone seeing her. Fairchild was standing, arms folded across his chest, listening intently to a man. She recognized him, it was Kamel Batami. She had just reached the swing doors that would take her into the main part of the hospital when she heard him call out to her, 'Fae, Miss Whiteman, are you all right?'

She turned back, setting her face in what she hoped were proper lines.

'Yes. Dad's tired. I'll come back later.'

It was Kamel Batami who took her arm, marshalled her back into the corridor. But not before the rat pack, ever faithful to the story, had crowded their way through the doors. Even the sick had to make room for them.

'Fae, Fae, how is he?'

'Did he tell you anything?'

'Why did he say all that stuff?'

'When is your stepmother coming?'

'There is nothing to say, gentlemen,' Batami said, 'not till later anyway.'

He hustled Fae out of a side door, into his own car.

'I can't reach him, Mr Batami. I can't say anything to him. He won't talk to me. And I feel so awful, and so guilty.'

'Don't feel guilty, Fae. I hope you don't mind me calling you Fae. Your father is in trauma – think of what's happened to him – but equally all your perceptions have been shot to pieces. You have to talk to each other.'

'If he'll let me.'

'You both need time and patience,' said Batami.

Patience Fae might have had, but there was no time – none at least for her and Sam. It seemed that everyone wanted a piece of her father. Batami's people, and the Americans – especially the Americans. There was the hostage counsellor, a psychiatrist, and of course the agents. The debriefing wouldn't wait.

Sam was hostile, unwilling to offer anything at all. Fairchild was anxious to move him, the psychiatrists felt he should stay in the womb-like atmosphere of the hospital. Sam wanted to go to Ichmet.

Fae just sat outside his room and waited. In the midst of all this Innessa and Fabrizzi arrived.

Innessa, as always, was blonde and beautiful – this time in a grey silk suit and matching shoes. Fae immediately became aware of her own dishevelled appearance, of creased trousers and white blouse. She hadn't bothered with herself since her arrival. She was suddenly conscious that she would like to have a shower and wash her hair . . . make herself look better. Fabrizzi limped to her, they hugged – tight.

'Listen, kid,' she said, fingering her brother's hair, 'he's tired.'

'Sure he is, he must feel odd too – suddenly back with us.'

Fae looked up at Innessa, who said, 'You know, maybe we should leave Sam to Fabrizzi. I think he'll sort him out.'

But even Fabrizzi couldn't help Sam. Oh yes, there was an emotional reunion, but Sam could not get out of the trough that separated him from the rest of them. Innessa could see that. She kissed his cheek.

'What do you want to do?' she asked him directly.

'I want to go to Ichmet. I need some time, Innessa, but they won't even let me ring him. Do this for me, please.' His wife nodded. She turned to William Fairchild.

'Please arrange,' she said, 'to transfer my husband to Ichmet Golabi's house. That's what he wants, and that's what he needs.'

Fairchild shrugged. He had no wish to make Sam uncomfortable. So he overrode the psychiatrists and made the necessary arrangements, after having first informed Langley.

'You can go tomorrow,' he informed Sam Whiteman and his family.

William Fairchild flew to a small military airport near Istanbul. A US diplomatic car with smoked glass windows collected and drove him straight to the home of Ichmet Golabi.

Fairchild made little attempt at pleasantries.

'Your friend Sam Whiteman is, I understand, coming to be your house guest.'

'That is correct.' As usual Golabi was essentially courteous, but there was no warmth between the two men.

'OK. We'll want you to let us know how he progresses.'

'No, Mr Fairchild. I will not file any more reports on Sam Whiteman. I have one more service to perform for you, and one which I admit serves my own purpose, but after that our relationship is terminated.'

'Now look here, Ichmet . . .'

'No, "look here" any more. This kidnapping of Sam Whiteman was not, as you know, an act which I favoured. I subscribed to it because my young associates needed some focus after the death of their friend, they wanted to do something to try to bring about the release of the other young people who had been arrested at that time. As you well know, I knew this was a politically naïve thing to do. But there are times when the older ones must step back. And Mr Fairchild, let's be honest, you were quite happy, yourself, to let this take place. You were having trouble with my friend Sam Whiteman. A little kidnapping did not worry you, "as long as he's eventually released". I believe those were your words. Your associate, Mr Marks, and indeed no one else in the Company knew that you were aware of the kidnapping. I knew that, and I waited, knowing that this information could buy my freedom from your services.'

'You've been happy enough to take the Company's money for all these years, Ichmet.'

'You blackmailed me, using a painful indiscretion of which I am most ashamed. You offered me gold, and I took it. It gave you information into our activities. It gave me freedom to pursue my own path. But now it is over. You have pulled in your markers, as you would say. And now I'm pulling in mine.'

'OK.' Fairchild offered his hand but Golabi did not take it. The slight was deliberate but conducted with courtesy.

'What's this last service?'

Ichmet Golabi glanced at his watch. 'In about ten minutes, my young friend Rashid, his sister, and two of Sam's closest guards, an older man – a kindly villager who played chess with him – and Hayri Gurbuz, will sadly meet with a car accident.'

'Excellent.'

'It's regrettable that young life should be lost in this way but I don't intend to have any witnesses to my involvement in the matter of Sam Whiteman's abduction.'

'For all your dignity, Mr Golabi, you are a cold-blooded bastard.'

'Like you, Mr Fairchild, I take my opportunities. And now I have to prepare for my friend, Sam Whiteman.'

Rashid's car was a steel-grey Mercedes. The four occupants were arguing.

'I say we should have killed him. He can identify us,' Faroud said.

'Ichmet Golabi instructed us to release him,' the older guard said.

'We should have ignored Ichmet. He's an old man, he doesn't know what he's doing.'

'There's no point arguing now. It's done. He's arranged for us to lie low for a period of time. He'll deal with Whiteman. It will all be all right.'

'You're soft, Rashid,' snapped Faroud.

'I'm not soft, I just trust Ichmet.'

'That's stupid . . . you should never trust anyone. He could betray us – even now.'

Those were the last words that Faroud remembered saying to her brother before the blast shot her clear of the car. Stunned, bloody from cuts from a thousand pieces of glass, she watched as her brother's car exploded in flames in front of her. She turned her head away, unable to look on the horror.

When Sam knew that he was going to Ichmet's house he briefly emerged from his private world like a snail out of its shell and talked . . .

First to Fabrizzi.

'I need some time, my boy,' he told him.

'I know, Dad. You need your friend.'

'Does it hurt you?'

'No, I understand. But you will see me, soon.'

'As soon as I'm better, come to me for a holiday.'

'No, Dad. Not here, you come to Italy.'

Sam nodded, he understood his son's fear of Turkey. He wished he could help him, he wished he could spend time with him, but he couldn't. Maybe, when he had healed himself, he could go to Fabrizzi. In the meantime he knew the boy was safe with Innessa.

Innessa was sitting quietly across the hospital room, her feet crossed neatly, her overnight bag packed.

'And Sam, you will let us know how you are.'

'Innessa, I thank you for your help.'

She cleared her throat, 'Fabrizzi darling, I need some moments with Papa, do you understand?' Fabrizzi minded, both parents could see that, but being a well brought-up boy, he went out of the room. Innessa waited until the door was shut before she spoke.

'You need time, Sam. I'm your friend, but not your wife. We both know that now. At first, when Fabrizzi was ill, I thought maybe . . . I remembered how it used to be, not how it had become.'

Sam nodded.

'We have to talk about Richard.'

Sam got out of his chair. He wanted to turn away from Innessa . . . he didn't want to hear her. But she was speaking again.

'I would imagine from your reaction that you know that Richard and I had a love affair. I am sorry about that. He was your friend, but for a while I loved him. He made me feel wanted. He's dead now, and I mourn him. You have to understand.'

'I can't, Innessa. They showed me photographs.'

'I won't defend myself.'

'Why not?' The anger flashed into the voice.

'You betrayed me too. Let's just leave it at that. You know, yesterday, when I heard of your release, I wondered if we should stay together – for a while . . .'

'No!' The answer shot back, like a cork bursting out of a bottle.

'I know. Take care of yourself.'

She offered her hand. Sam turned to look at her. He saw the small blonde woman he had once desired . . . he had no idea if he would ever want a woman again.

'I will go and get Fabrizzi,' she said.

She took Fabrizzi's hand whilst he hugged his father. Outside the hospital room, away from Sam and the photographers, her son stroked her hair. 'Let's go home, Mama. Give Daddy time, he'll get better.'

'Yes,' Innessa said. 'He'll get better and then you can see him.'

Fae took her father to Ichmet. The old Turk and his friend embraced each other. Fae felt a horrible jealousy.

'You will stay with us for a few days?' Ichmet asked her.

'No, I'm going to go back to England,' she replied.

She turned to Sam. 'I'm sorry that we can't talk to each other.'

Feeling better in Ichmet's presence, Sam could return to past habits. 'Princess, when I'm better . . .'

Fae could not.

'Firstly, I'm not your Princess, I'm your daughter – with all my faults, and you are my father, and I do love you. Dad, I know you've been through a terrible experience, but so have I

. . .' Fae screwed up her eyes as if she were in pain. 'I don't even know who you are; and I thought I did. I suppose all the therapists would tell me I'm being very selfish, I should give you time. To get over the trauma. But I want you to know how I feel.'

Sam stood still and looked at his daughter. He'd always thought of her as a defiant, small, female version of himself. Whilst he was a hostage he had clung on to her love of him. But now he wasn't looking at the love, he was looking at her anger. Because he failed her? Or because he built her an image of himself that wasn't there? He supposed it was both reasons.

He turned to her, to tell her that they would have to learn how to deal with each other, but there was sudden confusion outside Ichmet's house, and then a girl, bloody, dirty, burst in through the door. She was holding a gun.

Fae screamed . . . no sound, just screaming, but it meant no, not again.

Sam winced . . . he knew her.

'You bastard, Ichmet Golabi,' she said in English. She looked at Sam. 'This man – he's betrayed both of us. He was part of us, the group that kidnapped you. But after we released you, he killed my brother, he killed my friend, and now he will die. But first, Mr Whiteman, I will finish you off, as we should have done instead of bringing you back to your American masters.'

A gun fired. The sound ricocheted. The girl, Faroud, lay on the floor dead.

Kamel Batami stepped out of the shadow of the hall, and pocketed his gun. His policemen followed him in: they removed the body of Faroud. Batami looked sad.

'I knew her,' Fae said incredulously. 'It's Rashid's sister.'

It was Kamel Batami who responded: 'She was part of the group of conspirators that kidnapped your father.'

'But she said you were involved, Ichmet.' Fae spoke slowly, she reached out to her father. She was going to take him home.

Before Ichmet could answer, Sam spoke. His voice was frail again . . . the gunfire had frightened him.

'I'm not interested in investigating any wild claims from any wild girls. I just want some rest with my old friend. Please.'

'But . . .'

'I've told you, Fae. Now go home.' He looked at her – he smiled, but she could see that he didn't want her.

She could not accept that. Her father could not have understood. Ichmet, Ichmet Golabi, his friend had betrayed them all.

'Daddy, let me explain. The girl has just said . . .'

'I know what she said,' Sam interrupted. 'She claimed that my old friend kidnapped me. I don't want to know about it. We know who took me.' Sam turned to look at Kamel Batami, 'And they are dead, aren't they, Mr Batami?'

'They are.'

'I don't understand. This is ridiculous.' Fae was shouting, she couldn't help herself.

'We have no further interest in this case,' Batami said softly.

'But . . .' Fae started to say.

'And as for your father,' Batami continued, despite Fae's interruption, 'I think perhaps I should try to tell you that your father and Mr Golabi are friends.'

'Somewhat cancelled out by a little kidnapping, I would have thought.'

'But you are not me, Fae,' Sam answered. 'Ichmet is my friend. I've told you there is nothing else to know.'

'And you, Mr Golabi . . . what do you think?' Fae said.

The Turk stood up straight.

'I think, Fae, that your father is right. He has a home with me . . . we know each other.'

'And I don't.'

'Possibly not.'

Fae put her hand to her forehead. She was totally confused. But she would go, and without Sam.

She embraced her father, she shook hands with Golabi. As she walked to the door she turned briefly and she saw her father and his old friend sit down in two chairs – a chess board was near them . . .

In the car, on the way to the airport Fae spoke to Kamel Batami: 'It seems you understand why my father wants to stay with the man who actually betrayed him.'

'Your father observes different rules from you, Miss Whiteman. He only cares that Ichmet understands him. He, more than anyone else, knows your father's needs. He will not make demands. The kidnapping was part of the game.'

'Game?'

'For them.'

'I don't understand.'

'You cannot understand. Nor should you. The players in the world of espionage have their own rules. There are no baddies, and no goodies. Each one supports his own master . . . they accept whatever they do to each other. You should think about yourself now, Miss Whiteman.'

Herself, yes. For the first time Fae realized that was exactly what she was going to do. All her life she had shaped herself for others' approval. She supposed it was because she always wanted her father's approval. She had asked it from Nick too, that once unavailable passion who was in her life again now. With a sudden clarity she realized just how different her life was going to be: she was not the same person, safe in a womb, protected by Sam from the unpleasantness of life. There were no claps of thunder cracking across her mind emblazoned with the way to deal with herself. That was to come.

Kamel Batami was still speaking. 'What are you going to do?'

'I'm going home,' Fae said. Home to Nick? Beautiful Nick, who on a night when she had needed him, had slept with another woman.

At the airport, Fae was handed a message.

'Fae, my dearest girl. Your father is safe. I'm so glad. Please, please, always think of me as a friend. I will be in London on 21 October. Staying at Claridges. Can we meet? Lunch or dinner?' It was signed Robert Brockwell.

Fae folded up the note, and put it carefully in her handbag. On the plane she opened her diary at 21 October and made a neat entry. 'Robert Brockwell. Dinner, Claridges.'